Meet Me in the Greenhouse

A Novel

Kalyn Gensic

Staten House

Copyright © 2025 by Kalyn Gensic

All rights reserved.

No part of this publication may be reproduced, distributed, or transmitted in any form or by any means, including photocopying, recording, or other electronic or mechanical methods, without the prior written permission of the publisher, except as permitted by U.S. copyright law. For permission requests, contact through kalyngensic.com.

The story, all names, characters, and incidents portrayed in this production are fictitious. No identification with actual persons (living or deceased), places, buildings, and products is intended or should be inferred.

Book Cover by My Lan Khuc

Posthumously, to Bessie Marie Pierce
for being unapologetically eccentric.

~

And to her son, my father, John Pierce,
for keeping it quirky.

Contents

1. Prologue — 1
2. Chapter 1 — 6
3. Chapter 2 — 12
4. Chapter 3 — 22
5. Chapter 4 — 43
6. Chapter 5 — 48
7. Chapter 6 — 56
8. Chapter 7 — 61
9. Chapter 8 — 72
10. Chapter 9 — 80
11. Chapter 10 — 88
12. Chapter 11 — 98
13. Chapter 12 — 104
14. Chapter 13 — 123
15. Chapter 14 — 146
16. Chapter 15 — 168

17.	Chapter 16	177
18.	Chapter 17	188
19.	Chapter 18	194
20.	Chapter 19	201
21.	Chapter 20	213
22.	Chapter 21	223
23.	Chapter 22	238
24.	Chapter 23	256
25.	Chapter 24	263
26.	Chapter 25	279
27.	Chapter 26	289
28.	Chapter 27	296
29.	Chapter 28	303
30.	Chapter 29	321
31.	Chapter 30	337
32.	Chapter 31	349
33.	Epilogue	352
	About the author	359
	Acknowledgements	360

Prologue

Summer, 2002

"I'm still gay, Boone."

The acrid smell of deet-infused bug spray burned at the back of Boone Rutledge's throat as he listened to his brother's whisper. The discomfort of bug spray was preferable to the slew of bug bites that awaited them in the morning if they took a night off from dousing themselves. It always seemed to Boone that mosquitoes were more fervent in their pursuits at church camp than anywhere else.

Boone and his twin brother, Travis, laid on separate bunks in a cabin at Holy Hills Church Camp. Despite begging to spend the summer at their grandparents' house, the boys' parents had enrolled them at Holy Hills. Now, just a few days away from leaving, the brothers laid on their sides facing each other's bunks. Thankfully, their cabin mates had all fallen asleep, and they could steal a brief moment of privacy.

The Rutledge boys' parents, both of whom subscribed to the most fundamentalist branch of their conservative church, had one goal for the summer: turn Travis straight. Boone was single-mindedly focused on protecting Travis at whatever the cost. This was not the first time Boone and his parents had found themselves at cross-purposes.

When Boone first realized his parents' plan for the summer, he'd waited until he knew his father was watching and looked at another boy on the baseball team a stretch too long. His parents feared that Travis's gayness was somehow contagious, especially since they were twins. A seed of doubt was all that was needed.

Sure enough, he and Travis were both enrolled in a camp that advertised it could fix all manner of wayward boys, especially those who needed to be set back on a "straighter path." Boone suspected the pun was very much intended. Within a week of school letting out, Boone and Travis were deep in the woods of western Kentucky, surrounded by bracelet-braiding, gospel-preaching, hymn-strumming fundamentalists.

From the times they played dress-up in their grandparents' closet, Boone always dressing the part of the farmer while Travis found a vintage suit with a cummerbund or some of Grandma's Avon jewelry, Boone had known there was something different about Travis. It never bothered Boone that his brother was different. It never bothered their Grandma Rubie, either. All Boone had known was that he loved Travis just the way he was, and he could never understand why so many other people kept trying to change him.

The look of disappointment and despair on Travis's sweat-beaded face as he confessed his failure to change prodded a low-burning anger Boone had harbored on his brother's behalf for so long that he now suspected it was permanent and structural, like a kidney.

He could hear in Travis's voice that, on some level, his brother had hoped Holy Hills would deliver on its promises.

Boone said, "I figured. I mean, of course, you're still gay. You are who you are, Travis. There's nothing wrong with that."

The words were frustratingly inadequate, unlikely to change the dark, empty look his brother's eyes had taken on since the day their dad found him kissing the Miller boy from two blocks over.

Travis said, "That's not what people here think."

Boone thought back to the evening's gathering. Talk of abominations and denying the devil within and, of course, of hell's eternal fire - the really hot kind. Travis once slept in their dog, Duke's, bed in the laundry room for three full nights after the dog had a leg amputated following an unfortunate altercation with a Ford F-150. Boone might not be able to recite scripture to his parents' standards, but he knew enough to know there was no devil in his brother.

"Yeah, well those people are full of shit."

The curse word felt delicious as Boone spat it into the gummy night air. He'd never spoken one in the previous fifteen years, but he figured church camp was as good a place as any to begin.

Boone flipped onto his back kicking the sheet off his sweaty legs. Resting his head on his hands, he looked at the mattress of the top bunk above him. The blue-ticking cover squished through the grid of metal wires. Boone wondered just how many gay boys had lain on that old, worn-out mattress feeling they were the scum of the earth.

Despite the oppressive heat and humidity, Travis kept his sheet pulled up to his chin. He pulled a corner to his eye, wiping away moisture Boone suspected wasn't sweat.

"Boonie?" Travis used the pet name only Grandma Rubie ever used for Boone.

"What?"

"When we get back home-"

Travis paused, his voice shaking on "home."

"What is it, Travis?"

"When we get home, I'll understand if you need to keep your distance."

Boone asked Travis what he was talking about, embellishing with a particularly satisfying four-letter word.

"What I mean is that I'm no good, Boone. I'm sinful. You should stay away from me. We shouldn't both go to hell."

Boone pulled his hands out from behind his head and rubbed his eyes hard, trying to think what he could say to quell this nonsense.

"Travis, I'd just as soon burn."

Travis could no longer mask his tears as sweat. Sobs wracked his shoulders, and Boone feared his hiccups would wake the other boys. Boone turned back to face Travis, propping himself on one elbow. He reached across the narrow space between their bunks and grabbed his brother's hand. Holding it firmly, probably too firmly, Boone looked straight into his brother's wet eyes and spoke the words he needed Travis to hear and believe.

"Travis Rutledge, you are my brother, and I love you. There is nothing wrong with you. I will never abandon you, and just as soon as we're able to leave that abysmal place we call home, I will never again step foot in a building where people treat you like you're broken. Never again. Do you hear me, Travis?"

Travis said nothing as he struggled for composure.

"I said, did you hear me?"

Finally, Travis spoke. "I guess so since you're probably going to hell anyways for all those curse words you keep spoutin'."

Boone grinned, satisfied for the first time since arriving at Holy Hills.

Chapter 1

Winter, 2018

On the Second Sunday of Epiphany, Mother Miriam Howatch pulled on the sleeves of her clerical shirt, covering the tattoos that crept up each arm and around her shoulders, a flock of doves on one side flying to olive branches on the opposite shoulder. She always purchased her dog collar shirts with long sleeves and in dark colors. It was better for hiding the greenish-black ink. Not that Miriam minded, but it did seem to put the older church ladies at ease. Especially the ones in Altar Guild.

Once her shirt was on, the characteristic white tab had to be inserted in the collar. Miriam's stiff, cold fingers struggled to maneuver it into place. Even if the room hadn't felt like a walk-in refrigerator, Miriam would have struggled. For her, cold hands were an unfortunate by-product of nerves.

After considerable effort, the stiff, starched cotton of the tab collar slid into place. Next, she shimmied her way into the white cassock. Today, she was grateful for its warmth, the memory of the thick robe's oppressiveness in summer months distant. Miriam felt the nerves retreat ever so slightly. Her armor was almost in place.

Lastly, Miriam applied the finishing touches to her ensemble. Whispering a chant for mercy and grace beneath her breath, she lowered her head as she draped a white stole around her shoulders and tied a gold, threaded cord loosely around her waist. The repeating words of the prayers focused her mind, like a football team listening to Freddy Mercury belt out *We Will Rock You* in the moments before the big game.

At only thirty-three years old, Miriam had already served rice to children of war in two different countries. She'd been arrested for protesting the inhumane treatment of immigrants. The mugshot set in an elaborate frame next to the keyboard where she typed out the words of her sermons. She'd marched with hand-painted signs, advocated in capital buildings, and landed in some truly rickety planes on the tarmacs of countries where she was advised not to go.

Yet, in the small, quiet corner of Kentucky where she settled down a year ago, she still got nervous before stepping into a pulpit to deliver a sermon.

It was the first Sunday of the new year, and the chill of a Kentucky January left the large, open spaces of Trinity Episcopal Church impossible to heat. But damn warmth. It was a beautiful, old church.

Miriam adjusted her wooden cross necklace as she looked over her shoulder into the full-length mirror in the corner of the room. Even in vestments of the clergy almost as ancient as her faith, she was a striking woman. She had always had perfectly curled hair that, when cut correctly, sprung wildly but flatteringly around her face. The dark brown of her curls was the perfect frame for her warm, brown eyes. An old friend had once said they made him feel like he was looking into his morning cup of coffee.

Miriam's face was narrow, but not harshly so. Frequent smiles had etched subtle lines that no longer completely disappeared when she rested her face, but these foreshadowed wrinkles only added to her likability. She had a face that made people comfortable, that made them tell her secrets they hadn't dared to share with even their closest friends.

Somehow, none of these people ever seemed to notice that Miriam did not share in kind. The warmth and kindness and invitation her eyes perpetually extended were genuine. However, ministers didn't generally have people in their lives with whom they could confide. They were the confidantes, not the confessors.

And so Miriam had now spent many years of her adulthood apart - separated in some hard-to-define way from all but the most condensed group of friends, a small circle of people precious for their rarity and for their ability to remind her of her own needs. After all, the one who cooked the feast for a crowd often forgot their own hunger when it came time to eat. Luckily, Miriam had friends who insisted she take a plate.

Looking into her own attractive, young face was less satisfying than it used to be. She was beginning to sense that it wouldn't last. And while she was okay with the idea of aging, she wasn't quite done being young. With the protesting and advocating and flying to all the really scary places and trying her hardest to save the world,

Miriam was coming to realize she'd forgotten to tackle one small bullet-point on her bucket list.

She had forgotten to fall in love.

Over the past couple of years, wedding invitations from friends had stopped coming. Now the mail was pale pink or sky blue with baby rattles or stroller stickers affixed to the point of the envelope flap. Baby announcements dropped at rates that astonished Miriam. Her friends were starting families, becoming parents with their significant others, sinking roots wherever they had landed after the whirlwind of marrying and starting careers.

But she'd forgotten to fall in love.

Miriam had spent every moment of the past ten years preparing for and then being part of the clergy. As the Associate Rector for Trinity Episcopal Church in Paducah, Kentucky, Miriam loved the gig and couldn't imagine doing anything else with her life. But it wasn't always the best job for a social life. Or to be more blunt, one's love life.

The one friend who had always been single with Miriam, her dearest and oldest friend since their freshman year of college, had recently been engaged. It was a stark and unmerciful reminder for Miriam that she was about as close to being married and having kids as humanity was to colonizing Pluto.

Just as she was turning from the mirror and the thoughts it evoked of neglected bucket list items, Billy Finch pushed open the door. Billy was dressed in his own black robe with a white surplice on top, and his hair was gelled into place with such enthusiasm that Miriam suspected tornadic winds couldn't disturb it.

Miriam had forgotten it was Children's Choir Sunday. Billy was the son of one of the people who made up her small circle, Porter Finch. Porter was the Senior Warden of the church, so she worked with him in her capacity as a minister. But he was also one of her closest friends outside of work, and she was a regular part of his three children's lives.

"Mother Miri, this robe is itchy. Why are you always wearing these things?"

Miriam laughed as she walked over to straighten his surplice. It looked as though he had wrestled at least three other choir members that morning.

"It might be itchy, Billy, but you have to admit it's at least warm."

"Warm? It's hot!" He pulled down at the neck in a fruitless effort to let in cold air. "Mom's gonna have to wash this thing because I'm sweating plum through it."

Miriam squeezed his shoulders as she stepped back to examine her adjustments.

"Did you have something to tell me?"

"Yes." He wiped his nose on the sleeve of his robe. His mom would indeed need to wash the thing.

"Daddy told me to go burn off energy by running to tell you it's time."

Miriam looked at the clock.

"Oh no, Billy. You're right. I'm going to be late if we don't run."

"Good thing I'm good at runnin'."

Miriam grabbed her worn Bible with her sermon notes tucked between the pages, and she and Billy booked it out the door. She jogged behind Billy as his feet pounded down the long walkway that ran the length of the church. Miriam grabbed the brass handle and pulled with all of her weight on the solid wood door painted with the reddest of red paints. The groundskeeper had once told her the paint was called "Lipstick Red," a fact that always made her grin.

As the door opened, Miriam felt the organ's base tones vibrating through the walls of the church. She looked towards the entrance to the sanctuary and saw that about half of the choir was still in the narthex, the other half singing solemnly as they walked in the processional. She had made it just in time.

Bending over, she whispered into Billy's ear, "Go sit with your daddy until it's time for children's choir."

He looked over his shoulder to her. "Okay, Mother Miri, but this thing is so itchy I might fidget through your whole sermon."

"Thanks for the warning. Maybe you'll keep the people around you awake."

"Old man Johnson? Fat chance."

The last two words reverberated through the nave. The final few choir members turned to look at them, and a soprano's eyebrows raised disapprovingly. Unperturbed, Billy weaved around them to head to his family's usual spot, a pew three rows from the front.

Miriam took her place at the back of the processional, inhaled deeply, and stepped through the doors into the vaulted sanctuary lined with stained glass windows. The organ set the pace, guiding her slowly down the aisle.

CHAPTER 2

Boone Rutledge was tending the plants in his greenhouse, content to have quiet conversations with their leaves and spindly stems, when he discovered that he had an online dating profile.

Dating, especially of the swipe-right variety, was initially far from Boone's thoughts as he worked. Boone loved quiet like dogs love bones. He grabbed it where he could find it and hoarded it away, treasuring the snippets of peace so rare in his otherwise busy life. And few places are more suited to quiet than a greenhouse.

The greenhouse was Boone's place of refuge, a large structure he and his grandfather had constructed out of salvaged windows the summer after he first started college. An old schoolhouse had been torn down in town, and Grandpa talked the demolition crew into letting him have most of the windows. He was a master carpenter and had somehow turned the windows into a greenhouse with enough space for their food supply as well as his and Boone's vast collection of plants.

Now, almost fifteen years later, Boone was a Horticulture professor at the university in town, his grandfather had passed away a decade before, and Boone was living out on the farm with his Grandma Rubie. As much as he loved his grandmother, she did not share his reverence for solitude. One time when she had been talking for half an hour without so much as pausing to breathe, a bug flew into her mouth and bit her. Boone had regretted her discomfort, but he'd also had to conceal a laugh. After all, with the amount of time her mouth was open relaying gossip from her garden club meetings and church potlucks, it was only a matter of time before a bug got in there.

Needless to say, Boone was often grateful for a warm place inhabited by very quiet plants.

Boone moved down the rows with a galvanized metal watering can. Their little corner of Kentucky was now deep into winter, the January temperatures rarely making their way beyond forty degrees. Boone had spent his first summer back on the farm after receiving his doctorate winterizing the greenhouse. Hopefully, it would withstand the coming months, because *The Farmer's Almanac* was predicting an unusually nasty winter. A heating system coupled with a few fans that hummed overhead kept warm air circulating around Boone and the plants, making it almost hard to believe frigid temperatures surrounded their oasis. When he drove by the bank on his way home from work, it had said thirty-five degrees. The wind chill was bone-chilling.

As he turned down a new row of plants, Boone stopped at one of the raised beds and bent down to examine it. Even though the beds were built high, Boone's tall stature meant crouching at the knees to get a good look. An old girlfriend once told Boone she'd developed a crush on him solely because he looked like a hero from the cover of one of her historical romance novels. Boone supposed that with his imposing stature, full beard, and wavy auburn hair that always seemed to be due for a trim, there was probably some truth to what she said.

Reaching gently beneath a row of plants, Boone's large, calloused hands navigated the beds with surprising delicacy. The soil was just damp enough to stick to his thumb when he pressed firmly at the base of his heirloom turnips. He could skip watering this bed for a day.

Boone slowly and methodically moved to the next raised bed of plants. Mostly, he moved in this molasses-in-January fashion because it was his natural pace. He wasn't one to get in a rush. But today, he was even slower, hesitant to leave both the greenhouse's warmth and quiet.

Just as he tilted the watering can over a bed of kale and Swiss chard, he heard the door creak open. He should have taken WD-40 to those hinges months ago. Boone inhaled and held his breath, preparing for the silence to not simply be broken, but shattered.

A voice rattled by countless cigarettes smoked from the mid-1950s well into the 80s said, "Hello Boone. I've been looking all over the house for you and then I thought, 'Rubie, what are you doing? You know that boy is hiding from your yip-yappin' out in that there greenhouse.'"

Rubie wore what she would call a blouse but the rest of the human population would call a shirt. It had at least a dozen different varieties of flowers in all different colors against an emerald green background. Her pants were a different green, a green not close enough to the blouse's hue to make it match nor far enough to allow for coordination. Her hair, though gray, was still as thick as it had been in her high school senior portrait that hung in the stairway of the farmhouse, and as was the case in that particular photo, she had never learned to tame it. Though she combed it smooth each morning before heading to whatever luncheon or brunch or charity event she had that day, it was always tufted and standing on end by mid-afternoon. Coupled with her prominent nose and occasional chin hair that escaped both her notice and her tweezers, she was far from the elegant Southern church lady most women in their area aspired to be as they aged. Thank goodness, she had never held such aspirations.

Boone released the breath he'd been holding and growled, "I'm not hiding, Grandma."

"Oh, I know you're not hiding in a hateful way. You love your old grandma. You just weren't built for talking at my level. Few are, really. It's sweet how you tolerate all my prattling on about this and that. You've always been a sweet boy."

Now nearing ninety, Grandma Rubie had gained more self-awareness than most. Boone grinned with one side of his mouth. It took quite a lot to get a grin that stretched from one side to the other.

"Were you needing something, Grandma?"

She'd been suspiciously absent this Friday afternoon, and he was curious what she'd been up to. Regardless, his Friday classes always ended at noon, and he'd enjoyed the afternoon of stillness. Glancing up at Rubie from the plant he was tending, Boone noticed her eyes expand in a way that somehow made them look younger even as it exponentially multiplied the wrinkles of her forehead. Boone felt a prickle of distrust.

"I have some wonderful news to share. Marvelous, really. But you may not think it is wonderful at first. But I'm certain you will feel it is wonderful in time. It's going to change your life, my dear Boonie."

She typically only called him Boonie in a few specific situations, like when she was missing Grandpa and feeling nostalgic about the passage of time, or she'd left a light on in the car and run out the battery. More often than not, though, it meant she was up to no good and planning to convince Boone to go along with her antics. The last time she called him Boonie, he ended up driving her and Miss Hyacinth from the library club to a Bingo tournament in Nashville for singles over seventy-five.

"Rubie Elizabeth Rutledge, what are you up to?"

"That's Grandma Rubie Elizabeth Rutledge to you, young man."

"Grandma?" Boone didn't raise his voice. He rarely needed to raise his voice to convey his opinion.

"Me and Hyacinth..."

"Oh no."

"After our library club luncheon, well, we pulled aside one of the librarians and asked her to help us pull up the Internets."

"Why do you and Hyacinth need the Internets?" Boone decided to not ask when the Internet became plural.

"So we can get you a woman!" She was now clapping her hands together, clearly thrilled with her and Hyacinth's ingenuity.

"You what?" If there was an 85-year-old woman who could accidentally purchase a mail-ordered bride on eBay, it would be his grandmother. Boone immediately started calculating both the odds of her being in legal jeopardy and the possible ways to extricate himself from whatever scheme she'd concocted.

"We set you up a...oh, what do they call it? You know, when you have your own little spot on the Internets? On some web place?"

Boone couldn't even begin to grasp the meaning behind her gibberish.

"You know, a profile." She slapped her hand down with satisfaction on a nearby work table, clearly thrilled she'd come up with the jargon of kids these days. "We set you up a dating profile on that web place where you get to swipe this way or that if a girl piques your interest."

"You set me up a dating profile on Matchables?"

"Yes! You know about Matchables, too?" She sounded as though she'd just discovered she was second cousins with the person standing in front of her in the supermarket line, an occurrence that had happened more than once. Even the tuft of hair that was sticking out on the side of her head vibrated with excitement.

Of course, Boone knew about Matchables. Everyone knew about Matchables. It was as ordinary as meeting someone in a bar had been in the nineties. Boone couldn't seem to form words to answer his grandmother's question, though. Instead, he croaked the one word that seemed available to him.

"How?"

She straightened her shoulders, puffing with pride, and said, "With considerable help from the librarian. A sweet young lady named Krista, pretty as can be. Unfortunately, she isn't an option for you because she's a lesbian. I asked."

Boone rested his forehead on one of the support beams that stood every few feet down the middle of the greenhouse. He slowly tapped his head on the wood, saying with each light thwack, "What...were...you...thinking?"

Truly, going on dates with strangers was Boone's worst nightmare. He had a small handful, a very small handful, of close friends he socialized with, and he liked it that way. He hated small talk, get-to-know-you talk. He hated wearing shoes that weren't work boots and a little dirty. He hated trying to get his own thick hair to cooperate.

And as much as he hypothetically liked women (what straight, red-blooded man doesn't appreciate certain facets of women, after all), he was far more comfortable with plants. Plants didn't mind one-worded answers or a lack of direct eye contact or long stretches between laughter. Silence with plants was never awkward. It was just silence.

Grandma Rubie walked up to Boone and placed her ice-cold fingers on his forearm, turning him around from the beam he was abusing. Sternly, she said, "Now Boonie, I was thinking how nice it would be if you came home not just to your old Grandma, but to a nice young woman who loves you. I was thinking how lonely it must get for you out here on this farm with nothing but a couple of cows, a few barn cats, and a fairly eccentric old woman for company. And I was thinking how nifty these new web things are today. Did you know that they ask you over fifty questions to get a better sense of who you might be compatible with?"

"You and Miss Hyacinth answered over fifty questions about my romantic proclivities?"

"We sure did. And, boy, we made you look good!" She added far more syllables to the word *good* than Boone was comfortable hearing from her.

In a measured tone, Boone said, "What exactly were these fifty questions you answered about me?"

"Oh, you know, what type of pets do you like, do you want a family, what interests do you have?"

Each question made Boone cringe a little more deeply. He wasn't sure if he wanted to know how she'd answered these questions or if he should just try to forget this conversation ever happened. However, he couldn't seem to stop himself from asking one more question: "What are my interests, Grandma?"

"We just typed the things you seem to do the most. Carpentry, working with plants, baking recipes you find on Pinterest..."

"Baking recipes I find on Pinterest?" His tone was considerably less measured now.

"Yes, that was Hyacinth's idea. She read that women like that sort of thing in *Women's World Magazine.*"

"But I've never baked so much as a cookie in my entire life."

"Well, now, I can teach you."

Boone repeatedly rubbed the bridge of his forehead. Funny how he hadn't noticed having a headache all day up until this very moment. "Did *Women's World Magazine* have any other skills I'm going to need to learn in order to find a date?"

Rubie started slowly backing towards the door as if she'd just now realized that this interrogation might not go in her favor. "No, not really. Just, you want three children because, apparently, that is the new two-children family, and you hope to one day travel to the Middle East."

"Why the Middle East?"

"You're planning to promote world peace. Also, you should probably volunteer at a children's hospital soon. It would be awful to lie about innocent little children on a dating profile."

"Whose idea was the children's hospital?" His voice reached a pitch he hadn't heard since puberty.

"That would be Krista."

When Boone's face tilted in confusion, Rubie clarified, "The lesbian librarian."

With that, her diabetic shoes shuffled to the entrance of the greenhouse, one foot already out the door.

"Grandma, don't you leave this greenhouse until you have given me the username and password so I can delete this account."

She was already shutting the door, waving a dismissive hand in his direction. "Oh, Boonie, don't worry. Me and Hyacinth will manage the account. You don't have to worry at all."

As the door clicked shut, Boone grumbled, "Worried? I'm well on my way to a full-fledged anxiety disorder."

He then picked up his shears and began pruning, giving up on any conversation with his plants to instead simply say "that woman" and "I can't even" as he gave a cluster of herbs more trimming than was strictly necessary.

Chapter 3

Miriam and Porter Finch stood on opposite sides of the kitchen counter unwrapping chocolate bars. This would be the second tray heading out to the patio for party guests to make s'mores. Winter made people hungry.

Porter's large, pre-Civil War home was often the gathering place for their circle of friends, so it was only natural that the engagement party for Lucy and her fiance, Forrest Graham, would take place in Porter's backyard. As the Senior Warden at Trinity, Porter and Miriam had a horrible habit of falling into shop talk.

Miriam said, "Okay, we're here to celebrate our two best friends finally getting their act together. We waited years - and I mean *years* - for them to figure out they're in love, and now that we're finally here at their engagement party, we've got to stop talking church business. The roof won't cave in because we took one night off."

Forrest and Lucy had clearly been in love with each other years before they figured it out. Miriam and Porter, as well as the whole PSU English Department, had waited not so patiently for the two to realize what was so obvious to everyone else. Thus, the engagement party felt like a triumph for them all.

Porter said, "You're right. So what should we talk about?" He looked up at the ceiling, scrunching his forehead, and continued, "I know. Been on any dates lately?"

"Porter, that is not under your jurisdiction."

"Not as the Senior Warden, but as your friend…"

Porter knew he was one of the few people Miriam confided in, the others being Lucy and their close friend, Edith Rose, another PSU English faculty member. Unwrapping another bar, breaking it in half, and placing it on the platter, Miriam said, "How do you define lately? Like in the past month? Past year?"

"Either."

"In that case, nope. I haven't been on a date lately."

Porter's eyebrows rose as he said, "In the past month or year?"

"Either. Both. I haven't been on a date in the past month or past year or maybe even two years. It depends on if you count the time old man Jeffers grabbed my ass when I took the Eucharist to him."

Porter looked thoroughly unimpressed. "We won't be counting old man Jeffers. Also, don't ever go out to his house again."

Miriam popped a square of chocolate into her mouth and said, "Oh, don't worry. Father David nipped it in the bud and has taken over that particular shut-in."

Miriam was fortunate to have a rector at Trinity who did not suffer fools.

Plastic crinkled in Porter's hands as he balled up a few wrappers to toss, unsuccessfully, toward the bin.

Miriam said, "At what point do men outgrow treating every piece of trash like a basketball?"

Just then, Billy ran into the kitchen with his younger brother close behind, both screaming and laughing. He stopped just long enough to take his paper plate and toss it in the general direction of the trash can. It missed.

As the boys ran out of the kitchen, Porter said, "I have no idea what you're talking about."

Miriam just rolled her eyes and opened the final candy bar.

Picking up their previous train of thought, Porter said, "I only ask because I can't help but think it must get lonely wearing that collar, everyone dumping their problems on you and expecting you to not have any problems of your own."

Absent-mindedly, Miriam touched her collar. She'd not had time to change on her way to the engagement party after work. Even before the collar, Miriam had always been a person people confided in. Lucy used to tease her for knowing all the departmental gossip when they were undergraduate English majors. She still knew all the gossip. The only difference was that in her present situation, she was bound to confidentiality, both by the code of ethics of her profession and her own moral evolution.

She replied, "It would be terribly lonely if I didn't have a circle of friends to lean on. But lucky me..." She tossed a candy wrapper in his direction. "I'll let you make another almost-basket."

As another candy wrapper landed next to the trash can, Miriam picked up the tray of chocolates and headed out the door. She wanted to stay and ask Porter where his wife, Charlotte, was that evening, but the last time she asked, she sensed that he wasn't in a space to talk about it yet. Charlotte was a successful journalist, and her career had always taken her on the road. But for the past year, Miriam felt as though Charlotte was more often gone than present. They'd always been a strikingly autonomous couple, able to have their own social circles and careers without it seeming to negatively impact their marriage. However, with three children (including a toddler), Miriam had no idea how Porter was holding up on his own.

If Miriam had asked, Porter would simply have said the current election year was keeping Charlotte busy. It likely was. But something still felt off to Miriam. Unfortunately, with her many years acting as a confidant, Miriam could also tell when someone was specifically not ready to share. All in due time.

***

After cleaning up from working in the greenhouse, Boone informed his grandmother that he would be out for the evening. When she asked if she could iron his shirt for the date, he growled that it was not a date but, rather, an engagement party for a friend. He then kissed the top of her frizzy, unkempt head and headed out.

Boone wasn't sure what her sudden infatuation was with getting him a girlfriend, but he suspected it had something to do with the phone call they received the previous week from Travis. After ten years in the Big Apple, Travis was moving closer to home, Louisville to be precise. Most importantly, he would be making the move with his fiance, Paul. They were hoping for a quieter life closer to Boone and Rubie and to start a family of their own. Boone and Rubie were both thrilled at the news, but now Boone wondered if Rubie was harboring more complex feelings. Had it also made her question Boone's solitary existence? Maybe she worried that once she passed, he would become a hermit out in his greenhouse. Of Boone's possible futures, that was the odds-on favorite.

As much as he hated to admit it, Boone was intrigued by the possibility of Matchables. What if a search engine really could shuffle through the data of hundreds of women and present him with one who might just fit? Boone was awful at making introductions and initiating contact, which made it difficult to weed through the incompatible women to get to one who might tolerate his introversion and gruff exterior.

Boone's current romantic history would be defined by his fellow professors as a drought of Dust Bowl proportions. He'd hardly had a date since arriving in Paducah five years earlier. It wasn't because he couldn't find someone interested. The problem was that he'd never met a woman who seemed like she wouldn't run the other way the second she walked into his home to find an unruly almost-ninty-year-old woman with a hundred stories to tell, produce to pickle, and advice to administer to anyone who would listen. He loved his life, and he loved his grandmother with a fierceness that was evident to anyone who knew him, but honestly, how could he take a girl home to that?

For this evening, anyway, Boone would not be alone. His friend and colleague, Forrest Graham, had invited Boone to his engagement party, and while that was normally not Boone's scene, he wanted to support Forrest.

Three years ago at the annual faculty Christmas party, the Agriculture and English departments had been seated at adjacent tables. After an especially long-winded greeting from the chair of the Board of Trustees, Boone had whispered beneath his breath, "For the love of all that's holy, would someone bring out the food?" He had only intended to vent to himself, but the person whose chair backed up to Boone's own leaned back and whispered, "It's good to know I'm not the only person whose sole purpose for being here is the steak."

Before Boone knew what was happening, his chair was squeezed into the English Department's table, and he found in Forrest a friend, his first, really, at PSU. It wasn't that there was anything wrong with the Ag Department. They were nice enough, certainly all good at what they did. It was just that Boone had never fit into good ol' boy clubs, and the Ag Department tended to lean in that direction. Boone had always been a tad too cerebral, his approach to plants and animals a bit too philosophical, a little too quick to quote John Muir when making a point.

For Boone, working with dirt was more than a business proposition or career choice or field to be researched. It was something deeper; a way of connecting to something bigger than himself. And unlike the religion of his youth, this bigger something didn't require him to disavow his brother.

Somehow, Forrest, a specialist in 19th-century American Literature, understood this. A year after meeting, they'd devised a course for English and Ag majors that combined the ideas of conservation and horticulture with the writings of Thoreau and Muir. They'd now taught the course twice, and it was already popular among the students. For most, early registration was their only hope of getting a spot in the class.

So while Boone generally didn't venture off the farm for social gatherings, he would make an exception for Forrest.

Once he arrived at Porter's house, Boone walked through the gate into a beautiful, treed backyard with a fire pit roaring at full blaze in the center. People stood around the flames with steaming mugs and marshmallows on roasting sticks. A platter of already-prepared s'mores set to the side.

In the middle of the action stood the happy couple. When Boone first met Forrest and his fiance, Lucy, at the Christmas party, they weren't yet a couple. Regardless, Boone had been struck by how comfortable they seemed with each other. He couldn't imagine ever feeling so at ease with anyone or anything that wasn't vegetation.

Over the crowd, Forrest spotted Boone and waved a welcome. Boone returned the greeting and then headed to the marshmallows, hoping if his hands were busy rotating a stick over flames, he might not feel so alone even in this crowd.

***

Squatting low, Miriam held out a roasting rod with three marshmallows just a few inches over the flames of the fire pit. She liked her s'mores heavy on the marshmallows.

Miriam's puffer coat was zipped up tightly, and her neck was wrapped in a scarf she'd knitted during an abysmal stint on the Knits of Love ministry at church. It was much too crooked and knotted to give away in charity. Despite her layers, though, she was still shivering.

When Lucy first told Miriam they would be roasting s'mores on a January night for their engagement party, Miriam hadn't had the heart to tell her it was likely a terrible idea. Miriam was prone to getting chilled, and no amount of warm marshmallows in her tummy was actually going to keep her warm on a twenty-degree night. But Lucy and Forrest were glowing from within, infatuated with each other. Apparently, love made people impervious to cold. Miriam wouldn't know.

Just as she was starting to get a few light brown dots on her marshmallow, a man squatted down a couple of feet from her, two unblemished white marshmallows on his straightened coat hanger ready to be fired. She sent a passing glance in his direction but did a double-take when she realized she didn't know the person. She thought she knew everyone at the small gathering.

As Miriam took a closer look at the stranger, she was struck by the realization that he was profoundly handsome. He looked like a Scottish laird who'd strolled his way into Porter's backyard to roast s'mores. He had longish, wavy auburn hair that just grazed the collar of his flannel, plaid shirt, and a neat but not overly-groomed beard to match. Even through his coat, Miriam could see that his arms were solid and muscled, that he'd likely worked many long hours outside doing hard labor that would make a person sweat. His work boots looked like dust would puff from them if hit with a stick.

But what stood out the most, even in the night with only a fire and a few strung Edison bulbs for light, were his eyes. They were a strikingly pale blue, like looking into a frozen lake mirroring a clear, blue winter's sky. The flames reflected in them, dancing violently against their placid depths. Miriam could swear she'd seen those eyes before, but she couldn't place where.

For the first time in a very long time, Miriam felt a bolt of attraction rush through her. She was shocked by its presence, having not felt anything similar since the socializing and dating of undergrad.

It wasn't that she'd spent the past six years with blinders on, not noticing when she saw a man who had a passing resemblance to George Clooney circa his *ER* days. It was just that as she got older, more and more of the reasonably handsome men had suddenly been off the market. And when they were available, they were always spooked when the conversation turned to her profession. So Miriam had found it easier to just ignore attraction, to deem it not for her. People with Celiac couldn't have gluten. The poor souls cursed with lactose intolerance couldn't enjoy the milk chocolate Miriam was about to melt under her pound of marshmallows. And Mother Miriam Howatch didn't get to indulge in fantasies about being carried into a cozy, fire-lit hut in the strapping arms of the laird of a Scottish clan. Not that she normally had to suppress Scottish-laird-themed fantasies.

Just as she was trying to convince her mind that, no, really, she couldn't go into the hut and the only reason she was having visions of huts was because of stupid Porter with his stupid questions about dates and loneliness and her impending spinsterhood, the stranger's piercing blue eyes looked up at her. Miriam, who never was at a loss for words, felt the oddest sensation of her mouth going dry. She'd always assumed that was just a phrase used in books to demonstrate that a character was truly flummoxed, but it turned out to be an actual phenomenon that occurred when sexually starved women met handsome strangers over a fire pit.

Thankfully for Miriam, the stranger was not tongue-tied.

"The *Farmer's Almanac* predicts that it will get even colder come February."

Miriam squeezed the wool of her scarf tighter.

"That doesn't bode well for me, does it?"

He smiled gently and said in his quiet, gruff voice, "You look about five minutes this side of hypothermia."

Miriam laughed and replied, "I think I'll survive the night, but I've always been a wimp when it comes to the cold. Guess I'd better prepare myself for February." The stranger merely nodded his assent and refocused on the flames. Miriam wasn't finished speaking to him, though. With her voice once again strong, she continued, "Do you often use *Farmer's Almanac* for your forecasting?"

"Sort of. My grandfather always bought it. He'd read bits and pieces of it to me. I guess I've kept up the tradition."

He was both outrageously handsome and sentimental about old people. Miriam suppressed facial muscles that were threatening a goofy grin.

"We kept a copy in our house when I was growing up," she said. "I've always found that the families who still use the *Farmer's Almanac* tend to be a bit eccentric."

His eyes sparkled in the firelight, but he didn't outright smile.

***

Boone thought about Grandma Rubie going to a public library to create a Matchables profile for her grandson. He thought about his grandfather driving two hundred miles to hear a presentation on efforts to revive American Chestnut trees to their native forest - not exactly the normal interest of the average Kentucky farmer.

"Yes, I definitely come from a strange bunch."

The woman across from him laughed, seemingly comfortable in a crowd and sitting across from a complete stranger. Boone never felt comfortable in such settings, but he suspected she was one of those rare people who could make even the most stayed introvert feel comfortable.

Her companionable warmth enriched what was already a beautiful appearance. Boone wondered how anyone could have curls so perfectly sprung. One chestnut piece would wrap perfectly around his finger. The curls framed her face, cut flatteringly right below the jaw.

And once he looked past the striking hair, he found even more to hold his attention. People always waxed poetic about Boone's own blue eyes, but Boone was immediately captured by the rich brown of this woman's eyes. They reminded him of earth - of dried seeds and fertile soil. Blue eyes might look like the sky, but her eyes were the color of the soil sifting through his fingers as he planted tomatoes.

Around those mesmerizing eyes, Boone was left with the distinct impression that she would develop fine lines at a fairly young age from smiling far too often. He also thought she would look quite nice with a few fine lines.

She didn't wear much make-up, her tanned face glowing without the least bit of help, and her lips, slender but subtle, were naturally pink like the edges of the Impatiens Grandma planted in their window planters each summer. She looked like she could fit perfectly into any natural scene lush with vegetation. She looked like she could fit perfectly into his greenhouse.

Boone raked his eyes away from her, fearful he might make an ass of himself gawking at a pretty girl, and noticed that two of the three marshmallows on her stake were perilously close to melting off.

Pointing, he said, "Uh, ma'am, you're about to lose some of the marshmallows you have there."

The woman jerked, seeming to only just remember that she was roasting a row of marshmallows.

"Oh, goodness, how forgetful of me."

Her cheeks blushed as she pulled the marshmallows towards her plate.

Seeing only one graham cracker and a square of chocolate, Boone asked, "Do you need me to get you more crackers and chocolate? Looks like you have enough marshmallows for a few more."

"No, thank you. I like a little s'more with my marshmallows."

She was once again smiling as she slid the three marshmallows onto the crackers, creating a bulbous glob Boone doubted anyone could eat without making a mess and, likely, getting sick in the process.

Boone must have done a poor job of concealing his shock because she grinned sheepishly and said, "Don't you know roasted marshmallows are key to fighting hypothermia?"

"I see." Boone was surprised to find himself grinning in return. The fire crackled loudly, a limb snapping. Boone said, "My grandfather read the *Farmer's Almanac* because he was a farmer and needed to know when to plant. Since he died, I've leased out most of the fields to local farmers for corn and soybeans. A few even grow tobacco. But I still read the *Almanac* because when I do, I hear the words in my grandfather's voice. It helps me to not forget his voice."

Miriam looked up from the abomination she called a s'more. "That's a lovely reason to read it," she said, her eyebrows mirroring his own surprise.

Boone was astonished that he'd just shared something so intimate with a stranger. In fact, he'd never realized why he picked up an almanac next to the cash register in the Feed and Seed store each year. He hadn't realized the truth of the statement until he'd spoken it out loud to this woman with the earthen eyes. Wanting to move the conversation beyond his little confession, Boone said, "What was your eccentric family's excuse?"

"My dad was a history teacher, and my mother was an elementary librarian, so they both had their summers off. When I was little, they bought an ancient RV that smelled like a raccoon family had once nested there. After a good airing out, we spent our summers traveling all over the country exploring national and state parks with the occasional museum or Civil War reenactment thrown in. Now they're both retired, I don't know where they are half the time. But I like that they're still exploring."

As she spoke, her face clearly showed she was relaying fond memories, but Boone was still confused. "Traveling is great, but how does it pertain to the *Farmer's Almanac*?"

"Oh, it doesn't. I think he just fancies himself someone particularly in-tuned with nature, and the *Farmer's Almanac* seems like the thing a person reads if they want to be one with the planet."

"That makes sense, I guess."

"It really doesn't, but like I said, I also come from an eccentric bunch."

She grinned again. Did she ever scowl? Did she ever want to hide from the world in a small structure with nothing but plants? Boone had just met this woman, but he already suspected the answer to these questions was no.

Just as Boone was about to ask her which National Park was her favorite (a question that would veer him perilously close to an actual conversation with a stranger), Forrest called for everyone's attention. Even though many guests had helped themselves to s'mores already, the actual dinner food had just been delivered from a local Italian restaurant.

When Forrest was finished speaking, Boone turned back to continue his conversation, but the woman was gone.

***

As soon as Forrest made the announcement that the food had arrived, Miriam hopped up to go find Lucy and help with setting up the buffet line. Lucy had been in a panic about the food arriving later than expected, so Miriam wanted to make things go as smoothly as possible for the rest of the evening.

Smells of roasted garlic and sweet, simmered tomato, greeted Miriam as she opened the door. Taking off her coat and scarf, Miriam regretted again that she'd run out of time to change. She would've liked to leave the dog collar home for an evening.

Walking into the kitchen, Miriam gently grabbed her friend's shoulders, pausing Lucy's frantic darting about, and said, "Let me help. This is your party."

Lucy took a deep breath, smiled, and said, "I see you made a friend out there."

Miriam tilted her head in slight irritation. Why did people in couples get so excited every time a single friend showed even the slightest sign that they might not die alone in a house full of cats?

Lucy, unfazed, continued, "To be clear, the friend was of the boy variety."

Despite her irritation, Miriam was curious to learn more about the guy who didn't want to forget his grandfather's voice. She said, "Let's get people eating, and then we can sneak away and talk. That is, as long as you agree to not, under any circumstances, use the words boy or friend anywhere near each other."

It didn't take long for Lucy and Miriam to break away into Porter's study and close the doors. They'd been sneaking away to gossip and exchange secrets since Humphrey Dormitory their freshman year of college. Miriam hoped they'd matured some since then, but she also hoped they never totally outgrew whispering in a small room away from the crowd. It was sort of their thing.

Just as they were turning into the room, Lucy grabbed Edith Rose to join in the girl talk. Edith was an English professor with Porter and Forrest at PSU, but she specialized in Women's Studies. Over the past year, she'd become part of Lucy and Miriam's weekly girls' nights. Even though her domineering personality and self-confidence often rubbed people the wrong way (or made them down-right terrified of her), Lucy and Miriam knew Edith to be an exceptionally loyal friend who spread her own self-confidence in such a way that she boosted that very trait in the women who were lucky enough to call her friend.

As the door shut, Edith clapped her hands together and said, "Is it girl-talk time?"

It never ceased to amaze Miriam just how girly Edith could be when she wasn't being a hardass.

Lucy answered, "Yes, Edith. Did you see our girl here talking to the tall, dark, and handsome Boone Rutledge?"

Suddenly, Miriam placed the eyes, the captivating, blue eyes that had felt so oddly familiar. They were Rubie Rutledges's eyes, Miriams's very favorite church lady of all the little old church ladies at Trinity. Boone wasn't kidding when he said he'd come from an eccentric family. There was no one more colorful or outspoken or, in Miriam's opinion, endearing, than Miss Rubie. Of course, many disagreed with that last sentiment, finding Miss Rubie to be too blunt or loud or ostentatious for their tastes.

Miriam knew a little about the family through Miss Rubie. Her beloved husband had passed a few years before Miriam came to Trinity, something Miss Rubie regretted because she felt the previous rector had been overly stuffy for the funeral. She'd once told Miriam, "You would have been vastly superior. Roger would have loved the idea of a tattooed, female minister throwing the ashes on his coffin."

Miriam also knew that Miss Rubie was estranged from her son, but she didn't know why, and she knew that the woman worshiped the ground her two grandsons walked on, one of whom lived with her and taught at PSU. If memory served, the other lived in New York City.

Edith interrupted Miriam's thoughts. "Boone's a good one. I mean, as far as non-English professors go, he's the best. The last article he got published in a journal was about the conservationist, Rosalie Edge. So, you know, he's actually aware that people without dicks have contributed to his field, which is more than I can say for the vast majority of male professors at PSU."

Miriam grinned. "That is quite the glowing endorsement from you."

"Absolutely."

Miriam shook her head as she said, "It was just a few words exchanged, you two, and anyways, he has family who goes to my church, so it's out of the question. I don't need that kind of drama in my work life."

"Well, bummer," Lucy said. "I'd been thinking about setting the two of you up. He and Forrest have been teaching a class together, some hybrid course about environmental literature, and we've grown fond of him."

"Sorry, girls, but don't worry about me. I'm making peace with my spinsterhood. Even if this Boone was a possibility, I'm sure my collar and random people calling me 'Mother' on the street would scare him off."

Edith said, "Everything would be so much easier if we were lesbians. Then we wouldn't have to worry about not scaring off men. They scare so damn easily. It's one of the great regrets of my life."

Miriam had a hard time not laughing at the beleaguered look on Edith's face as she bemoaned her heterosexuality. Instead of laughing, she simply said, "You would have made a great lesbian."

"I really would have."

Lucy and Miriam smiled at each other as Edith went to open the door. It was time to rejoin the party.

As they walked into the adjoining room, they came across Porter, Forrest, and Boone. Forming a little circle in the living room, they were seated with beers in hand and heaping plates of lasagna. As they passed, Forrest grabbed Lucy around the waist, hugging her to his side, and said, "You girls hiding from the party?"

Edith, sighing deeply, responded before Lucy, "Just regretting our straightness and the necessity to deal romantically with the opposite sex."

Forrest raised an eyebrow at Lucy.

She smiled innocently and said, "Yes. Something like that."

Shrugging, he didn't seem too concerned as he released her, and the three women headed to the kitchen to finally eat.

As Miriam passed by, she permitted herself a glance at Boone. Were his eyes really as identical to Miss Rubie's as Miriam suspected? What she saw in those eyes shocked her.

His gaze was locked on her collar, and the corners of his eyes had narrowed in a way that looked decidedly unpleasant. Miriam had seen many reactions to her collar over the years. Surprise, curiosity, disappointment, a subtle raising of some barrier people were compelled to keep between themselves and the clergy. But this was different. He looked angry, the color drained from his cheeks.

Within moments of their eyes meeting, Boone looked back to Porter, commenting on which team he thought most likely to win March Madness that year. Miriam followed Lucy and Edith into the kitchen. As she went, she thought to herself that there was some merit to what Edith had said. Men really were a pain in the ass.

#

Boone set his half-eaten meal to the side, no longer hungry. As the conversation around basketball wound down, Boone leaned closer to Porter and Forrest. "So who is the curly-haired woman with Lucy?"

Porter said, "I'm surprised you don't know her. That's Mother Miriam. She and your grandmother are thick as thieves."

"As in Mother Miriam of Trinity Episcopal?"

Porter answered, "That's the one."

Forrest said, "She and Lucy have been best friends since college."

Boone took in the information, letting the pieces fall into place. During his time in Paducah, he'd heard of Mother Miriam from their various shared acquaintances. And his grandmother did indeed love the woman, talking about her like she was God's gift to Western Kentucky. Between Boone's avoidance of all things religious and his hermit tendencies, he'd managed to avoid meeting her.

Until now. But no matter. Whatever interest her pretty face and easy conversation had stirred, Boone would simply extinguish like a fire after the last marshmallow was roasted.

After all, he'd happily avoided interacting with anyone who worked for a church for well over fifteen years. Why stop now?

Chapter 4

Boone walked towards the house heading back from the barn. After the party, he headed home to do a few chores before bedtime.

Boone was really more of a plant man, but he and Rubie kept a few animals on the place they butchered for fresh, organic meat. He'd just finished checking on the cows, a pig, and the chickens when he walked into the kitchen to find Rubie sipping on something steaming from a mug.

"What are you doing awake, Grandma?" Boone asked as he kissed the top of her head, the frizzy hairs tickling his nose. He walked over to the olive green stove, one of the first purchases his grandparents had made after they said "I do" in 1958, and lit the burner beneath the tea kettle. He had no idea how the Magic Chef gas range was still working, but he suspected Rubie's stubbornness had something to do with its longevity.

Really, the kitchen looked like it should be on exhibit in a museum. The lower cabinet had no doors, instead shuttered by red-and-white gingham curtains. Rubie would make new curtains for the cabinets about once every decade so it always looked clean and crisp.

The uppers were just open shelves lined with Rubie's dishware, mixing bowls, and tea sets collected over the past sixty years. She'd always been attracted to prints and patterns, so everything was colorful and cheery, nothing elegant or understated about their farmhouse. It was Boone's favorite room in the old house.

Rubie said, "My tummy wasn't wanting to let me sleep tonight, so I'm sipping on a cup of warm milk."

"What has your tummy upset?"

She took another sip. "Oh, probably the two convenience store burritos I ate for dinner."

Boone closed his eyes and shook his head. "This is why I can't leave you home alone, Grandma."

She just grinned at him mischievously, and he went ahead and smiled back. She really was too old to change her ways, now. But goodness, Boone was pretty sure that even he was too old for convenience store burritos.

"Enough about my stomach and abysmal eating habits. How was the party?"

The image of a smiling face framed by the glow of flames flashed into Boone's mind. She'd been kind and smart and had made him want to tell her things, things he generally kept to himself. Boone was still in shock that he'd been fooled by her, that in reality, the person he'd confided in was a minister.

Since throwing off his cap at high school graduation, Boone had kept the promise he made to Travis that hot, sticky night at church camp, the promise to shun any organization that treated his brother like he was broken. Boone left his parent's house and never looked back, putting as much distance between himself and religion as was possible.

The only religious people he ever trusted were his grandparents, but their faith was different. Unlike most of the people Boone had known through his childhood, their faith didn't demand they hate people. His grandparents had always accepted Travis just as he was, never trying to change him, never asking him to hide who he was to make other people more comfortable, and they'd made their home available as much as possible, thinking up any excuse they could to have the boys come stay with them.

Boone would never understand how someone as close-minded and sanctimonious as his father had come from parents as gentle as his grandfather or as radically accepting as his grandmother.

But despite Boone's trust in his grandparents, he still distrusted religion. This was especially true for anyone who became part of the clergy, who devoted their entire career to churches. Growing up, he'd had some significant run-ins with the hell-fire-and-brimstone ministers his parents followed. Regardless of whatever prejudices Boone might harbor, he'd heard his grandmother sing the praises of Mother Miriam since she'd arrived. If he didn't tell Rubie he'd met Mother Miriam, someone else was sure to.

"It was a fine night. Nice seeing Forrest and Lucy so happy." He opened the doors to the antique hutch where Rubie kept the teas and coffees, grabbing a bag of Sleepy-time tea. Turning around, he continued, "And I met that Mother Miriam of yours. Turns out, she's Lucy's best friend from college."

Looking up from squeezing honey into a teacup, Boone saw his grandmother perk up.

"Oh Boone, isn't she just divine? She's the first rector we've had who doesn't take that prissy Evelyn Dougherty's opinion over mine at every Altar Guild meeting. And she doesn't seem to care who she offends. She just gets up in that pulpit and talks about justice and love and…oh, I don't know what all. She's just brave. That's all I know."

Boone reached into the fridge, another olive green appliance from a bygone era, and said, "I don't know about all of that." Seeing Rubie squint in disapproval, Boone added, "But she did seem nice."

On these words, Boone noticed a gleam in Rubie's eyes that he both recognized and feared.

"Don't go there, Grandma. It isn't going to happen."

She set her mug down a little too hard, milk sloshing out.

"But Boone, she's so pretty. You've got to admit that at least."

"She isn't awful to look at." Boone inwardly cringed at the understatement. Before seeing the collar, he would have happily stared at her curl-wreathed face for hours. "But she's clergy, Grandma. So it's a hard pass."

Slumping her shoulders, Rubie replied, "I can hardly blame you, seeing as how a fair chunk of them are assholes."

As if trying to bleep out his grandmother's profanity, the tea kettle chose that moment to squeal. Boone shook his head and grinned, pouring the steaming water over his tea bag and honey.

As he sat down with his cup, Rubie reached across the table and squeezed his forearm. She said, "If you can't ask out my Mother Miriam, you can at least go out with one of those nice girls on Matchables."

"How do you know they're nice?"

"I've always been an optimist."

Boone thought about how Rubie wanted him to go on a date, any date. And he thought about all the times she'd gone out of her way to bring a smile to two miserable little boys who only found love in her old farmhouse.

Taking a sip of tea and grimacing from the burn of the hot liquid, Boone said, "Okay, Grandma. I'll set up a date with one of those nice girls."

Chapter 5

Miriam sat at a round table in the church's fellowship hall staring at the crumbs left on her plate from an almond cookie. She hadn't been hungry. She'd only eaten the cookie to break up the monotony of the Altar Guild meeting, but now she wondered how inappropriate it would be to press on the crumbs with her finger and lick them off, perhaps noisily.

The Altar Guild held their meetings on the third Sunday afternoon of each month, which also happened to be the week Miriam was always slotted to preach. Unfortunately, this meant that she was usually spent by the time she arrived to discuss floral arrangements, the conditions of various banners, and which fine citizen of Paducah, Kentucky, was fornicating with which fellow fine (and oftentimes married) Paducahan.

Apparently, the citizenry of Paducah was on their best behavior, because it was a particularly boring meeting. Maybe it was just too cold this winter to go fornicating or to find people with whom to fornicate. Miriam wouldn't know. She hadn't been in the fornicating business for quite some time.

Miriam decided to damn decorum and was licking crumbs off the tip of her finger when none other than Rubie Rutledge came up and took the seat next to her. Ever since meeting Rubie's grandson, she'd been curious to see Miss Rubie, to compare her to the face Miriam had seen across the fire pit. Also, there was the simple fact that in a profession where one was strictly forbidden to have favorites, Miss Rubie was Mother Miriam's favorite.

In a voice shaky with age, Rubie said, "If fingers weren't made for collecting cookie crumbs, I have no idea why we have them. Well, except for holding a cigarette, but the damned doctors haven't allowed me to do that in decades."

Miriam smiled as she said, "Miss Rubie, you caught me being unladylike."

Rubie's eyes glinted conspiratorially. "All my favorite people just so happen to be unladylike. Besides, I can think of few things less ladylike than you wearing that collar."

Miriam guffawed at Rubie's cheek. Rubie remembered the days when women wouldn't even dare to dream of ordination in the church. Rubie had watched the tides change and had supported every female member of the clergy who had come through Paducah's pulpit for the past fifty years. The same couldn't be said for all members of Trinity.

And Rubie was the sort who would lick the plate without thinking twice about whose sensibilities she might offend. Really, she was the most unlikely person to be a member of an Altar Guild, a group that tended to attract the primmer members. While the other ladies wore pearls, kitten heels, and cardigans in muted tones,

Rubie was sporting paisley-printed pants in shades of blue, a floral satin top that was two sizes too big, and costume jewelry. Her hair was frizzy and wild but still oddly charming. She always gave the impression that a strong northern wind had just blown her into whatever meeting or church service was in session.

"The jello salad was extra yummy, Rubie. The green kind is my second favorite." After three years of full-time ministry, Miriam was an expert on potluck fare. Jello salad was a dish with Cool Whip, jello powder mixes, and various nuts and fruits depending on the flavor. In any other location on earth, it would be placed on the dessert table. But in the American South (or adjacent-south as Miriam liked to call Kentucky), jello salad was a side dish sitting right alongside green bean casserole and potato salad. After all, the word "salad" was in its name.

Rubie was the master of jello salad, and few church functions passed without her adding a bowl of pink or orange or green "salad" to the table. As far as Rubie was concerned, its place on the table was just as valid as any vegetable. And since she made it with so much love and joy of life, who could help but enjoy it?

"Next time, I'll make the orange one." Rubie winked as she made the promise. She knew it was Miriam's favorite.

Miriam said, "It has been far too long since we've had the chance to talk. What is going on in your world, Miss Rubie?"

Rubie's hand shook almost imperceptibly as she raised a cup of coffee to her lips. After swallowing a sip, she said, "Well, just this past week, I learned how to use Matchables and I made a lesbian friend."

It was fortunate Miriam had not joined Rubie in sipping on coffee. The contents surely would've spewed across the table.

Miriam knew what Matchables was. Every single person under the age of fifty knew what Matchables was, and most had probably tried the dating app. Miriam had considered it. However, the fear of anyone even loosely connected to the church seeing her on a dating website made Miriam tug at her collar. What Miriam couldn't figure out was why a woman in her 80s was using Matchables and how a lesbian friend figured into the equation.

Rubie's eyes sparkled. She was clearly relishing the shock she'd caused.

"You young people get to be young in such fun times - dating at the tip of your fingers, and people able to be open about who they are. I hope you're enjoying it, eating up every bit of life, Mother Miriam. Have you tried out Matchables? Ooh, and are you a lesbian? If you are, I have the nicest young lady friend for you."

Miriam wished she could rewind and play back the conversation at half speed.

"Um, no on all accounts. Not on Matchables. Not a lesbian."

"That's too bad."

Rubies shoulders slumped an inch.

"Too bad I'm not on Matchables? Or too bad I'm not a lesbian?"

"Both."

Miriam wished, not for the first time, she could convince Edith to come to some church event just so she could meet Rubie. Truly, she would find her soul sister from another era in the woman.

The coffee cup rose again to Rubie's lips, its rim now stained with her Avon lipstick. She continued, "But really, you can only fix one of those."

"How's that?"

"Well, you can join Matchables. Hyacinth and the lesbian librarian and I can get you set up on there if you'd like?" Rubie's voice brightened at the prospect.

Miriam groped in her mind for some way to make sure this suggestion never materialized. After a considerable amount of sputtering, Miriam managed to croak, "I'll get back to you on that."

Ever since Friday night's engagement party, Miriam had been thinking of Boone. Not of his eyes or towering build or Scottish laird-ness. Well, only a little about those things. No, mostly she was thinking about some of the things Lucy had told her about Forrest's friend later in the evening. How he was a horticulture professor who focused on sustainability and protecting native species. How he was oddly literary in his outlook, and that is why he and Forrest had bonded and built their unique course. How Forrest always marveled at how Boone, with his perpetually muddy boots and work-roughened hands, could pull out a Walt Whitman or John Muir quote at a moment's notice.

Miriam was in the process of making an old idea of hers into reality, and she felt Boone might be a piece in the puzzle for how to best proceed. She'd been wondering how she could teach her congregants to care for creation, their most fundamental duty. And who better to add to this conversation than a local conservationist? According to Lucy, Boone had a reputation within the Paducah community. As a professor in the Agriculture Department at Paducah State University, he regularly promoted environmental causes in the local news. Miriam would love to hear Boone Rutledge speak on creation care.

Of course, she hadn't forgotten the odd look on Boone's face when he'd spotted her collar, but she was hopeful that her eyes had deceived her, that what she'd seen in him was not hatred or distrust but simply shock that the marshmallow enthusiast was a woman of the cloth, so to speak.

Regardless, Miriam was willing to take a chance to see if her plan might work. Leaning towards Rubie, Miriam whispered, "I have a question for you, Miss Rubie."

"Yes, ma'am."

"I want to do a class on what the Bible has to say about our responsibility to care for the environment and how that relates to climate change and pollution and the general mess we have made of things."

"I'd go to that class," Rubie said as she patted Miriam's hand.

"Good. Well, what I was wondering was if your grandson might be willing to come speak to the class about the impact climate change and pollution are having on the environment here in Kentucky and ways we can lessen our impact."

Rubie patted Miriam's hand again, this time to soften a blow.

"That is a wonderful idea, and Boone would be perfect for it. I'm biased, of course, but no one knows more about what you're talking about than my Boone. But I'm afraid not even I could talk him into it. He'd almost certainly say no."

"Why?" Miriam was not one to take no for an answer without making an effort at persuasion first. Maybe if she knew why, she could better hone her plan of attack.

"Oh, well, because he has sworn to never step within ten feet of a church door ever again in his life."

"Oh." Miriam leaned back in her chair and digested the information. "That's easy. We'll hold it somewhere else. The library or the community center."

"But that's not all, dear." Rubie wore a pained expression like she was about to tell Miriam she should try wearing deodorant.

"What else is there?"

"Now Miriam, please don't take offense at this."

Rubie's patting of Miriam's hand was edging towards frantic.

"Okay?"

"But Boone also considers all members of the clergy, regardless of denomination or theological beliefs or anything really,..."

"Yes?"

"Well, he hates every last one of you."

Apparently, Miriam had not misread his look.

"Oh."

Miriam chewed the inside of her cheek, processing this information. It was rare for Miriam to meet someone she couldn't convince to come around to her side. But this time, she might've met her match. She said, "I don't suppose there is anything I could do to change his mind?"

Rubie tilted her head sympathetically. "I wish there was, Mother Miriam. And I assure you, if there is a minister out there who could change his mind, it's you. But I just don't know if it's possible, dear. I'm afraid he has had a few run-ins with the worst sorts of ministers, and I'm not sure what it would take for him to decide you aren't all rotten."

Miriam sighed. Few could do more damage than ministers, and she'd counseled many parishioners through old traumas acquired at the hands of churches and their leaders. Miriam wondered what Boone's wounds were that they cut so deep. And what would it take to change his mind, if not about all ministers, at least about her?

Chapter 6

"And so it was against this backdrop of industrialization that Whitman worshiped nature down to the individual leaves of grass."

Boone sat behind the desk at the front of the lecture hall listening to Forrest piggyback off the lecture Boone had just delivered on the effects of industrialization on plant life in North America. It was his final class for the week, and then he could head home for a couple of hours in the greenhouse before heading out again.

"If Dr. Rutledge doesn't have anything to add, I think we'll leave it there for today."

Boone, standing up and stretching, said, "Nope, I'm good."

"In that case, have a fantastic weekend."

As the class dismissed, several students came up to ask Boone or Forrest followup questions. It took about ten minutes before they could finally pack their briefcases.

"Another successful class. We make a good team," Boone said as he slid his notes into place.

"Yes, I couldn't be happier with how this course is going. Thanks for being willing to do something out of the box."

"You don't have to thank me. It's nice to get out of Morris every once in a while."

Morris Hall housed the Agriculture Department, Boone's second home for the past few years. He'd been teaching at a university further South after he earned his Ph.D., but when a position opened up at PSU, he'd jumped on it. Although Grandma Rubie was in good shape, he knew it wouldn't last forever. He'd always known he'd eventually move to the farm to be with her.

The two men walked out of the lecture hall to the central mall of the PSU campus, the early-February air so cold it shocked Boone's lungs. Regardless, the campus was gorgeous. Where there weren't sidewalks or old, Georgian-style buildings, PSU's campus was covered in trees as old or older than the university, which had just celebrated its centennial a few years ago. At this point of the year, the trees were bare, their gray-brown branches criss-crossing above Boone and Forrest, creating a dramatic maze against the gray sky.

As if by rote, both men turned left at the water-fountain that stood in the middle of campus with a bronze bulldog hunched at the top. An afternoon this cold desperately needed kiosk coffee, and everyone at PSU knew the kiosk by the campus center had the strongest brew. Forrest's polished leather loafers and Boone's dusty work boots turned in unison like a practiced marching band.

"Well," Forrest said, "what are your big plans this weekend?"

Usually when Boone was asked about his weekend, his answer involved nothing more titillating than working in his greenhouse and grading papers. But this weekend was different. Boone felt the slightest blush rising, and he damned his ruddy complexion. Fixing his gaze on the white, peeling bark of a sycamore opposite Forrest's direction, Boone shrugged and said, "Oh, nothing too exciting."

Boone considered these words to be perfectly true. His plans for the weekend weren't exciting. They were mortifying.

Forrest, observant as ever, said, "Funny, because I'm about to marry a blusher, and she usually doesn't turn the color you just turned over unexciting plans."

"Yeah, well, my plans for this weekend happen to be absolutely ridiculous. I don't know why I ever agreed to them, and I really just want to spend the next two days documenting growth rates in several plants I'm trying to propagate. That and grading the stack of 50 papers written by farmers' sons trying to describe the state of soil in Kentucky farming land. Spoiler alert: it's bad." Stress had the unfortunate effect of making Boone even more surly than usual.

The two arrived at the kiosk and placed their order. Then, Forrest continued, "But instead of measuring plants and grading papers, you are..." Forrest left the sentence hanging in mid-air, waiting for Boone to fess up.

"Instead..." Boone ran a hand down his beard. "Instead, I will be going on a date with some complete stranger I met through a dating website my grandmother, her best friend, and a public librarian signed me up for."

Forrest started laughing. Boone stared at him unamused.

"Forrest, if you don't stop laughing, I'm going to seriously question our friendship."

The laughter didn't even slow down, not even for the barista to hand them their coffees.

"I'm sorry, Boone. It's just your grandmother? A fellow senior citizen? And a librarian?"

"A lesbian librarian, to be precise. Not that it matters, except that Grandma really wishes she could set us up."

Forrest wiped at an eye while taking a deep, calming breath.

"So, a little observation here; you don't seem thrilled about this date. Tell me why exactly you're going. Surely, two old ladies and a librarian aren't running your profile and accepting requests, are they? You could just shut it down."

Boone was at a loss for words. Why hadn't he canceled the profile the first night? And why was he meeting @catsandcoffeegirl at the local bar for drinks that evening? He said, "Thankfully, they haven't logged onto my account since the initial set up...that I know of. I honestly don't know why I didn't cancel it right away. It's just..."

"It's just maybe it wouldn't be so bad to meet someone?"

Boone shrugged. "Maybe."

"You know, if you're interested in dating, Luce and I could set you up with her best friend, Miriam. You seemed to hit it off last month around the fire pit at the engagement party."

Boone took a long sip of his coffee, buying himself time to formulate a reply. All he came up with was, "She just isn't my type."

Nope. Tall and slender with thick, curly, chestnut hair framing a face that always seemed to be smiling wasn't his type. Chocolaty brown eyes that warmed with nostalgia at the mention of the *Farmer's Almanac* certainly wasn't his type. A gorgeous woman bearing Grandma Rubie's stamp of approval - not his type.

Boone sighed. It was a damn shame she was a minister.

As they arrived at Forrest's building and said goodbye, Forrest insisted he wanted all the juicy details come Monday.

Boone said, "Juicy? You might want to lower your expectations."

"Keep your face always toward the sunshine, and shadows will fall..."

The door closed on Forrest before he could finish the Walt Whitman quote. Pretty sure he'd gotten the point, Boone headed to Morris Hall.

Chapter 7

Several hours after parting ways with Forrest, Boone sat across from @catsandcoffcegirl in a cafe housed in a narrow stone building. The structure had been erected around the time Ulysses Grant was sitting on Paducah's stretch of the Ohio River waiting to make his move.

Boone enjoyed the atmosphere of the restaurant, and as he waited for his food, the smells of garlic and lemon and wine-laced sauces made his mouth water. Guiltily, Boone wished he was sharing the experience with someone who shared more common interests with him or who, at the very least, talked less.

"So that's when I decided George really did have to be neutered despite my misgivings. I mean, the smell. And the urine on the walls. It was a lot of urine. Urine everywhere."

Boone tried to focus on the pleasant smells in the restaurant. He tried not to listen so much that he actually pictured what she was saying but still enough that he could administer the occasional "hmm" or "I see." He went with a slightly drawn-out "hmm" this time.

"I mean, he had the potential to be a really great stud - a real money maker. He has dramatic lynx ears that Maine Coon fans go ga-ga over, but when he sprayed my Anthropologie curtains, well that was snip-snip for him."

Boone clenched as she made a scissor motion with her hands.

It was the Matchable app and its ridiculous notification sound that was to blame for his being here listening to stories about cats and flagrant urination. He and Rubie had been sitting in the living room passing a quiet Tuesday evening - Boone reading the newest issue of the *American Journal of Ecology and Viticulture* while Rubie read *Fried Green Tomatoes* for what had to be the hundredth time - when Boone's phone started twittering in what he could only assume was a nauseating impression of lovebird mating calls. It was the Matchables notification alert, and Rubie had already developed a Pavlovian response to its chirping. Within seconds, she was looking over his shoulder gushing at the pretty face in the photo while dictating his response. Yes, he would love to meet that Friday night. Rubie had tried her hardest to convince him to schedule the date for Saturday evening, Valentine's Day. She'd found out fairly quickly that a first date on Valentine's Day was the line Boone wouldn't cross. So Friday the 13th it was.

Scheduling a date with one's grandmother peering over one's shoulder wasn't the most auspicious way to start a relationship, so Boone figured he shouldn't be surprised that the evening was going so wretchedly slow. Finally, the waiter headed towards their table balancing a tray of food. Boone's stomach grumbled, and he hoped it wasn't audible from across the table. However, on the bright side, she didn't seem to be squeamish about bodily functions.

The waiter laid out the meal, and Boone picked up his fork and knife, ready to dive into the juicy Parmesan chicken and pasta that might just resurrect the evening.

"Unfortunately, after his procedure, George got an infection where they removed his testicles. Thank God for antibiotics, right?"

Boone set down his utensils, lifted the glass of Chardonnay to his lips, said an extra-long "mmh-hmm," and took a sizable gulp.

Just then, he heard a familiar laugh coming from the bar. It wasn't shrill or inappropriately loud or off-putting. It was just joyful, and it tugged at him. Turning, he saw sitting at the bar Forrest's fiance, Lucy, the chair of the English Department, Dr. Edith Rose, and next to them, the unmistakable curls of Mother Miriam Howatch. She was laughing along with Lucy, probably at something outlandish Edith had said, and he could see her face in profile looking happy and confident and graceful. He had no idea how she could convey so much while sitting with a few friends at a bar, but he saw it all in her.

Her collar was missing. She still wore black, but it was a simple black sweater, black slacks, and, surprisingly, red flats. In the dim lights of the restaurant against the raw stone backdrop of the walls, she cut a striking figure.

Boone picked up his knife again, determined to eat and enjoy his meal regardless of whatever George-themed stories might follow. The evening must truly be abysmal if he was being struck dumb by a woman with the honorific of "Mother." Reminding himself of her true identity, Boone swirled pasta onto his fork and did not glance back towards the bar for the remainder of the evening. Mostly.

***

Miriam, Lucy, and Edith usually had their girls' nights at one of their homes, and it rarely involved anything more elaborate than microwaveable popcorn, wine, and a movie. At most, Lucy would add baked goods. But tonight was special.

Scrolling on her phone, Edith said, "So if we're celebrating your birthday on none other than the day before Valentine's, that makes you Aquarius, right?"

Miriam said, "Yes, but I don't know much about my sign. Are Aquarius people charming and kind and unnaturally intelligent?"

After a few taps on her phone, Edith said, "Try rebellious, eccentric, and sporting a nonconformist attitude."

Lucy chimed in, "That sounds about right."

Miriam guffawed, "I'm a minister. How much more conformist could I be?"

Lucy just grinned. "But your parents are agnostic."

"There is that."

"And you hardly manage to get through a single sermon without stepping on some toes," Lucy added. She knew Miriam far too well.

Edith said, "I love stepping on toes. Maybe I should've been a minister."

Lucy, who had worked in the English Department with Edith for many years, just patted her hand and said, "Don't worry, Edith. You manage to step on lots of toes all the time."

As Miriam laughed, she felt the most peculiar sense that someone was looking at her. Looking across the dining room, her eyes scanned countless couples. Turning thirty-two while single the day before Valentine's Day was adding insult to injury. Judging the room, Paducah was chock full of happy couples getting a jump-start on their romantic weekends. Her eyes landed on a man who seemed in the process of turning back towards his date, and it only took Miriam a few seconds to identify the auburn hair, broad shoulders, and (she leaned over a smidge for a better look) muddy boots as belonging to Boone Rutledge. Well, even if he'd been looking at her, it was probably just to register dislike.

Lucy, always perceptive, followed Miriam's gaze. When Lucy turned back, she was grinning. "Looks like somebody managed to get Swooney Boonie on a date."

Miriam nearly spit out wine. Swallowing hard, she croaked, "Swooney Boonie?"

Edith laid down her phone and said, "Oh, yeah. That's the nickname we gave him in the English Department when all the female students started lingering after class to ask him their most pressing questions instead of asking Forrest. I'm pretty sure Boone loves having his own nickname."

Lucy said, "I'm pretty sure he does not. But Forrest loves getting a break from the attention."

Miriam rolled her eyes and said, "Boone Rutledge doesn't strike me as the type who would enjoy being called Swooney. Or Boonie, for that matter."

Lucy was laughing. "It's amazing he puts up with all of you." Lucy had only recently left her position as the English Department secretary, but she spoke with fondness even as she shook her head.

Just then, the waiter brought the three women the pizza they were sharing. Written out in pepperoni on top of the bubbling cheese was the number "32."

Miriam grinned and looked at Lucy. "This was your doing, wasn't it?"

Lucy only shrugged, but it was just the type of thoughtful gesture she was known for.

As they dug into their pizza, Miriam's thoughts annoyingly returned to Boone Rutledge. She said, "Can you believe that even on a date, he's wearing old muddy boots?"

Edith pulled at the slice of pizza she'd bitten into, a string of cheese refusing to break. Finally getting it unattached, she said, "It's sort of endearing, isn't it? In a stray dog sort of way."

Miriam gasped, "Dr. Edith Rose doesn't use the word 'endearing.'"

"True enough," Edith said. "Except for people in my inner circle. And he has sort of wiggled his way into our department."

Edith was right. She was capable of great affection and loyalty even if only for a small circle of people. Miriam was glad to be among the chosen few.

Lucy said, "I do wonder what the story is behind the date. Forrest hasn't mentioned Boone seeing anyone."

Grumbling as she raised her slice of pizza to take another bite, Miriam said, "Can we talk about something, anything really, that doesn't involve the word 'date'."

Lucy and Edith looked at each other significantly. It was out of character for Miriam to sound so surly.

"What has you so anti-dating this evening?" Edith asked. She had more questions to add: "Is it dating in general? Or is it a particular person who happens to be on a date tonight in this same establishment?"

Suddenly, the wine hit Miriam, causing a warm flush to rise from the v-neck of her sweater to her hairline. Or at least, she wanted to believe it was the wine. "If you are referring to Swooney Booney over there, it has nothing to do with him. I barely know him, and we definitely aren't each other's type. I just mean dating in general. It has been years, ladies - years - since I went on a date."

Forgetting momentarily that she wasn't in her collar, Miriam raised her hand to her neck. When it wasn't there to pull on or readjust, her hand dropped to her lap. Miriam could see in both of her friends' faces their thoughts spinning. If she were guessing, she would say Lucy was carefully choosing words to make Miriam feel confident and secure, and Edith was probably formulating a plan to get Miriam laid within a week.

Ominously, Edith lit up first. "I know. After we're done here, we'll go back to one of our places and set up a dating profile for Miriam on that popular one, oh, what's the name? Matchees? Matcharoos?"

For the second time in a week, Miriam found herself in the uncomfortable position of trying to convince someone to not set her up an online dating profile. Swallowing the hot bite in her mouth too quickly, Miriam's eyes watered as she said, "Really, that isn't necessary. And it's Matchables."

"That's it," Lucy said, clapping her hand on the table. "Edith is right. That would be the perfect after-dinner activity."

Looking into their formidable faces, Miriam knew resistance was futile. Calling the bartender over, Miriam said "If we're doing this tonight, I'm going to need something a bit heavier."

***

An Uber pulled up to take the three tipsy women to Edith's house just as Miriam realized she needed to run to the lady's room. After a quick dash to the bathroom in the rear of the restaurant, Miriam rushed around a corner on her way back to the dining room. It was then that she ran straight into a wall of flannel.

Sputtering I'm-sorries over the emphatic I'm-sorries of the other person, Miriam looked up into icy blue eyes. She inhaled, realizing Swooney Boonie's hands were clutching her arms as if he'd been steadying her. Even more startling, her hands were lying on his broad chest, and she could feel taught muscles beneath her fingertips.

Having finally ceased saying his sorries, Boone said in surprise, "Mother Miriam? I believe that's what you go by."

Miriam flushed again, frustrated that wine always made her more blushable. "Just call me Miriam. Or Miri. Some people shorten it to Miri." She couldn't begin to imagine why she'd shared that detail. Only her closest friends called her Miri.

Then, silence fell over them as they stared at each other for a length of time that could only be attributed to considerable amounts of alcohol. It couldn't be anything else that kept their eyes glued to each other. Finally, Boone said, "Miri."

The single word broke the spell, and each took a step back as their hands dropped.

Miriam said, "I need to head out to the car. Lucy and Edith are waiting for me."

"Tell them I said hello." He hesitated for a moment and then said, "Do you all need a ride? Looks like you were helping yourself to a few of their generous beverages."

Miriam bristled at his tone. Was she not supposed to drink because she was clergy? When would people finally remember that Jesus's first miracle was creating a bottomless vat of wine? With an edge to her voice, she said, "No, don't worry. They cover the concept of a designated driver in the second year of seminary. We have a ride."

Boone squinted his ridiculously lovely eyes into a scowl. She'd hit her mark. But, goodness, men shouldn't have eyes that pretty.

Miriam was turning around to leave when, recklessly, the wine began manipulating the strings, turning her back around to face Boone once again. Then, the blasted wine spoke as if to test what Rubie had confided to Miriam that week: "I've been wanting to ask you if you'd ever consider coming and talking to my church about the environment, maybe some information on sustainable gardening, that sort of thing."

When Miriam first met Boone at the engagement party, she'd thought she spotted warmth beneath the surface of those ice-blue eyes, but if it had ever been there, she'd done a superb job of getting rid of it. He said, "No, I don't have time for talking to people who don't want to listen."

"What makes you so sure they don't want to listen to you?"

"Let's just say I've been around church folk plenty in my life. They only listen to people who keep them comfortable. I have no interest in being that guy."

Maybe it was her state of semi-drunkenness, but Miriam couldn't turn away from the brewing argument. Stepping towards him and looking up into his stern, set face, Miriam said, "It's just gardening tips, Boone. I'm not asking you to start a revolution."

Still quiet, Boone said in a tone for only her ears, "I said I don't want to have anything to do with your damned church."

Without a word, Miriam jerked around, walking toward the door.

"Miri."

Miriam paused, trying to decide if she should turn around or keep walking, hating that someone who clearly hated her had used her nickname. How could he be kin to Rubie?

"Yes?" she said, without looking back.

"I was just going to say watch out for yourself. The weather is supposed to start turning tonight. It's going to get ugly."

"Will do."

With that, she left, wondering why he cared how she got home or whether she watched for some winter storm or not. The heavy, solid wood door of the restaurant slammed behind her, muffling the sounds of the chattering diners as she crossed into the frigid night.

Her ride was waiting parked at the curb right in front of the doors. She climbed into the back seat, squeezing in next to Lucy. Taking a deep, fortifying breath, Miriam said, "Who's ready to make me look good online?"

Chapter 8

Boone left the same bedroom he and Travis had used throughout their childhood. While he usually slept peacefully in the room he still associated with safety, last night was the exception. He was almost looking forward to a few days snowed-in on the farm. Surely he'd shake off his run-in with Miriam after some good, old-fashioned isolation.

As it was, Boone had spent the night tossing and turning under the patchwork quilt made by his grandmother's hands. How could he both want to talk with someone and want to have nothing to do with them? Boone considered himself a simple man who was pretty content just playing in the dirt, but suddenly, he was confounded.

Walking downstairs into the kitchen, Boone looked over Rubie's shoulder to see what she was whisking so fiercely.

"Mmh. Cream of wheat?"

"You bet," she said. "Nothing like beating the clumps out of cream of wheat to get an old woman's joints loosened up in the morning."

"We wouldn't have chocolate chips to throw in there, would we?" Boone asked.

"Would your old grandma serve you Cream of Wheat without chocolate chips on Valentine's Day morning?" Rubie asked.

Boone had forgotten it was Valentine's Day. Hopefully, @catsandcoffeegirl wouldn't expect a message for the occasion. Admonishing himself to put the previous evening behind him and focus on what would be a busy day ahead as he continued to prep for the storm, Boon hugged Rubie's shoulders on his way to the coffee maker.

"Happy Valentine's Day to you, too, Grandma. I'm glad you did all of the grocery shopping yesterday afternoon. It has been drizzling for an hour, and it's freezing the second it lands. After a few hours of this, we're supposed to get heavy snow. We may not be leaving this farm for days."

Rubie took the pan off the flames and set it on an old, stained hot pad she'd crocheted years ago. She added a few generous scoops of brown sugar and a couple of pats of butter to the pot while continuing to stir. As she worked, she said, "Hyacinth and I each left with a cartload. We really put the bagging boy to work, but we should have everything we need to eat just fine for however long we're iced in."

Silently, Boone hoped Rubie had been reasonable in her shopping. Sometimes, their definitions of essential didn't line up, but he figured they wouldn't starve. Even if she'd bought Little Debbies instead of canned beans - a scenario that was firmly within the realm of possibilities - they wouldn't starve.

The two worked around the kitchen getting bowls, spoons, glasses of juice, and cups of coffee. Rubie poured the chocolate chips into a jadeite dish with scalloped edges. Boone couldn't figure out why they couldn't just pour the chocolate directly from the bag into their bowls, but he knew better than to ask.

As they sat down, Boone wanted to delay the inevitable questions about his date the previous evening, so he distracted her the best way he knew how: "Travis called this morning right as I was getting out of the shower."

Predictably, she lit up. "How are he and Paul?"

"Doing great. They just got the moving truck booked for the beginning of June."

Rubie scooped up a spoonful of cream of wheat with a chocolate chip perched on top. Before taking the bite, she said, "I can't believe they're going to only be three hours away."

"And they're already talking to an adoption agency in the area. Looks like they might be able to start the process soon after they settle in."

Rubie reached over and squeezed Boone's hand. "Can you imagine, Boone? A child in the family again."

Lifting a steaming cup of coffee to his nose and inhaling deeply, Boone admitted, "I really can't imagine it, Grandma. I've never been around kids."

"Well trust me, Boone, they're wonderful, and you're going to be a natural. You can teach 'em about growing plants and taking care of the animals. Yes, you'll make a fine uncle."

Just as Boone was getting comfortable with the conversation and almost forgetting about the previous evening, Rubie said, "Don't think I've forgotten last night was your date. I do expect a few details, Boone."

Despite preferring not to revert to the communication skills of his adolescent years, Boone groaned.

"And don't worry, Boonie," she assured. "I won't ask for all the details. I don't need to know if there was any kissing, hugging, groping,..."

"Alright. Fine. I'll talk."

Boone would do anything to end Rubie's list-making. She took a smug sip of her heavily sugared coffee.

"Go on, dear."

"She was a great gal if you don't mind talking about cats for a full two hours. And not just cats. Cat-mating rituals. Cat urination. Cat spaying procedures. Cat socializing. Cat everything."

Rubie straightened, saying firmly, "I have lots of friends who live with lots of cats..."

His gregarious, open-minded grandmother would be friends with the local cat ladies.

She continued, "And really, the stigma is unfair."

Boone stared blankly at Rubie. "She detailed the three-month process she used to train her cats to use the same toilet she uses."

"So there was no groping, I take it?"

"Perceptive, Grandma." Boone stood to clear away his dishes. Passing by her on the way to the sink, Boone squeezed her bony shoulder. "I'm sorry, Grandma."

She patted his hand and said, "It's okay, Boone. Maybe next time."

After his coffee cup and bowl were washed, dried, and put away, Boone headed out to the barn to feed the livestock. He left without telling his grandmother that he had seen a beautiful woman in the restaurant, one who didn't talk overly much about cats that he knew of. One to whom, if he were being honest, he'd been an ass. Boone could admit to deserving the bit of fight he'd gotten.

When she'd stepped towards him, Miriam had been flushed - whether from the wine or her anger at him, he wasn't sure which. Either way, she'd left an impression that stayed with him long after he'd parted ways with the minister. He couldn't recall the eye color of his actual date, but the fierce flecks of gold that dotted Miriam's eyes as she'd stood up to him were ingrained in his memory.

No, Boone kept the story of his little run-in with Miriam to himself, and as he opened the door to leave the house, he called back to his grandmother, "Maybe you're right, Grandma. Maybe next time."

***

"Today's weather is going to be a doozy. Watch out, Paducahans, for-"

Miriam's hand found the snooze button and hit it clumsily until the damned weatherman shut up.

A single strip of light glared through the window beneath the blinds. It was inconveniently placed directly at her eye-line, making her alcohol-pickled brain feel like it was undergoing a lobotomy. What had she been thinking drinking another two glasses of wine after they returned to her place last night? Oh, yes, it was to steel her nerves for creating a Matchables profile. Miriam slapped herself on the forehead at the memory and immediately regretted doing so.

Trinity Episcopal Church had a small cottage on their property that had only ever been used for the odd scholar in residence. However, when they hired Miriam, a single person with no children, they offered it to her. They were happy to have the home occupied, and she was happy for the short commute. Also, she loved being in the midst of Trinity's beauty.

Just like the church, the cottage was from another time. Built in a classic style with stone siding that matched the gray church, it was inconspicuously hidden away on the property behind the elaborately manicured grounds to the south of the church. Inside, it was all hardwood floors and vintage wallpaper that Miriam had personalized with art she'd picked up on her various adventures around the world, rugs in rich red and gold tones, bookshelves she'd built after watching YouTube videos, and furniture her parents dropped off when they'd downsized so they could travel uninhibited. Thankfully, they hadn't bought into the gaudiest trends of the 80s and 90s, so their furniture worked well in the cottage.

As charming as the place was, Miriam was not in the mood to enjoy it this morning. Instead, she rolled out of bed, stumbled to the kitchen while ricocheting from side to side down the hallway, and, finally, upon arrival, mixed up the hangover cure of choice for Miriam and her fellow seminary classmates: tomato juice mixed with pickle juice. The vinegary scent of the pickles made her gag even as it brought back memories of post-finals revelry. Seminary students were generally a well-behaved crowd until they were isolated among themselves with no outsiders to impress. Miriam choked down the repugnant concoction.

As the fog lifted, the quiet voice of Boone Rutledge telling her to essentially stay away intruded on her thoughts, as if the memory had been waiting at the periphery to reemerge as soon as the alcohol wore off. With the clarity that came with morning, Miriam heard the words with less hurt and more curiosity. What horrible thing had happened to Boone to make him so distrustful - to make him hate? Boone, a man who spoke sentimentally of his grandfather and was adored by his grandmother. It didn't fit that he would hate. It didn't fit unless something at some point had been seriously broken.

Part of Miriam wanted to sit down in the quiet of her kitchen and analyze his behavior, how he could ricochet from words shutting her off to seeming to care for her well-being. Unfortunately, Miriam didn't have time to ponder the mystery that was Boone Rutledge. She had a long list of stops to make.

Even though it was Saturday, Miriam had committed to delivering Valentine's Day baskets to the older members, mostly widows and widowers. Anytime jobs needed to be done that were exclusively for the elderly, Miriam was the first to volunteer. Simply put, she liked old people. They had good stories. She could listen for hours to them reminiscing about World War 2 and hiding under desks at school and how much a soda used to cost. Oddly enough, she also found the oldest members to be less critical than the middle-aged crowd. Maybe it was because they'd retired from their leadership positions in the church long ago, but they were content to let people be, Rubie Rutledge being the prime example.

After the unorthodox hangover cure, a steaming hot shower, and putting on her armor of a long-sleeved black shirt and crisp, white collar, Mother Miriam headed out into the freezing February morning.

Chapter 9

A few hours later, Miriam found herself wishing she hadn't cut off the weatherman before he delivered the full forecast.

It was nearing two o'clock when she pulled into the Rutledge driveway going only about ten miles an hour. Her small, compact car had slipped once about a mile back, and she'd feared getting stuck in a ditch on the rarely-trod rural road. Thankfully, she'd been able to regain control before the worst had happened.

She begrudgingly admitted to herself that saving the most rural, middle-of-nowhere members for last had been a grave error. The thing was, Rubie was her favorite, and Miriam was a save-the-best-for-last kind of girl. Plus, Rubie was a talker, so she learned early in her time at Trinity to make Rubie the last stop or she would inevitably be scolded by other members for her tardiness.

In all the times Miriam had come out to visit Rubie or deliver something from the church, she'd never seen Boone. Of course, she was usually out on weekdays when he was busy at PSU. Odds were he'd be far too busy taking care of farm things to notice her presence this Saturday afternoon. Miriam had no idea what a person did to prepare a farm for snow, but, hopefully, it was time-consuming.

As she crept down the driveway, one side buttressed by a deep snow drift along the tree line, Miriam found it almost impossible to conceive that so much snow had fallen in a single morning. And unfortunately, before the snow had fallen, the region had been soaked by several hours of freezing rain. Having been preceded by a week of freezing temperatures, the wet, slushy mix froze quickly to the already-cold tree branches, sidewalks, and roads. Everything on the farm was glistening with a coat of ice as Miriam gingerly parked her car, but she couldn't appreciate the beauty because she was too worried about the drive home. Miriam reminded herself that she was a Northern girl, having spent most of her childhood in Northern Indiana. Driving bravely in wintry conditions was a cultural identifier.

Getting out of her car, Miriam grabbed the gift basket filled with chocolates and fruits and small crafts made by the church's children. She started walking towards the house, slipping once and barely catching herself with her one free hand. Before she proceeded, she picked up a couple of cards that had fallen out and shook the snow off of them, returning them wet and soggy to the basket. As she arrived at the front porch that stretched the full length of the old farmhouse, she paused to stare at the steps. Four steps. Four steps that glistened with ice. Four very slick steps.

Miriam desperately wanted to scoot up the steps backward on her hind end, but her pride would have none of it. Grabbing the equally frozen handrail in a death grip with her free hand, Miriam took one step at a time, looking very much like the geriatric church members she'd been visiting that morning.

Once Miriam made it to the porch, the weathered wood planks were relatively safe terrain. She loved the board and batten siding of the house, painted in a white as white as the snowy landscape. The door, though, was a sunny yellow that seemed out of place in the current scenery but perfectly fit the personality of the house's mistress. Miriam used the old brass knocker for two loud, decisive taps.

It didn't take Rubie long to answer. As the door opened, the smell of coffee and cinnamon made Miriam impulsively breathe deeper.

"Nice muumuu," Miriam said in greeting.

"Thank you, dear. I bought it on the island itself on my 50th wedding anniversary trip with Rupert." The red hibiscus print clashed jarringly with Rubie's fuzzy purple socks, blue fur-trimmed slippers, and pink housecoat. But clashing or not, her wrinkles rearranged into a grin of pure joy opened the door to Miriam. "Come in, my dear. Come in. You'll have to excuse my slippers. As you know, I'm usually far more put together."

Miriam seriously doubted any of the other church ladies had ever considered Rubie to be put together. Rubie continued, "But on a cold day like this, you just want to stay in your most comfy clothes. Right?"

"Absolutely."

Before Miriam knew it, she was sitting in a kitchen that looked like it should have museum ropes at the door. Miriam had been to Rubie's house many times, but it never failed to charm her anew. Sitting across from her, Rubie placed a cup of coffee so pale with cream it would be called a latte anywhere else. Miriam took a sip and let the warmth suffuse her cold body. She hadn't realized until that moment just how tense she'd become driving in the less-than-ideal conditions.

Rubie said, "So I'm assuming I'm not the first to receive one of these lovely baskets this Valentine's Day?"

Peeking over the rim of her cup, Miriam said, "You would be the twelfth."

"Oh dear," Rubie said. "You didn't go out to old man Jeffers's place, did you? The old pervert."

Miriam smiled. "Let's just say some members had their baskets left on their front porch. I've learned how to keep my ass as far out of reach as possible."

"I swear. Sometimes being older than dirt is such a relief. I can't remember the last time I had to evade unwanted attention. And believe me, I'm not complaining."

Miriam looked around the place, listening for another set of feet. Despite how rude he could be, Miriam was curious about what the laird looked like in his natural habitat. "You aren't alone today, are you?"

"No, no. Boone is just out in the greenhouse, probably making sure he has everything ready to withstand this storm. Sounds like we could be in for a stretch."

"Well, I'm sure he got his own Valentine's surprise last night. His date looked lovely, and they seemed to be having the most wonderful time." Miriam had no idea what had possessed her to say such a thing. Had they seemed like they were having a good time? Did Boone Rutledge ever seem like he was having a good time? All he had ever offered in front of her were grunts and frowns and the occasional scowl. Except for that time at the party. That one time. Looking up from swirling her coffee, Miriam registered the surprise on Rubie's face.

Rubie said, "How did you know about his date?"

"I was at the same restaurant celebrating my birthday with a couple of friends."

"How odd Boone didn't tell me."

Miriam was just about to comment that, really, it wasn't that odd, that she would hardly stand out to him, when she heard footfalls coming towards the kitchen. Miriam's hearing wasn't above average, but she could swear she heard dirt sifting off of boots as the person came closer.

Then, a low voice from the hallway said, "What did I not tell you, Grandma?"

***

Boone was surprised to hear his grandmother talking. She might be old, but she was far from senile. She'd yet to start having conversations with invisible people, but, surely, no fool would be out in this weather.

As he came into the kitchen asking Rubie what he'd forgotten to tell her, he froze in his tracks. There, sitting at the old farmhouse table was a pink-cheeked, red-nosed Mother Miriam. She cradled her coffee in both hands right beneath her chin, greedy to collect what warmth she could from the steaming liquid. Last night's sweater and jeans were gone, and she was back in the dog collar.

Boone spoke the first words that entered his mind, not pausing to consider how one treats a guest or how short he'd been with her the night before or how quickly she'd exited the cafe on account of him. "What the hell are you doing out in this weather? I told you it was going to get nasty."

Miriam's eyes narrowed. "When I left this morning, it was just a drizzle."

"Yeah, a drizzle that has been accumulating into a layer of ice and then topped with a few feet of snow. As the weathermen predicted, I might add. So I go back to my original question: What the hell are you doing out in this?"

"I slipped a bit, but the salt trucks will be by in no time."

Boone looked like he might pop a blood vessel, but the volume of his voice still didn't rise. "Do you know where you are? Yes, the salt trucks will be on Interstate 24 in no time. But you, Mother Miriam, do not take Interstate 24 to leave our property. The road that runs by our property is Farm to Market Road 102978. Do you know when they get to FM 102978? My guess is late next week."

It wasn't until he'd played this trump card that he looked at Rubie. She was glaring at him with an expression unseen since childhood summers when he and Travis would forget to shut the screen door and let the flies in. Being the only Rutledge in the room who seemed to remember there was a guest in the house, Rubie turned solicitously to Miriam.

"I'm afraid my brute of a grandson is right. These roads will be impassable soon if they aren't already there."

Miriam's jaw worked as she processed what they were saying. In the silence, a loud cracking noise reverberated from somewhere outside, sounding like a gunshot. Miriam startled, sloshing coffee.

"What was that," she said to Rubie, ignoring Boone's existence.

In a moderately softer tone, Boone answered, "That was a tree limb snapping. They're getting heavy with ice. All the roads between here and town are canopied in trees. It won't be safe to drive them while limbs are coming down."

"Well, that's just ridiculous. I have to go home. I'm sure I can drive around a few limbs."

Boone ran a hand down his beard. "That isn't how storms like this work, Miri. It won't be a limb here and there. You could have a whole damned tree fall on you."

"Which means..." Rubie's hands clapped together as she spoke, "...that you absolutely must stay with us. Possibly for days."

Miriam's gaze darted between Rubie and Boone.

Boone shut his eyes in grimacing defeat as he said, "That is unfortunately true."

Rubie took Miriam's hands in her own, and faced her squarely. "Let me speak with less assholery. Really, Boone?" She spared a quick look at Boone and then returned her solicitous gaze to the minister who was now quite pale. "Here's the situation. I just went and bought enough food to feed a small army, not to mention all the winter greens Boone grows. We have firewood and plenty of blankets and shelves full of paperback romance novels from the past sixty years. Really, you could be stuck in far worse places. And I'm tickled pink to have another girl around for a few days. As you can see, Boonie here sometimes forgets his manners."

Boone rolled his eyes.

"Okay, Miss Rubie. If you feel it isn't safe."

"It's clearly not..." Boone stopped talking when both women sent glares as sharp as ice picks.

Turning from him, Rubie said, "It's really not safe, dear. And besides, we're going to have the best time."

Miriam smiled for the first time since Boone walked into the kitchen. The smile was most definitely not directed at him. Which was fine with him. He had no reciprocal smiles to give. How was it that he, Boone Rutledge, would be living under the same roof as an actual minister for only God knew how many days?

Miriam said, "I'll stay. But you have to let me help around here with the cooking and such."

As the two women discussed what should be for dinner that evening, Boone couldn't exit the kitchen fast enough.

Chapter 10

The events of the past hour couldn't possibly have happened. Miriam couldn't possibly have landed herself in this mess. Had she really just agreed to live under the same roof as Boone Rutledge for however long this ice took to melt?

Rubie turned to Miriam, her hands clutched beneath her chin like a child, and said, "Oh, goody. Let's go upstairs. You're going to need warmer clothes to get you through these next few days, especially if the power goes out like I suspect it will. I have the perfect idea."

Miriam followed Rubie to the narrow staircase with more than a little trepidation. She'd seen Rubie's eclectic taste in clothes, and it was a bit ostentatious for Miriam who was accustomed to black from head to toe.

The wood stairs creaked beneath Miriam's feet as she climbed behind Rubie. The tops of the stairs were painted red, and the front facings were white. The wall of the staircase was lined with plates in all varieties of floral patterns. It felt as though Rubie had spent the entirety of her sixty years in this house making sure no spot was neglected, no corner or hallway forgotten. Every wall was an opportunity to display a cherished collection of colorful crafts and antiques.

Once they reached the second floor, the scent of rose and lavender soaps wafted from the bathroom at the end of the short hallway. She could see a claw-foot bathtub with a faded, floral towel draped over one side. On each side of the hallway, two bedroom doors faced each other.

"Here, my room first," Rubie said.

As Miriam walked into the older woman's room, the smell was no longer only floral but, mixed in, was also leather and sawdust. Looking around, Miriam saw touches of the former Mr. Rutledge all around. Rupert. Rubie peppered his name into conversations regularly. Miriam wondered if Rubie had kept so many of his items out so that she wouldn't lose that faintly masculine scent in the room.

Rubie walked around the bed. It was an adjustable bed one would expect to see in a nursing home room, but Rubie had adorned it with a cheerful patchwork quilt and throw pillows that helped camouflage it into the homey space. Opening the door to a small closet, Rubie grabbed an old corduroy barn coat from inside.

"This was Rupert's, but he only used it on the coldest days, so it's still like new. That flimsy trench coat of yours isn't going to stand up half so well as this coat will."

Miriam took the article of clothing as Rubie handed it to her. Running her hands over the ridges of corderoy, Miriam said, "This isn't necessary, Rubie. I'll be fine." Even as Miriam said the words, she regretted the slight mistruth. It was an insubstantial thing she'd bought far more for its sophistication than for its ability to keep her warm. Continuing, she said, "And I'm sure Rupert's things mean a lot to you. I don't want to use them."

"His things do mean a lot to me, and so do you, so I'd say it all works out quite neatly."

Following the surprisingly spry steps of Rubie when she was on a mission, Miriam crossed the hallway into the opposite bedroom. Its walls were covered in white wallpaper with a thin, blue pinstripe and adorned with old snowshoes, antique fishing gear, and a collection of paint-by-number landscapes. Seeing Miriam's eyes take in the boyish room, Rubie said, "I used to spend my evenings doing paint-by-numbers back when they first became popular. I've always had the artistic temperament without the actual artistic talent, so that was my compromise."

"This room is charming," Miriam said.

"I decorated it when the boys were around ten, when I first started to realize they'd need to spend more time with us."

As Rubie spoke, Miriam walked up to a framed photograph sitting on the end table sandwiched between the two Jenny Lind twin beds. Two young boys stood, each with an arm draped over the other one's shoulder. One was in a plain blue t-shirt, and the other wore a button-up with geometric shapes in the neon colors so popular in the early nineties. Their cheeks were red from what Miriam guessed to be hours playing outside in the Kentucky summer humidity. Miriam was struck by how incredibly joyful the two looked side by side. Picking up the frame and bringing it close,

Miriam realized that the one in the t-shirt had the tell-tale eyes of Boone Rutledge.

"There's my boys." Rubie had walked up behind Miriam and was looking over her shoulder. "That was during the summer. They'd just gone fishing with Rupert and caught a good haul for me to fry up. They were beaming."

Miriam couldn't take her eyes off Boone. "Boone looks happy. I've never really seen him smile. At least not with his whole face."

Instantly, Miriam regretted having said anything. Here Miriam was insulting Rubie's beloved grandson after she'd opened her home to Miriam. Rubie didn't seem put out by it, though.

"Life has a way of beating a person up. But when Travis visits, we still get a few full-face smiles out of Boone."

"It seems like the boys spent a lot of their time here. I've never really heard you mention their parents."

Rubie took a deep breath. "Let's just say the boys begged to be here as much as possible, and sometimes it seemed their parents preferred to just look away, not see their sons. Not really."

Miriam was quiet, fearing she'd been too presumptuous bringing up the topic. But Rubie kept sharing.

"Rupert and I tried to raise our son to be a loving person, but he met that wife of his in college and seemed to change overnight. Suddenly, I was an embarrassment and nothing we did was good enough. Then the boys came along, and they thought Rupert and I hung the moon. That was bad enough, but then, well, the rest of the story isn't mine to tell."

Miriam gingerly placed the frame back in the space, lining up its edge against the faint dust line where it had stood. The rest of the story would answer so many questions, Miriam knew. Like why Boone never smiled. Miriam could almost imagine what an untethered smile would look like on Boone's mature, bearded face with eyes that were startling under any circumstances.

Rubie squeezed Miriam's shoulder. "I think you're beginning to thaw him out."

A snort escaped Miriam before she could compose herself. "Rubie, I just got a tongue-lashing from him. He hardly seems thawed out to me."

Waving her hand dismissively as she circled to the room's closet, Rubie said, "Oh, that just shows he cares whether or not you get stranded in a ditch and die of hypothermia. If it were any other minister, he probably would have offered a polite wave goodbye."

"So I should be happy he didn't quietly send me off to an icy death."

"Baby steps, Miriam. Sometimes you just gotta focus on baby steps."

Digging around in the closet, Rubie pulled out a few hangers from the very end.

"Here they are. These are old, thick flannel shirts the boys would wear over Christmas break back when they were string-bean teenagers. They should be just right for you." Shuffling some more, Rubie continued, "And here are some jeans Travis left behind years ago. He said he could never wear Wranglers in New York City. He's never bulked up the way Boone has."

Miriam took the offered clothes. Miriam didn't think "bulked up" was the correct phrase for what Boone's body had done since his adolescence. That phrase made Miriam think of men who had added thirty pounds or so after leaving their high school athletics behind. From what Miriam could tell, Boone's bulk was the muscles of a man who worked the land. If she were to run her hands over him, Miriam suspected she would find no unnecessary bulk.

"Are you coming?"

Miriam startled and blushed, realizing she'd been lost in thought as Rubie had made her way out into the hallway.

"Yes, I'll just use the bathroom to change. You're right. I'm not really dressed for this weather."

"Alright, dear. I'll be downstairs."

***

Boone sat in an empty stall in the barn trying to think of a few more tasks to do to delay reentry to the house. Unfortunately, the animals were all fed and warm, the greenhouse plants would surely die from over-watering if he headed that way again, and the weather made any tasks in the field untenable. The most sensible thing to do was to return to the warm house, get out the stack of papers his Introduction-to-Horticulture students had just turned in, and start grading. Boone liked to grade on the old buffalo plaid sofa in the living room with his feet propped on the coffee table. But last he'd seen, Mother Miriam was curled up on the wingback chair next to the sofa with one of Rubie's vast collection of paperback novels. Rubie's taste in books very much paralleled her taste in burritos: she was happy to buy them at a convenience store.

Just then, he heard the barn door open and a soft, feminine voice call his name.

"Boone? You in here?"

Boone briefly considered ducking down in the stall, but his pride wouldn't allow for hiding from people in his own damn barn. If he and Miriam were going to coexist on the same farm for who knew how many days, he would face her at some point whether or not he felt awkward about their previous encounters.

Standing straighter to crane his neck over the stall's gate, Boone said, "I'm in here."

Miriam caught his eye over the stall door and came over. She was bundled up in Grandpa's corduroy coat, the wooly collar flipped up around her ears, and wore a pair of jeans he was pretty sure Travis had left behind. Travis had always been skin and bones compared to Boone's brawny build, leaving people shocked to discover the boys were twins.

Peaking through the wool collar, Boone saw that she didn't have on her clergy shirt, but instead, she was wearing a thick flannel shirt in a red plaid. With a jolt of awareness, Boone recognized the shirt as one of his own, an old one from his adolescent days before his shoulders broadened and upped his shirts by two sizes.

In her new clothes, Miriam looked warm and earthy and at home in the barn. She smiled as she stepped onto the bottom slat of the gate to the stall, her arms crossing in front of her on the top slat.

"I'm here to tell you dinner will be ready in about five minutes." She looked around the barn, taking in the row of stalls and the hay loft in the back. "What are you up to out here? Doing farmer-type things, I suppose?"

"Farmer-type things?" Boone repeated.

"I really don't know anything about agriculture, so yeah, 'farmer-type things' is the best I can do."

"Yes, I guess I was doing farmer-type things. I added some pine shavings to the chicken coop floor to give them a little added insulation, brushed the horse, and fed the two cows we have right now."

"What are you up to now? Maybe I can help."

Boone looked down at the hay-covered floor and shuffled a boot until he found dirt. What was he supposed to tell her he was doing in an empty barn stall? Avoiding being alone with her? He finally decided vagueness was his best bet.

"Just cleaning up a bit. But I'm finished now."

"Well, I offered to help in the house, but Rubie is insisting that I rest after driving around in treacherous conditions - her words not mine. So I've been reading, and let me tell you what, Boone, your grandma has quite the book collection. I mean..." Miriam just shook her head, smiling. "I just read a book from the early 80s that only took about fifty pages to go all HBO on me."

There was a glimmer in her expression that told Boone she hadn't minded. Nothing about her joviality or the words she was saying matched what Boone was expecting from Mother Miriam, and she barely paused for breath.

"Of course, if someone were to ask me which of the old ladies in my church was most likely to own an archive of decades worth of Harlequin publications, I'd have picked Rubie."

"She was still pinching Grandpa's butt every time he walked by up until the end." Boone told the memory without embellishment. He was simply agreeing with Miriam's assessment of Rubie, but Miriam threw back her head in laughter, her short, curly hair mingling with the wool of her coat collar. Without a dog collar hiding her, Boone noticed how slender and smooth her neck was.

Miriam said, "That sounds exactly right. I know it's my job to try to push people to be better versions of themselves, but sometimes I just want to point to Rubie and tell everyone to try to be more like her. Less uptight and have a little fun."

Boone was used to side glances and skepticism when it came to his grandmother. For the prudish, Southern sensibilities of most Kentuckians, she was far too inelegant and open-minded and loud. Miriam's recognition of Rubie's deep, abiding goodness touched Boone. He wanted to say something kind in return, something affirming, but his tongue felt tied. Instead, he asked, "Are you going to finish the book, or were the first fifty pages too scandalous?"

"Oh, believe me, I'm going to finish it. That fragile schoolmarm from the east is going to win over the burly, crude Texas rancher who, underneath it all, is just a man needing love after the disfiguring injury he received on the battlefield. Yes, I'm going to read every last word."

The two of them started heading towards the front of the barn, wordlessly agreeing the five minutes were almost up.

Boone said, "Sounds pretty good. I might have to read it after you're finished."

Miriam turned, surprised, to look at him. Now surprising himself, Boone winked at her and grinned, but only with the left side of his mouth.

A smile slowly spreading across her face, Miriam said in astonishment, "The man makes jokes."

Boone pushed the door open, pressing his weight against it to move the snow that kept building up at the base. Miriam walked ahead of him towards the house. As Boone followed, he had the ominous feeling that given enough days and enough flannel shirts, he might just forget Miriam Howatch was a woman of the cloth.

Chapter 11

Boone opened the door for Miriam, his arm stretching out as he stepped to the side. Walking by him into the house, Miriam felt his proximity with an awareness that was unnerving.

Before going out to get Boone, Miriam had sat in the kitchen chatting with Rubie as she glazed a ham and peeled potatoes. Now, returning to the cheerful, cozy room, Miriam was inundated by the scent of ham and brown sugar in the air.

"I'm almost finished, kiddos. Just let me drain the potatoes and mash them, and then we'll be ready to sit down and eat."

Boone walked over to the oven and cracked the door open.

"That ham looks amazing, Grandma. And it's a good, practical idea. It'll work for breakfasts and in sandwiches."

Practical was not a word frequently associated with Rubie, and Miriam could almost hear Boone's relief at seeing that his grandmother had picked ham over dinosaur-shaped chicken nuggets or gummy worms.

Just as Boone was turning from the oven, Rubie opened the vintage refrigerator and pulled out an ornate glass bowl with a pedestal base. Immediately, Miriam recognized the contents of the bowl. It was the extra naughty cousin of jello salad, a potluck dish the people in the area called Pink Fluff. If Miriam remembered right from the cookbook their church had assembled for a fundraiser, Pink Fluff was mostly Cool Whip, canned cherry pie filling, and marshmallows.

Miriam lifted a hand to cover her mouth. She wouldn't laugh, but she couldn't keep her eyes from looking at Boone. His mouth was set in a straight line, and his eyes were closed in the elongated blink of the long-suffering.

Rubie noticed none of it.

Within five minutes, the three sat in the dining room off the kitchen with a feast before them. There was a beautifully roasted ham, mashed potatoes, homegrown green beans pale from canning, hot rolls, and Pink Fluff. Miriam spent a brief, awkward moment wondering if she should offer to say grace since she was Rubie's minister, or if Boone or Rubie would do it since it was their house. Boone cleared up the confusion almost immediately by reaching around the Pink Fluff to grab the mashed potatoes.

Just as their plates were filled, the room turned black.

"There it is," Boone said, showing no surprise whatsoever. He stood up and walked towards the kitchen. "I knew those power lines couldn't hold up to this ice accumulation."

Rubie, also seeming unfazed, said, "This happens every few years, but we always make it. In fact, Miriam, could you thank God for me that we have a gas stove and oven? We certainly won't go hungry."

Miriam's heart raced. She'd been in storms before that took out electricity, but this storm already seemed more devastating than those past experiences. She heard another gunshot-like snap as another limb broke beneath the pressure. Finally, processing what Rubie had said, Miriam replied, "You know you can thank God directly? You don't need to go through me."

"Yes, but it just feels like he'll hear it better coming from you. And I've never lived with a minister. Seems like an opportunity I shouldn't waste. I'll let you know if I think of anything else I need you to tell him."

Miriam knew that the warmth of the small dining room wouldn't immediately escape just because the heat had shut off, but she still felt grateful when a sudden warmth suffused her back. For a brief, illogical moment, she wondered if the prayer she'd silently delivered on Rubie's behalf had resulted in this heating glow. But then an arm reached around her, and Boone's hands placed a candelabra with several candlesticks on the table in front of her, lending the whole room an amber glow. As soon as he walked away, the warmth of his body heat vanished and Miriam felt a chill run down her back.

The flowers and birds on the dining room's wallpaper moved with spring-like energy under the candlelight's flicker. Miriam took a deep breath, banishing the initial adrenaline surge from those first moments without electricity. She was stranded in an ice storm without power, yes. But she was stranded with Rubie, who had lived through this many times and showed no fear, and Boone, who, for reasons she couldn't articulate, she trusted implicitly.

Miriam knew as surely as the sun would rise that Boone would know what to do in whatever situation they found themselves in. He'd already done work to prepare for what he'd identified as a threat since reading some passage in a *Farmer's Almanac*. It was likely much, if not all, of Paducah would lose power from downed lines. Miriam could certainly be in worse places to endure the storm.

Finished lighting candles, Boone sat down at his spot and picked up a fork, digging into his plate of food. He exhibited an air of nonchalance even as the flames danced wildly in his eyes.

Boone said, "Personally, I like having to rough it every once in a while. We've got plenty of candles and firewood. There's a kerosene heater for Grandma's room and enough quilts for half the state. No need to worry, okay?"

Miriam thought she'd masked her initial bolt of concern, but perhaps he was more intuitive than she realized. Trying to reassure him that he wouldn't have some damsel in distress on his hands for however long this storm lasted, Miriam said, "I know, Boone. I'm not worried."

From across the table, Rubie said around a mouthful of ham, "You know, Rupert and I conceived your father one dark, icy night when the power had been taken out."

Miriam spewed Pink Fluff across the table. Boone coughed violently. He'd taken a sip of sweet tea at a very unfortunate moment.

Weakly, Boone said, "That's nice, Grandma."

"Although, maybe it wasn't at night. We were snowed in for days, and there was only one really good way to keep warm. So it could have been day or night. Who knows?"

Miriam couldn't keep the laughter from her eyes as she glanced at Boone. His eyes were on her, and she could swear he was also suppressing a laugh.

Rubie continued, "I'm not sure what it was about a cold storm that made us so fertile. God knows we'd tried for years before and years after without a bit of luck. We did have fun trying, though."

"This Pink Fluff sure is tasty, Grandma," Boone said, making a valiant effort to change the subject.

"Yes, I didn't think we should only have beans and rice and potatoes to get us through. Life can get dreary without a little Pink Fluff sprinkled throughout. Not to mention it being Valentine's Day!"

"Good call, Rubie. I keep forgetting it's Valentine's Day," Miriam said to Rubie even as she glanced back at Boone to see if she could catch one more of those knowing, laughter-lace looks. This time, he was focused on cutting a slice of ham. Miriam turned back to her plate, wondering why she was disappointed.

For a moment, the only sound in the room was the clinking of forks and knives on Rubie's floral-trimmed plates. Then, Rubie said, "Boone, do you want me to sleep downstairs?"

"No. You need your adjustable bed. Especially as stiff as cold weather makes your joints."

Miriam said, "And I can take the other bedroom or the living room."

Boone paused a fork of ham mid-air as he said, "No one is sleeping in the other bedroom. The only heat we have now is the kerosene heater in Grandma's room and the fireplace in the living room. That other bedroom will be in the teens or twenties if we're lucky. No, I'm afraid you and I will be in the living room."

A bite of food lodged in Miriam's throat. Taking a gulp of tea, Miriam limply said, "Sounds good." The words lacked conviction, but Miriam had never been one for acting. The thought of sleeping within a few feet of Boone did not sound good at all. It sounded panic-inducing and painfully awkward, but she would never voice her complaint in front of Rubie.

Boone continued eating, seemingly unfazed. His eyes darted to her again, but this time instead of shared humor, Miriam saw a little of her own apprehension mirrored in his glance. She reached up to her neck to adjust her clerical collar. Finding none, her hand fell to the table. Suddenly, a bowl was being passed to her.

"Here, dear," Rubie said. "Have some more salad. Nothing like a little sugar rush to keep you warm."

Miriam took the Pink Fluff, not sure how she'd eat another bite.

Chapter 12

"Goodness, Rubie. How can I already be a hundred and fifty pages into this book?"

Miriam, Rubie, and Boone all set around the warmth of the fireplace in the living room with patchwork quilts draped over their laps and shoulders. While the house was habitable, it had dropped several degrees without the central heat. Between the fireplace and a few candles, there was plenty of light for reading. Boone's book looked terribly responsible with plants and birds beautifully illustrated on the cover. Rubie and Miriam each held paperbacks with scantily clad figures embracing in windy conditions.

"Oh, that's the fun part, dear. These books just fly by without you even realizing you've been sitting for two hours doing nothing but reading."

This was certainly the case for Miriam. Somehow, the day was a blur. Delivering Valentine's Day baskets seemed like ages ago. Back then, she didn't even know about Flossie Johnson's spunk in the face of the rugged, unsettled Texas countryside or Houston Johnson's soft underbelly once a person got to know him. Miriam hadn't read a book that wasn't a theological treatise in far too long. She might just need to visit Rubie's bookshelves more often.

As far as the previous evening when Miriam celebrated her birthday with Lucy and Edith, that seemed like a different season entirely. The weather this winter had largely been mild for their little corner of Kentucky, but it had certainly found its bite. Miriam's head was still spinning at how quickly the storm had come and turned her life upside-down.

Interrupting Miriam's thoughts, Rubie asked, "Any news from town today?"

Miriam wasn't sure who the question was addressed to, but Boone seemed absorbed in his book, so she answered, "Most of Paducah is blacked out. Apparently gas stations are even shut down. The church is in one of the neighborhoods without power, so I'd be pretty chilly if I was there tonight."

"It's a good thing you're not. For lots of reasons." Rubie's attention returned to her book, and she continued reading for another fifteen minutes. Then, with the clock almost hitting ten but not quite, Rubie placed a crocheted bookmark into her copy of *Lustfully Yours* and slowly stood up. Miriam was surprised she didn't hear popping knees given the effort it took Rubie to stand. Through a yawn, Rubie said, "That's it for me, kids. I'm plum worn out from all the excitement today. Time for me to head up to my old-person bed."

"Are you sure you want to put that book down? Looks like a page-turner." Miriam hoped that her attempt to stall the moment when Rubie left wasn't too transparent.

Boone spoke for the first time in what seemed hours, "Yes, Grandma. Don't feel you have to go to bed on account of us. Stay down here and read as long as you like."

At least Miriam wasn't the only person feeling hesitant at the impending night in this small living room. Really, it was an exceptionally small living room. How had she never noticed just how microscopically small this living room was?

Boone continued, "It's not like you need to go to bed early. We shouldn't have any excitement tomorrow. Surely, no one will be foolish enough to get out tomorrow."

Any budding sense of camaraderie Miriam might have felt towards Boone died at his words. With all of Rubie's warm words of welcome and enthusiasm at having a guest, Miriam had almost forgotten that Boone must be seething with blame towards her for their predicament. After all, she'd been the one to flaunt weather forecasters and go out driving. She was the one who had saved Farm to Market Road 1029-something-something for last, a road that the county apparently also saved for last when dealing with winter weather conditions. Yes, Boone had not invited her out to his home. The fault lay solidly at Miriam's feet.

Rubie dismissed both of their protestations with a simple wave of her hand toward the book. "When you're my age, Boone, you need sleep even for a day holed up in a house. And that book will wait 'til tomorrow just fine. I've read it at least half a dozen times. This old lady needs her sleep."

As Rubie spoke, she walked over to Boone and kissed the top of his head, wishing him a goodnight with an affection and comfort that could only be born of years of familial bond. Miriam, who was by far the most affectionate person in her small family, had never received such casual displays of love. It wasn't that her parents were cold or unloving. It was just that they were the standoffish sort who showed their affection to their only daughter by reading to her long after most children's bedtimes or taking her on grand adventures. Miriam suspected that it was still a mystery to them how they had sired a child so gregarious and openly affectionate and verbose. Sometimes she feared it was her own alien-ness that kept them traveling.

After wishing Boone a goodnight, Rubie circled the coffee table to the wingback chair where Miriam was curled up with her book. Much to Miriam's surprise, Rubie bent down once again, and, just as she had done with her grandson, she kissed the top of Miriam's curly head. After the stress of the day and the feelings of shame at her foolishness for getting herself into this predicament, Miriam felt mortifyingly close to tears. Swallowing, she said, "Goodnight, Rubie. Thank you for the shelter from the storm."

Rubie patted her shoulder and said, "Thank you for making the storm more fun."

Walking to the base of the stairs, Rubie held firmly to the handrail as she climbed slowly to the second floor.

In Rubie's absence, the fire sounded much louder, a crackling sound filling the space between Miriam's chair and the opposite side of the sofa where Boone sat. Miriam didn't think sounds from the fire could be more jarring if popcorn were being popped on it. Just when she thought she couldn't possibly be more aware of her surroundings and all the noises filling their deafening silence, her phone made an appalling sound that almost sent her jumping from her perch.

If it were spring and sunny outside, Miriam might have assumed there were birds just outside the window wrestling each other to a bloody demise. Snapping up her phone, she saw love birds facing each other and making what must be intended to be mating calls. Beneath the birds in bold, pink letters, it said, "Check out this birdie!"

In the twenty-four hours since signing up for Matchables, Miriam had completely forgotten it existed. She'd been far too busy transversing ice and snow to think about the previous evening with Lucy and Miriam giggling as she tried to describe what she was looking for in a man. It wasn't their most mature moment. Now, fully aware of her thirty-plus years of age and the nauseating sound coming from her phone, Miriam repeatedly tapped the notification trying to get it to shut up. She managed to freeze her phone for a few seconds before it finally caught up to her persistent tapping and shut off.

Barely glancing up from his book with zero couples embracing on the cover, Boone said, "You need to turn that thing off. We might not have power to charge it for days."

"But someone might need me." Ministers were on call at all times.

"To borrow your snow plow?"

"I don't have a snow plow."

"Salt truck?"

Miriam sighed. "Not one of those either."

Still looking down at his book, his eyes moving steadily across the page, Boone said, "Then trust me, no one in Western Kentucky is going to need you anytime soon. Anyways, if you turn your phone off now, you can turn it on for a few minutes each day to check for messages. If not, it'll be dead way before this mess is over."

Miriam turned back to her phone, knowing he was right but too overcome with curiosity to care. Pulling up Matchables, Miriam found the face of Boone Rutledge looking back at her. If she was seeing him, that meant he hadn't seen her first on the app and passed on her. If she passed on him, he'd never see her profile. At least, she didn't think he would if the app worked how she thought it worked. Obviously, accepting him with the "nesting" icon wasn't an option since he wasn't exactly her biggest fan.

Before she passed, his profile picture paused her thumb. Even on social media, the man didn't smile fully. But in the context of a dating app, his subtle half-grin looked mysterious in the most alluring way, making a person wonder what it would take to make a man so reserved let down his guard. If Miriam were honest, his half-smile on their way out of the barn tonight had certainly elicited that response in her. Why were the most unavailable men always the most intriguing?

"Miriam, I'm serious. You might need that phone later."

Miriam jumped guiltily at his words.

"I'm just checking a couple of things, then I'll turn it off."

She didn't have to "pass" or "nest." She could just turn the phone off. But first, she could take a peek.

Scrolling down the profile, Miriam read at record speed. She'd always assumed Boone had his fair share of women fawning over his broody demeanor. But here he was, joining the ranks of online dating. She hoped that as she scrolled down the rows of survey-like information, Boone didn't see her eyes expanding in shock.

***

Boone didn't think he'd ever sat so long with a book in his hands while reading so little. Miriam's book was holding her attention enough that her eyes rarely left the page, giving him far too many opportunities to look at her over the edge of *Endangered Species of the Midwest*.

With rhythmic regularity, Miriam mindlessly wrapped the curls at the nape of her neck around one finger, pulling outward gently, and then releasing the curl to spring back into place. Over and over, her hand found a curl, twisted it around, and released it. Perhaps, if he wasn't on the endangered bat species chapter, his book would have held his attention better. They had never been a particular interest of his. But as it was, Miriam's curls were winning his attention with the book barely putting up a fight.

Although he hadn't read a damn word the whole night, Boone did have the presence of mind to periodically turn a page. And the few times she looked up, Boone had moved his eyes in a passable imitation of reading.

Now that Miriam had sat down her book in place of her phone, Boone was more hesitant to do what he was pretty sure could be classified as ogling. Turning a page that he hadn't come close to reading, Boone tried to process the fact that the world's worst app notification had just come from not his, but Miriam's phone.

His first gut response to the cloying mating calls of Matchables love birds was mortification that Miriam would come across his profile. After all, Paducah wasn't a huge city, and the area's online dating presence was likely a small pool. There, Miriam would not only see that Boone was single and lonely enough to take a chance on Matchables, but she would also discover Boone as seen by Rubie Rutledge and her intrepid side-kick, Miss Hyacinth.

After processing this terrifying possibility, Boone's second response was total dismay at the revelation that Mother Miriam Howatch was on Matchables. A minister was participating in online dating? Boone had somehow never considered that Miriam was a potential date for any man. Certainly not him. Boone wasn't one to make small talk with a minister, much less date one.

The ministers of Boone's childhood were all cast from the same mold. They had all been middle-aged men with wives who either seemed sickly thin or like they lived lives full of reasons for emotional eating - there rarely seemed to be an in-between. The men were usually in a suit no matter the weather or the occasion, and they seemed to sweat anger and contempt.

Boone's parents had thought any minister must be respected because he'd been noble enough to choose the most important profession. They'd accepted every word spoken from the pulpit as a solid fact, even when the words told them they should despise their own son.

After a potluck when Boone was seventeen, just a few months before he was going to escape the claustrophobia-inducing small town where he and Travis had endured years of small-minded thinking disguised as good old-fashioned values, Boone found himself alone in a classroom with the minister of the church his parents had raised him in. The church tended to go through ministers every few years. This one was particularly plump, stretching the limits of the brown polyester suit he'd probably purchased straight out of Bible school twenty years before. His wife had the bedraggled lankiness of a woman too busy long-suffering in the kitchen to actually eat the potluck-style recipes that fattened her husband.

Boone had escaped into the classroom during one of the never-ending potlucks his church hosted on the first Sunday of every month. Travis had made himself throw up that morning to get out of going, leaving Boone more free to hide out. When Travis came, Boone never left his side, guarding him from predators like an Old English Sheepdog guards a flock of sheep.

The room was in the basement of the church building, and it had slit windows along the top of one side of its shallow walls. The windows were at ground level, but he looked upwards, there was a decent view of the maple trees across the church's property. Boone went back and forth from the windows, looking at the trees, examining their red and orange leaves, and thinking about the process that turned maples into such stunning displays of fall's power.

He had already decided that he would spend his life working and studying nature even if he hadn't settled on the specifics yet.

Into this quiet space, Brother Paul Jones walked in and found Boone pacing. Boone wasn't sure what had brought the minister to that particular room, but the man's beady eyes took on an ominous scowl the moment they landed on Boone. Speaking in a manner particular to Southern ministers where the most unlikely of syllables are emphasized, Brother Paul said, "Ah. One of the Rutledge boys hiding away, I see."

Boone answered, "No, sir. I was just finding a bit of quiet. As Christ said, 'Come ye yourselves apart into a desert place, and rest a while.'" No one could ever accuse Boone of not learning each memory verse his parents had demanded of him. Failure to do so would lead to a whip with his father's belt, and if his father took the time to remove his belt for Boone's transgressions, he usually whipped Travis for good measure. After all, Travis always had a devil in him that needed to be beaten out. Unfortunately for Boone, Brother Paul was unimpressed with his Biblical knowledge.

"Don't speak the Lord's words to me, boy. I know what you are, you..." The minister spit out a slur that stung Boone more viscerally than any slap ever could. Brother Paul inched towards Boone, his face red with pent-up contempt. "I don't say much to you and your brother because I know how hard your parents have worked to try to turn you boys towards righteousness. I don't know how such good and faithful servants ended up with you devils. But I just want you to know that as soon as you two graduate and leave their house, you are no longer welcome in the House of the Lord."

Boone lifted an arm to wipe off his face as Brother Paul spit out the final words. Of course, Boone wasn't going to argue. As soon as the tassel flipped sides at his graduation cap, he had no intention of ever again stepping foot in his parent's house or Brother Paul's House of the Lord. But he also didn't intend to give Brother Paul the last word.

Straightening his back, Boone looked into the eyes of the red-faced, perspiring minister and quietly said, "If a man says, I love God, and hateth his brother, he is a liar: for he that loveth not his brother whom he hath seen, how can he love God whom he hath not seen?"

The verse had never been assigned to Boone for memorization. In fact, it was rarely mentioned and usually glossed over because it didn't bolster any of the battles the church was waging. If a word couldn't be weaponized for their causes, what was its purpose?

But Boone had memorized the verse on his own, taking a short break from verses on various abominations and the fates that befall the wicked. He'd never suspected that a small act of rebellion would provide such satisfying returns.

Before Boone could process what was happening, Brother Paul reached up and grabbed the sensitive, nervy area of Boone's neck and rammed his thick, strong fingers deep into the ligaments. Boone buckled, his shoulder collapsing in pain. Boone was younger, stronger, and more agile than Brother Paul, but while he was considered a rebel by his parents and church, Boone was naturally a rule follower. His teachers had taught him to respect those in authority. His grandparents, who he trusted implicitly to guide him, insisted he be respectful. So Boone simply buckled, the shame of his weakness keeping his eyes to the ground as Brother Paul growled into his ear, "You're going to burn in hell, boy. You're going to burn in hell with that brother of yours, and it will be better than the two of you deserve."

Throwing Boone against the wall, the minister left the room. Boone slid to the floor, rubbing where the minister's hand had twisted into this neck.

Sitting in front of the fireplace, lost in thought, Boone's hand came up to the same spot, massaging the muscles that no longer ached but still held the memory of pain.

Miriam's voice broke into his thoughts, "I turned off my phone. I'll just turn it on once a day or so to see when the church gets back its power and the roads get cleared."

"God forbid a church closes its doors for a few days."

With an edge to her voice, Miriam bit out, "Yes, I hardly do anything in my job. They just pay me to look pretty in a pulpit."

Their eyes were locked for the first time after a long day of stolen glances and giving each other wide berths. Boone had crossed a line and found her limit. He knew he'd sounded harsh, even dismissive.

Finally, Boone broke the silence, although not the tension. "I'm going to go upstairs to get ready for bed. You can use the downstairs bathroom. Maybe the fireplace will have kept it from getting too cold."

Tossing his book on the table knowing he'd have to figure out later where he'd actually read to as opposed to where he'd pretended to read to, Boone stomped up the stairs forgetting to tread gingerly so he wouldn't awaken Rubie. After grabbing a thermal shirt and flannel pajama pants that he hoped might lend warmth, Boone went to the bathroom where he shivered his way through his nighttime routine.

As he splashed the icy cold water in the single most unpleasant sponge bath of his life, Boone wished the discomfort would take his mind off the other sensations coursing through him. He was angry at Miriam for thinking her job was so important she would forsake safety to deliver a few old people baskets of chocolate, and he was angry that she was now his problem. He was ashamed of himself for hurting her and dreading a long night of hearing her breath a few feet from him. At the same time, he wanted to be close to her and to hear her breath. Also, he was damned confused.

As he made his way out of the bathroom towards the stairs, he heard a voice from his grandmother's room.

"Boone?"

Cracking open her door and sticking his head in, Boone was relieved to feel that the little heater was sufficiently heating the space.

"You called, Grandma?"

"I just wanted to say goodnight."

"Goodnight, then," Boone said as he started to close the door.

"Boone?"

Opening the door again, the old hinges protesting loudly, Boone said, "Yes?"

"She's nice, isn't she? It's nice to have someone else around, don't you think?"

"Sure, Grandma. It's nice. Goodnight."

Boone didn't even get the door shut before he heard, "Boone?"

Taking a calming breath, Boone ground out, "Yes, Grandma?"

"I wouldn't love her if I thought she wouldn't accept Travis. She's different from the ministers you knew growing up. You know that, right?"

Boone stepped into the room and walked to her bed. Bending over, he gently placed a goodnight kiss on her frizzy gray hair. It tickled his nose as it had done every embrace since he was a sad, hurting child.

"I know, Grandma. I love you."

Rubie patted his hand and snuggled back beneath the covers, closing her eyes. Boone left the room, closing the door to ensure the precious heat wouldn't escape, and headed downstairs to the long night ahead.

***

Even as the cold of the tiles lifted her onto her toes, Miriam was solidly grounded in anger.

The downstairs bathroom was smaller than the one upstairs with only a sink and toilet. The tight quarters coupled with the Arctic-like conditions gave the impression she'd walked into a refrigerator. She shook from head to toe, either in cold or anger or an invigorating blend of both. It was like a triple shot of espresso right before laying down to sleep, or at least pretending to sleep.

Miriam should've been accustomed to people dismissing her career. It had taken her parents, neither of whom shared her faith, iron wills to not balk when Miriam informed them she would be attending seminary. Their words of encouragement couldn't mask the disappointment on their faces. At the time, Miriam found their reaction amusing. Every kid, though, wants to make their parents proud, and despite Miriam's commitment to the path she'd chosen, it sometimes irked her that her parents would never truly understand or support her work.

She'd withstood significant skepticism from her undergraduate community at PSU, as well. Both from fellow students and some of the faculty, there was an outcry over someone with so much natural talent for academics and English Literature leaving the field. People had assumed she'd go on to be a professor, and several in the faculty had offered to write her references to various Ivy League graduate schools. Instead, she'd asked that the letters be sent to seminaries.

The exception to the wall of resistance she'd faced was Lucy. Throughout undergrad, Lucy watched Miriam's blossoming faith as she became a part of the Trinity Episcopal Church. While other students were sleeping off hangovers until noon on Sundays, Miriam was kneeling in prayer beneath the vaulted ceiling of Trinity, feeling in its beauty a connection to something bigger - something she'd always suspected was out there but was only just seeking to understand.

Miriam's grandmother was a devout woman of faith, and Miriam had been drawn to the aspects of the divine she'd sensed in and around her grandmother. On family trips to her grandmother's house, Miriam would sneak away to the prayer corner her grandmother kept in her bedroom and light the candles. Kneeling in front of the flickering flames, Miriam would pray. She'd pray for her cat, Charlie, who always seemed to barely miss getting run over. She'd pray for the little boy from her class named Beau who everyone picked on and who never wore clean clothes. She'd prayed for her grandma who always seemed to be missing Miriam's grandfather, a man Miriam had never met because he died only days before her birth. Looking back, Miriam could see that her mind ran far too fast and felt far too deeply for such a young child. No wonder her parents seemed perplexed by her. But in all the praying, Miriam found a peace that hinted at something real to her grandmother's beliefs.

So when she was on her own at college, Miriam took the independence so intoxicating to young adults and stepped into Trinity. There she rediscovered her grandmother's prayer corner.

Of course, as a woman going into the clergy, she'd encountered her fair share of resistance even after her education and completing the extensive ordination process. For two years, Miriam didn't settle into a single congregation, instead traveling around the world doing various mission projects. Fearing burn-out without a place to call home, Miriam accepted her first full-time position in a rural part of Kentucky that had only had electricity since the mid-twentieth century. From the moment she'd first walked into the small church in Bethel, Kentucky, Miriam's gender had been a barrier. Within a few months, tensions were rising as a cohort of older men took offense at every sermon regardless of how benign it seemed when she wrote it. They were looking for the quickest way to once again have a man in their pulpit.

With guidance from mentors who'd been in the ministry far longer than Miriam, she came to the conclusion that she should seek a transfer. Sometimes, one just has to admit defeat and move on.

In the months leading up to her move, the more contentious members of the congregation only increased their combativeness, picking arguments over issues they knew would be points of disagreement. Although the situation ultimately ended with Miriam leaving on her own terms, it did mean that the parting was only bitter, lacking the sweetness one hopes for when closing a chapter. The experience shook Miriam's confidence in her calling, causing her to wonder if, perhaps, the skepticism she'd faced from friends and family had been justified after all.

Just as she was hitting a low point in her ministry, Miriam got the call that she was being offered the position as the Associate Rector at the church she still considered home, Trinity Episcopal in Paducah. She was going back to the place where she had first been able to embrace the faith. Also, she was returning to Lucy, to the friend who had stuck with her no matter how many miles separated them over the years.

It only took Miriam a few months to sink into the close-knit community around Lucy. Her friend had spent the years since their graduation working as the secretary for their English department, and that department had coalesced around Lucy into a unit that acted more like a family than an office. Miriam was back in the fold, spending time with Lucy and Forrest. Porter had been a fresh, young professor when Miriam attended PSU, but now she had come to value his friendship both as a member of her congregation and as a close, personal friend. And of course, Edith, the chair of the English department, had become one of Miriam's dearest friends.

The church, being made of humans as it was, had its issues and its dramas, but Miriam found a solid core of congregants who were either like-minded or tolerant of differing opinions and who valued her contributions. She loved serving the older people, participating in the various ministries for the poor and the sick that Trinity supported, and conversing with the other staff about theology, sermon ideas, and new ministries.

As Miriam thought about the life she'd built in Paducah and the calling she was fulfilling at Trinity, she felt renewed resentment towards Boone for his dismissive statements. Sometimes, she would watch his gentle affection towards Rubie and think that he might be a pretty nice guy. Lucy and Edith certainly thought highly of "Swooney Booney." Even Forrest and Porter liked Boone, adding him to their guys' nights as if he taught Shakespeare instead of horticulture.

So if he was such a good coworker and friend, if he was such an attentive grandson to a grandmother who was quite the handful, why was he so rude to Miriam? What was different about her? She hated the middle-school tone of the questions running through her mind, but why didn't Boone Rutledge like her?

After spitting out and rinsing, Miriam pulled on the flannel pajamas Rubie had found for her from when Travis visited. Her whole body protested when she removed the clothes that had kept her warm all afternoon to pull on the pajamas. Miriam looked at her bra. This late in the day it felt positively oppressive. But Miriam opted to keep it on. The sleeping arrangement was awkward enough without worrying about cold nipples.

Dressed and freshened up, Miriam headed back around the hallway to the living room. The coffee table was moved to behind the couch. Where it normally stood in front of the fireplace, there was now a palette made of sleeping bags and blankets. On the palette, Boone lay either asleep or doing an impressive opossum act, his chest rising and falling in slow, deep breaths.

Parallel to the palette, the couch was made into an inviting bed that looked like it might just be toasty. There was a thick pillow, sheets already tucked into the cushions, and at least three quilts. Miriam didn't need to do anything. She could just climb into a bed made by Boone's rough hands.

Slipping silently under the covers, Miriam turned towards the back of the couch and buried her face into the cushions to hide the fire's light. To her great surprise, the anger that had energized her only moments before diffused almost immediately beneath the comforting weight of the many quilts. Closing her eyes, Miriam fell into a dreamless sleep.

Chapter 13

Boone woke up long before it occurred to the sun to rise. He usually did. His grandfather had kept farmer's hours, and Boone developed the habit during his many stays at their house. Quietly climbing out from his covers, Boone suppressed a groan from the stiffness caused by a night on the cold floor. Boone wasn't old, but mid-thirties was old enough to want a mattress.

Tip-toeing to the kitchen, he found Rubie sipping a cup of coffee with a plate of scrambled eggs in front of her.

"Eggs are on the back burner. Without electricity, I had to make coffee in that fancy French press of yours. I hate to admit it, but it's actually pretty good."

"I've been telling you it makes good coffee." Boone poured himself a cup and sat across from Rubie with his eggs. The liquid in his cup was black as night. Rubie's was the light tan of moth wings, syrupy with cream and sugar. "Have you peeked outside yet?"

"Yep, the snow is coming down heavy."

Boone shook his head. "This is going to be one for the record books."

"Yes, it could be a while before they get electricity out to those of us deep in the country."

"We'll be fine."

"Oh, I know. The longer it lasts, the longer I get to have another woman in the house with me, so don't think I'm complaining."

Boone smirked in between bites of egg.

"What's so great about having another woman in the house when you get to live with a great conversationalist like myself?"

Rubie threw a kitchen towel at him.

After cleaning dishes, Boone bundled up and headed out to do his chores. Even taking it slowly, Boone slipped a few times. The ice beneath the snow made for treacherous terrain.

Once in the barn, he was relieved to find that the collective body heat of the animals made the interior livable. Taking a shovel, he broke up the thin layer of ice that had collected on each watering trough. Then, he moved to feeding and caring for each animal. As he worked in the barn, Boone whispered words of comfort to each one, stroking them as he spoke. It was to soothe the stressful situation for them, but it worked to ease the tension he was holding in his shoulders, as well.

Boone hadn't fallen asleep until late into the night. He'd done a decent job acting unconscious, but he heard every step Miriam made across the cold wood floor to the couch. Then, he heard the quiet sigh of satisfaction she exhaled when she crawled into the bed he'd meticulously laid out for her only minutes before her arrival. Within no time, he was listening in both envy and fascination as her breathing took on the slow, deep pattern of the sleeping.

In comparison, Boone was wide awake and flipping through a card catalog of thoughts coursing through his mind. And every damn card was Miriam-themed.

She was just so beautiful. Not in the supermodel, made-up kind of way. Her beauty, so unadorned and lacking pretensions, was somehow more authentic. She was like the fields of purple deadnettle that cropped up around Western Kentucky in the spring. Those fields of weeds lacked refinement, but their beauty rivaled the most elaborate bouquets in a florist shop.

By the time Boone was finished working in the barn, it was hardly even mid-morning. Long hours in the same house with Miriam stretched before him, and he wondered how many gaffes he would commit, if he would accidentally hurt her again with his surliness.

Boone hadn't always been so brooding. He'd had long summer days of laughing and teasing with Travis and his grandparents throughout his childhood. When he would arrive home, though, he would lay his head low and try to get through the long months before he could head back to the farm.

Even now after life had thrown him a few curve balls, Boone could still relax and enjoy time with his friends. It was simply when he got around people he didn't trust, people who in any way reminded him of his parents and the people he'd grown up around, that Boone retreated. And while it was like a bad game of "Seven Degrees to Kevin Bacon," Miriam did bring up thoughts of those people. She, too, let faith guide her. It had determined her whole career. In her strange clothing and steepled workplace,

Boone didn't see how she could be categorized as anything but a religious zealot. As such, he did not trust her.

But Rubie did. It was one of the great paradoxes of Boone's life that his grandparents, the two adults he'd loved and trusted most, actually shared the same faith as his parents, the two adults who had sown seeds of fear and distrust and shame in Boone from such a young age. Boone hadn't spared too much thought for this oddity over the years. He'd decided Rubie and Rupert were the exceptions that proved the rule, but the rule was still ironclad.

Making his way back through the heavy snowfall, Boone opened the door and rushed in, hoping to preserve as much precious heat trapped in the drafty house as possible.

The kitchen was deserted, so after taking off the snow-caked boots he'd been wearing, Boone walked into the living room where he found the women chatting animatedly as they each worked on separate tasks.

"I'm convinced that if I try canning, I'll end up improperly doing it and kill someone with some deadly bacteria that will creep into my poorly processed jam." Miriam spoke the words around a nail that was sticking out of one corner of her mouth. She was on her knees on the floor with the heirloom kitchen table from Rubie's grandmother lying upside down, its spindled legs looking flimsy in the air. Boone's eyebrows rose in surprise as he watched her fixing the loose leg he'd assured Rubie he would get around to. Eventually.

Rubie sat on the sofa with an afghan she was knitting draped over her legs. It served both as warmth and as a way to keep her hands limber in the cold. Not noticing that Boone had walked in, Rubie continued the conversation, "I've been canning for almost seventy years, and I haven't killed anyone yet. If you get a can that doesn't seal, you just pop it into the freezer."

"Maybe if you're standing by my side watching every step like a hawk, I'd give it a try."

"Then it's settled. We're canning this July. Mark your calendar."

"Yes, ma'am."

Boone stepped further into the room. "Maybe we'll get torrential rains and you can spend several days canning together."

"Ooh, ask God for that, Miriam."

Miriam hit the tip of a near-empty bottle of wood glue against her thigh as she said, "I think I'm done with Biblical-level storms for this year, thank you very much. But I'll happily come hang out at your house anytime, girlfriend."

Rubie cackled in delight at Miriam's playful words.

"Here, can you hold this?"

It took Boone a second to realize Miriam was talking to him. He jerked to attention and bent down next to her. She gave him a few instructions, and he held the leg firmly while she tightened clamps.

Watching her hands move deftly over the tools, Boone said, "Where did you learn how to work with furniture?"

Miriam bit down on one side of her bottom lip, concentrating hard on the task at hand. "How do people learn anything these days? YouTube. I've watched lots and lots of YouTube videos."

"What all did these videos teach you to do?"

"I built custom bookshelves in Lucy's apartment. I've helped Porter fix the banister on his staircase. It was improperly done and dangerous for the kids - especially his crazy crew. I made a board meeting table for the church offices."

"Wow. I had no idea YouTube held such a bounty of information."

Glancing at him from the top of her eyes while she was still leaning over the leg, Miriam said, "Everyone in our generation has used YouTube to learn something. How to get a muscle knot out. How to make a sourdough starter. How to fix a car. What has Boone Rutledge learned on YouTube?"

"I'm afraid not much, but I do teach on there. PSU had me make a series of videos on sustainable gardening, composting, how to create spaces that feed bees and butterflies. That sort of thing."

Miriam paused what she was doing and looked at Boone with a blank expression. The conviviality of their conversation seemed to have abandoned them, but Boone couldn't understand why.

Suddenly, Rubie's voice cut into the awkward silence. "Are peanut butter and jelly sandwiches okay for lunch? I have a jar of the strawberry jam I canned last summer that I can use. Then, you'll definitely want to learn to can this summer."

"Sounds delicious," Miriam said as she twisted one more time on a clamp, picked up her tools, and headed to the kitchen to help prepare lunch.

***

It was without a doubt the best peanut butter and jelly sandwich of Miriam's life.

"Alright, Rubie. Even if I accidentally kill someone, it is worth the risk to learn how to make this jam."

"Told you so," Rubie said smugly.

Boone had already scarfed down two sandwiches and left for the greenhouse before Miriam and Rubie could even get one down. Miriam barely contained a roll of her eyes as he grunted a goodbye and left the women to eat daintily. Yes, he could eat twice as much twice as fast. Yes, he had very important work to do in some greenhouse out back. And yes, he could make YouTube videos on all the things Miriam asked him to speak about with her church. But he couldn't possibly cross Trinity's threshold.

Between the condescension the previous evening and this renewed sense of being thoroughly snubbed, Miriam was charged up for a confrontation. She could be a very nice person while visiting old people and attending meetings about floral arrangements and leading adorable children's worship ceremonies, but she had her limits. If she was going to coexist in the same house as Boone until the sun decided to come out of hiding and melt some ice, they needed to clear the air.

After helping clean up, Miriam said in her best imitation of a casual voice, "I think I'll step out and see this greenhouse your grandson is always hiding in."

"You should do that."

The snow had finally stopped over the lunch hour, but the sky was still ominously dark for mid-day. Miriam wore Rubie's Wellies over a double layer of socks. Even with the knee-high protection, she had to lift her knees awkwardly to traverse the path to the greenhouse without getting a boot full of snow. Finally arriving after a walk that reminded her of high school gym class and angry coaches demanding more high knees, Miriam opened the door to the greenhouse.

Stepping in, Miriam froze in place. Perhaps it was the minister in her, but Miriam knew immediately that she had stepped into someone's sacred space. This was a church just as holy as the one where she stood each week and preached. Even if the Lord's Prayer had never been uttered nor a hymn sung into the vaulted, windowed ceiling, worship happened within its glassy walls. Of that, Miriam had no doubt.

Everywhere Miriam turned, lush greenery abounded. There was no spot for the eye to land where there wasn't a healthy, thriving plant. Miriam recognized some of the varieties, but there were far more that were foreign to her. Even if she hadn't known the owner of the greenhouse, she would have known it was not cultivated by the average person with a green thumb. This was a place of expertise. It was an elite greenhouse.

As Miriam rotated taking in the full wonder of the space, Boone appeared. He'd been crouched down working by a row of plants. Startled, Miriam's hand jumped to her chest.

"Were you not expecting me to be here?" Boone asked, a wry grin on his face.

"I was, I just got lost for a moment in this space. This is divine, Boone, and I don't use that word lightly. You must spend hours out here. I've never seen anything so beautiful."

If Miriam wasn't absolutely certain Boone was a man who lacked the capacity to blush, she'd swear the skin above his beard had tinged like a half-ripe tomato on the vine.

"Grandpa and I built it the summer before I went to college. We used windows from an old school they tore down in town. It was too large for what Grandpa needed, but I think he sensed I would need it to be bigger when I took over the farm."

"Well, I'm impressed." Miriam delivered the compliment acutely aware that Boone was entirely unimpressed with her, that he had so far found virtually nothing on which to compliment her and plenty to criticize.

As she moved farther into the greenhouse, she felt Boone's icy eyes on her. Running her hands over her hair, Miriam tried in vain to tame the curls she hadn't even combed that day. With each step she took into the center of the greenhouse, she was only more amazed by its abundance. Suddenly, she realized that for the first time since dinner the previous evening, she wasn't cold. In fact, she felt positively toasty.

"It's warm in here," Miriam commented.

"Yep."

"Like, weirdly warm."

"I have a generator hooked up to the greenhouse. There's a little heater keeping the place ideal for the plants."

Miriam processed this information for a moment. "So let me get this straight. You have a generator to keep your plants warm, but the humans just have to fend for themselves?"

"Pretty much. I figure we have the fireplace in the house and gas for cooking in the kitchen. Overall, we're doing okay."

"I guess you're right. But this is the first time in my life I've ever been jealous of vegetation."

"Welcome to my family's life," Boone said with a fondness in his eyes.

"What does that mean?" Miriam asked.

"Just that Travis and Grandma used to always complain that Grandpa and I spent too much time with our plants and not enough time with them."

Miriam laughed, thinking how Travis and Boone seemed to reflect the personalities of Rubie and Rupert, respectively.

Stopping at a short row of rose bushes, Miriam leaned closer to the blooms, vivid and lush even in the middle of a winter storm. Suddenly, Boone was behind her reaching around. Gingerly grabbing a portion of a stem without thorns, he said, "Here, smell this one. No flower on earth smells better than the Madame Alfred Carriere. They almost never bloom outside of summer, but this one unexpectedly gave me a Valentine's Day bloom."

Miriam touched her nose to the pillowy petals, inhaling the pepper and sugar scent. She could feel his warmth. Boone's nearness coupled with the humidity of the greenhouse and the intoxicating scent of the rose left Miriam heady with unexpected sensations.

Turning around, she came face to face with Boone's blue eyes which were always so serious, and his longish beard which was always as perfectly kept as these plants, and she realized with startling clarity that it had been many years since she'd stood so close to a man. And whoever that last man had been (she couldn't recall the details), he hadn't filled a space like Boone. The last time she dated, she'd still been seeing men in their early twenties, hardly out of puberty in the grand scheme of things. Boone was like another species.

Whispering because the air felt too heavy to carry anything louder, Miriam said, "Is the Madame Alfred Carriere a native of Kentucky you're researching or something professorial like that?"

"Nope. Grandma just likes how they smell, so I grow them for her."

It was such a simple, logical answer, and it didn't surprise Miriam in the slightest. But it also didn't line up with the Boone who was so standoffish, so quick to dismiss her.

Still whispering and with more insecurity than she'd felt since middle school, Miriam said, "Why don't you like me?"

Boone's eyes registered shock, and Miriam turned away quickly, mortified that such a childish question had escaped her filter. Ministers typically had very good, dependable filters. One didn't make it far in the clergy without heavily editing thoughts before they became spoken words.

Boone's whisper sounded rough, like sandpaper, "Don't like you? What do you mean?"

"Most people like me. I'm generally a very popular person." Miriam wanted to dig a hole in the snow and burrow away like some survivalist on television. But instead, her filterless mouth kept going. "In high school, I was voted most likely to replace Oprah. In college, every person in the English department knew me and stopped me to chat, even the awkward ones that chose English as their major specifically so they could spend more time with books and less time with people. In seminary, my apartment was the gathering ground for group study sessions and the after-finals party. And, yet, despite this stellar record, you seem thoroughly unimpressed."

"I'm not unimpressed. You're clearly intelligent and Grandma loves you, and generally, she has pretty good taste. I mean, overlooking Miss Hyacinth, of course."

"Okay, then let me reword the question. Why don't you respect me?"

***

Miriam's eyes, always so bright and slightly crinkled with smiles, looked too dark, as if the barista had forgotten to add the creamer. Boone turned away from her, running a hand through his hair and down his beard, not wanting her to mistake the anger he was feeling towards himself as anger towards her for asking.

After the way he'd acted since they met, she had every right to question his respect for her. Boone felt ashamed for making an intelligent, capable woman feel less than she was. Truthfully, if Miriam were in any other profession, he would likely have felt only fascination and respect for the beautiful, funny, charismatic woman in front of him. Boone had never won any popularity contests, usually opting to fade into the scenery. And he'd never particularly cared for the popular crowd, but Miriam was different. As much as he distrusted her, he was overwhelmed with an urge to be near her, to be in the presence of so much warmth and humor and strength. Honestly, if it weren't for the collar, he would be trying to date her knowing good and well she was out of his league by miles.

Finally, feeling pressure to respond, Boone turned around and said, "It's not you. I've got some baggage when it comes to religion, and I've taken that out on you. Which is completely unfair, and I'm sorry."

Miriam was just about to wave an absolving hand in his direction when Boone said, "No, really, Miriam. I sincerely apologize. You're wonderful. It's easy to see why you were voted as Oprah's obvious successor."

Their eyes locked as he waited to see if his little stab at humor would bring back her glow, if she heard his genuine remorse within the words of his apology. He exhaled a sigh of relief when the corners of her eyes crinkled once again and she said, "Does this mean you want to be my friend?"

Boone chuckled softly while reaching out for a handshake. "Friends sounds damn good to me."

Miriam placed her hand within his own. It wasn't a particularly feminine or delicate or smooth hand. After all, she was a carpenter in her off-hours. Boone realized then that he, too, had joined the ranks of those who couldn't help but like Miriam Howatch. He even liked her hands.

"I have a confession to make," Miriam said, immediately transforming from cheerful to contrite, although Boone still sensed a gleam of mischief in her expression.

"What is it?" he asked warily.

Miriam removed her hand from his and placed both hands behind her back as she spoke. "You know how the English Department calls you Swooney Booney?"

"I was aware of that unfortunate moniker."

"Well, in my annoyance last night, I may have referred to you in my thoughts and in a few discreetly growled rants as Broody Booney."

This time Boone's head leaned back and his eyes shut as his entire face broke out in laughter. Exhaling, he said, "I'm a little surprised Travis never thought of that."

"I don't know how fitting it is after all. Now that I've seen you smile with your whole mouth, broody seems less appropriate."

"What do you mean 'with my whole mouth'?"

"You only ever smile with this side of your mouth."

As she spoke, Miriam reached up and gently tapped her finger just to the left of his lips. The two taps sent awareness through Boone that he hadn't felt in a very long time. He had certainly not felt it Friday night with @catsandcoffeegirl. Before he could turn his head into her palm or take her hand in his, she removed it and placed it once again behind her back.

Boone didn't know how to respond to the admission that she'd noticed something as intimate as his smile. The silence verged on the uncomfortable when Boone finally said, "Can I show you around the greenhouse?"

For the next hour, Boone walked along the rows of his carefully cultivated plants explaining what made each special, where they had come from, how various specimens fit into his work at PSU, and which held sentimental value. The latter were usually in connection with his grandfather. He couldn't help but notice how closely she walked beside him, asking intelligent questions, displaying genuine interest in his work, and even requesting he teach her more while she was stuck on the farm. By the time they headed into the house, Boone feared that he liked Miriam Howatch entirely too much.

***

Later that night, Miriam lay in her couch bed reading the very thorough education Flossie was receiving from the ruggedly handsome Houston on all things pleasurable. As Houston kissed his way down Flossie's abdomen, finally reaching her most intimate place and shocking Flossie to the core with all the wonderful things a mouth could accomplish down there, Miriam's eyes darted periodically to the broad shoulders of the man only a couple of feet from her. Boone faced the fireplace and was engrossed in the same book he'd been reading the night before.

Miriam's body was almost hot beneath the cocoon of quilts Boone's hands had smoothed out as he'd insisted once again on making her bed. Miriam had only been intimate with two men, one a college boyfriend and the other from seminary. The college boyfriend had been inexperienced and nervous, and they'd broken up soon after. The seminary boyfriend had known what he was doing, but he had the woeful habit of writhing in guilt and shame every time he so much as brushed a hand against her breast. Purity culture had done a number on him. It took less than a year for Miriam to decide the relationship wasn't worth the anguish.

This rather depressing history left Miriam wishing for just a moment as Flossie. Just one night when she could try all the things boyfriend-one had been too inexperienced to even fathom and boyfriend-two had felt too ashamed to indulge. Due to basic inexperience, Miriam didn't know what kind of sexual partner she would be to someone who was fully engaged and had a basic understanding of the process, but she suspected she would have all sorts of fun learning.

By nature, Miriam was deeply relational, always most invigorated when she was with others. She'd never suffered a shortage of people who were drawn to her energy and happy to spend time with her. Yet, here she was envying a twenty-year-old schoolmarm from a paperback romance.

Unable to bridle her mind, Miriam placed the bookmark within the pages of her book and rested her eyes firmly on Boone. After all, he didn't have eyes in the back of his head.

A tree snapped in the distance, the first snap they'd heard in a while. The trees that remained were mostly the ones that could hold the burdensome ice. Boone didn't budge at the sound of the snap beyond turning the page of his book.

If Miriam were to guess, she would suppose that a man with such a gentle, patient touch with plants would bring those same traits to the bedroom. Miriam imagined what his calloused hands would feel like sneaking beneath her shirt. She imagined how his lips that rarely smiled would soften while administering rows of kisses down her neck. She imagined the scratch of his whiskers if he were making his way down her abs as Houston had so artfully demonstrated.

Miriam needed to stop thinking about Boone's hand and mouth and whiskers. She needed to engage in conversation. She wanted to know more about the man next to whom she would once again sleep. Before she'd considered the wisdom of her words, Miriam asked, "So, what's your baking style? Cakes? Pies? Cookies? Nah, I bet you're one of those artisan bread guys."

Turning around to face her, Boone said, "I'm sorry. Did I miss the intro to this conversation?"

"I read on a certain unmentionable website on which we both appear to have profiles that you bake. I hadn't pegged you as a baker, so I'm trying to figure this out."

Boone's face scrunched in shame as he settled on his elbow, his head resting on a hand. "I've never baked a thing in my life. I didn't actually write a word of that God-forsaken profile."

Miriam couldn't disguise her surprise, so she decided to not even try. "Then who the hell wrote it?"

His face still distorted in what looked like actual, physical pain, Boone said, "Grandma…"

"Miss Rubie?"

"…and Miss Hyacinth…"

Miriam gasped.

"…and a lesbian librarian?"

Oh, this was too good.

Boone continued, "Not that the lesbian part matters. It just always seems to come up."

Suddenly, the conversation Miriam and Rubie had at the Altar Guild meeting resurfaced in Miriam's mind. The dawning understanding led her to exhale a long, "Oh." Sitting up further on her pillow, Miriam said, "So when Rubie said that she'd set up a Matchables profile, it wasn't for Rubie. It was for you."

She pointed directly at Boone and then descended into a fit of giggles.

"I thought we weren't going to say the name of that dadgum website." Boone turned to his back, crossing his arms over his chest and scowling at the ceiling.

Miriam sobered just the slightest bit. "So judging by who created your profile, I can safely assume that you don't bake?"

"Nope."

"And you don't have a gift for speaking with horses?"

His eyes shut. "I missed that one."

"And that you've never trained service dogs for the disabled?"

Rubbing his eyes, Boone muttered, "You must not have been trying to preserve your phone battery too hard if you had time to read all of that."

"You have to give her and Miss Hyacinth credit for their creativity, right? I would've never thought to claim I spoke fluent Portuguese or that I'd once backpacked across South America."

"That part is partially true."

"You speak Portuguese?"

"No, but I did travel through Brazil. Deforestation is endangering up to half of the tree species in the Amazon. I wanted to see them before they're gone."

Miriam was quiet for a moment. "That's a sort of depressing vacation."

"Yep. Not great online-profile material."

"I once traveled to an orphanage in Somalia to serve at a refugee camp, and I've worked in an orphanage in Tanzania for children whose parents died of AIDS."

"So you've also taken some pretty depressing vacations?"

"Yes. After seminary, I took a couple of years to try to save the world before I settled into a position here in the States."

Boone stared contemplatively at the ceiling for a few more moments before he returned his eyes to Miriam. Even in the dim firelight, she was blown away by just how light blue they were.

"How was saving the world?"

Miriam thought for only a moment before she said, "I didn't do much of anything except see my own privilege and feel deep shame. After a while, I came back to the US and protested and marched and, having failed to save the world, tried to at least make home a more just place."

"Did that go better?"

"I got arrested once, so now that I'm leading my comfortable middle-class existence, I can at least keep a mugshot on my desk to remind myself that not a day goes by when I don't fail to do enough."

His eyes hadn't moved from Miriam's face in a disconcerting span of time while she'd rambled about her adventures. He turned back to his side, propped on his elbow, and asked with profound seriousness, "Is your arrest record on your dating profile?"

Miriam smiled cynically. "I took the approach of trying to make myself look normal. But surely, with our little area of Kentucky so small, Matchables has sent you my profile on the wings of their nauseating love birds."

Boone's lips twitched on one corner in the faintest impression of a grin. "I've happily used the storm as an excuse to hide from my phone and its less enduring apps for the past two days, so no, I haven't stalked your profile yet."

"I'll spare you the trouble. I'm a career woman who works in pastoral care. I'd like to one day have a husband and children, but I'm not in a rush. I prefer dogs to cats but currently do not have either. I like my wine red and not too sweet but not too dry, either. I'm a carpenter hobbyist, and I like to spend time with friends.

I don't cook much, but I'm happy to eat Lucy's baking. When I get antsy, I hike. I don't have a green thumb, but I have a small collection of books on houseplants that I set around in the hopes that I will develop one at some point. That is actually a little bit more than I put in the real profile."

"Pastoral care?"

"With everything I just regurgitated, that's what stood out?"

Boone shrugged. "You sound normal enough. I'm guessing you're not going by Mother Miriam Howatch on your profile?"

Miriam flipped to her back and covered her face, wondering why she'd initiated this humiliating line of conversation. She moaned, "Can you imagine? I'd say my odds of getting a date are already abysmally low without that tidbit of information."

"I doubt it," Boone said so quietly the words barely registered above the crackle of the fire. "Most men ignore the content and focus only on the picture. You'll get plenty of attention."

Miriam thought she might have just been called pretty. Her voice quieting to match Boone's own, Miriam said, "If women were ogres who only paid attention to pictures, you would do quite well yourself. But since most women are, in fact, literate, your profile is intimidating. You should change the answers to the truth. A man who can grow anything, who tries to bring dying species back to life, who travels the world to see exotic, endangered trees. Women would eat that stuff up."

At this point, Miriam expected Boone to end their conversation and go to sleep. After all, he'd be waking up long before her to do whatever chores needed to be done before the sun could rise.

Instead, Boone seemed to settle in for more conversation. "So why don't you have a dog if you like dogs?"

"I don't own the house where I live. It's a parsonage owned by Trinity. I don't feel like being responsible for the damage a puppy might inflict. Plus, I have Lucy's dog, Clark, at my place all the time. How about you? Ever had a dog?"

"My old dog died last fall. I keep meaning to look for another puppy, but I guess it's just hard to move on. Bear and I, well, we went through a lot of life together."

Miriam smiled softly. "I do believe you're sentimental, Boone. I hadn't pegged you for a sentimentalist."

Boone raised a skeptical eyebrow. "If I'm sentimental, it's only for animals and plants. I don't particularly care for humans."

Miriam chuckled even as a yawn escaped. "Humans are sort of pains in the ass."

"Says the minister."

"Exactly. I should know better than anyone."

Now Boone was the one laughing, and Miriam cuddled deeper beneath her cover, self-satisfied that she'd made the beast laugh.

As his laughter subsided, Boone yawned, too, and said, "I'd best get some sleep."

"Me, too," Miriam said even though she had no early morning chores. For some unknown reason, she felt lingering energy pulsing through her system. She suspected she wouldn't sleep for some time.

Within a few minutes, Boone's back was rising and falling in the slow, steady ebb and flow of sleep. Feeling like she'd just downed a double shot of espresso, Miriam flipped to her other side, her face coming up against the back of the couch. Shutting her eyes stubbornly, she tried to forget how very close she lay to Boone. The more she tried, the more she failed.

Chapter 14

Boone trudged through the deep snow towards the greenhouse. He'd just finished eating dinner, but he couldn't stomach another evening spent staring at his book. He should go grade, but he wouldn't be able to focus, anyway. So instead, he headed out to water plants that were in no need of water whatsoever.

It was now Miriam's fourth day at the house. Temperatures remained well below freezing, giving the ice no chance to even begin thawing. This weather event was truly of historic proportions for Western Kentucky. Boone had turned on his phone earlier that afternoon just long enough to know that power was being restored to Paducah and other nearby towns, but most remote areas still had several days of waiting ahead of them. The downed trees had done considerable damage to the power line infrastructure of the area, and many roads, including their own, were still impassable. Rubie was thrilled at the news.

While he'd been trying to use his phone quickly and efficiently, Matchables squawked a notification that let him know they had potential love birds for him to peruse. Miriam's photo popped up on the wings of two birds with little hearts tweeting from their beaks.

He'd expected to see her float across his screen at some point after hearing the shrill tweets coming from her phone. While everything about the app was hideous, Miriam's picture was predictably beautiful. She'd chosen a casual, unposed photo where she was laughing. A curl fell over one eye, and her hand looked as though it was in mid-reach to swipe the curl behind an ear. Boone stared at the photo for several minutes, forgetting that he was supposed to be preserving his phone battery.

His thumb hovered over the "pass" bar. If he understood the app, a "pass" would prevent the app from recommending them to each other in the future. Clicking "nest", a button in the shape of an actual bird's nest, would send his information directly to her. Clearly not an option.

There was a third option, though. Boone closed the app without touching a thing and shut off his phone, tossing it into his desk drawer.

During the brief window when his phone was on, Boone let Travis know they were doing fine. He'd also sent word to Porter and Forrest that Miriam was still safe and sound on the farm, although sound was really not the right word. Sound insinuated peace and calm.

No, Miriam was not a calming presence in their little world. As she became more accustomed to their house, she'd found ways to occupy her time. Now, at least three pieces of furniture had been repaired, and the quilt top Rubie made several years ago was stretched into a frame with the two women happily applying small stitches along all the seams. Rubie beamed with pride telling Boone how quickly Mother Miriam had learned to hand quilt. She'd also joined him a few times in the greenhouse to watch how he trimmed back plants and let others go wild. She was fascinated by how he knew exactly how damp the soil should feel and exactly how much dirt should cling to a finger when pressed in a perfectly moistened environment. Miriam even managed to befriend the barn cats. It took Boone a good while to convince her that, no, really, they weren't too cold in the barn, and they didn't need to become house cats.

And through it all, through all the activity she had rustled up in their formerly quiet home, Miriam chatted cheerfully, laughed freely, and never displayed a shred of boredom. She seemed endlessly engaged in each task, fascinated by learning new things and appreciative of the talents she saw in Boone and Rubie. Boone felt he should be annoyed with the sudden onslaught of sound, the relentless chatter and gaiety. After all, as Rubie loved to point out, he was known for seeking solitude among his plants. But, surprisingly, he kept finding himself drawn to Miriam and the stir of activity swirling around her.

As Boone opened the door to the greenhouse, warmth immediately engulfed him. Four days without heat in the house had left the interior painfully cold except for right around the fireplace. The greenhouse with its generator and the barn with its animals were both warmer than parts of the house.

Boone smiled at the thought of Miriam's outings to the barn, probably seeking warmth. When she first befriended the barn cats, he'd brushed the horse long past the time that was necessary so that he could listen to her silly ramblings to the cats. She asked them how they liked the barn mice and if they knew how pretty their orange coats were. She petted them each and gave them more human interaction in an hour than they normally received in a week.

The cats weren't the only recipients of Miriam's constant questioning and curiosity. Once when Boone came in from the greenhouse undetected, he'd stood quietly in the hallway listening to Miriam ask Rubie a million questions about when she first fell in love with Rupert and what their early years had been like. They were all questions Boone wanted to know the answers to, all questions he wished he'd thought to ask himself. By the time he walked into the room, he'd learned that his grandparents met on a blind date in high school, that they'd written to each other weekly while Rupert had served in Korea, and that his grandfather was apparently a "boob-man," a fact Rubie declared advantageous since she'd always been generously endowed. That was the point in the conversation when Boone decided eavesdropping wasn't the best idea.

Perhaps what surprised Boone the most about Miriam was that when she came to the greenhouse, he didn't feel she was imposing on his space. He didn't mind her questions, and he let her help even when she was clumsy and lacked finesse with his beloved plants. Astonishingly, her presence felt natural in the space.

And then there were the nights. At night, Boone and Miriam would each stretch out on their makeshift beds, parallel with only a couple feet of separation, and they would read their books. They were four nights into this routine, and Boone had yet to get past the bat chapter. Miriam, on the other hand, had burned through at least three paperbacks from the eighties and had gleefully recounted to Boone a plethora of sappy moments.

As they lay by the fire either reading or pretending to read, their books would be laid to the side every few minutes as Miriam thought of some little something she wanted to tell Boone. She'd share something about her book or a funny story Rubie had told her that day or ask a question about some plant they'd worked with in the greenhouse. Each time she spoke, Boone would feel relieved to be able to stop the reading charade and, instead, focus on her.

When she spoke of her book, her lips would purse in a mischievous smile. When it was a story about Rubie or one of their mutual friends, she would lean forward, like she was presenting an offering they could share. Boone always wanted to mirror her movement, to lean towards her as well, but he'd maintain his position, allowing himself only to look, never to lean.

Finally, when Miriam closed her book and shut her eyes, Boone would face the fireplace and find sleep tortuously unattainable deep into the night. Since moving out of his college dorm, he'd rarely slept in the same room as another person. When he had girlfriends, he'd always gone home after their dates, even when the dates ended in sex. There was something about sleeping with someone, the actual literal act of sleeping, that felt shockingly intimate. And yet, here he was doing it nightly with someone he would never date.

Rubie had now commented on more than one occasion that Boone was looking tired. He could have sworn she hid a giggle when he'd yawned repeatedly over breakfast that morning.

As Boone walked among his plants, he didn't really do anything. He didn't water or prune or check the soil. They'd all been tended to more than usual. Instead, he strolled through the aisles thinking about the past few days, about how quickly and radically Miriam had integrated herself into the rhythm of his and Rubie's life. The conclusion he came to was quite simple: it was nice to have her around. Of course, she never really stopped talking, but still, it was nice.

The couple of light bulbs that hung naked from the ceiling shone brightly off the snow-lined windows. The bright white contrasted sharply against the areas of windows without snow that were now pitch black in the winter night absent of any security lights. It created a chessboard effect all around Boone and his green menagerie. As Boone slowly turned in place enjoying the beauty of the greenhouse covered in snow and darkness, the door creaked. He'd forgotten to grease the hinges. He wouldn't be surprised to find Miriam taking a can of WD-40 to the old door before she left.

Miriam's curls appeared around the edge of the door.

"Need company out here?"

***

Miriam had been sitting in front of the fire reading for about thirty minutes when she decided to search for Boone. The chill in the house was feeling oppressive. Rubie headed up to her room early that evening, probably to warm up with the little kerosene heater and the stack of quilts on her bed. Miriam would do almost anything for central heating. Figuring Boone was also seeking relief from the cold, Miriam headed out to the greenhouse.

Several times a day, Boone could be found in the greenhouse. Rubie assured Miriam this was his normal routine, not a by-product of Miriam's stay. Apparently, he gravitated to the greenhouse like a cat to a catnip bed.

It only took Miriam her first trip out there to understand why. She, too, found herself gravitating to the glass walls and ceilings, to the vivid presence of life and to the quiet man walking between the rows.

So here she was in the black of night, her hand around the ice-cold door handle, finding Boone standing in the center of his masterpiece. He didn't have shears or a trowel or any evidence of work in his hands. She immediately intuited that he had simply been soaking in the space. In essence, she was doing the same thing. However, Miriam preferred not to admit that Boone's presence was, for her, part of the greenhouse experience.

She said, "Need company out here?"

Boone sputtered, probably trying to come up with some task that would explain why he wasn't in the house or would give them something to occupy their hands. Finally, he said, "Sure. Would you like to help me cut Rubie some roses? I have a few that have bloomed under the grow lights. I'm sure you'd be better at arranging them than me."

Miriam was already familiar enough with the layout of the greenhouse to know where to go. She stepped over to the small section of roses, the ones he grew not for some research project but only for his grandmother's enjoyment. Boone followed behind her, quieter than normal. What had been on his mind when she entered his sanctuary?

As Boone stepped beside her in front of the roses, Miriam took off the heavy corduroy coat that had been his grandfather's and set it on a nearby table. She unbuttoned the cuffs of yet another flannel shirt Boone and Rubie had lent to her. Slowly, she rolled up her sleeves, enjoying the feel of the greenhouse's damp air on her skin. She'd stayed bundled up all day, even in the house. Without the weight, she felt light enough to float.

"What are you doing?" Boone asked as he watched her roll a sleeve.

"I don't want to snag one of your shirts on a rose thorn."

"But I don't want you to get a scratch. A few holes in that shirt will be no great loss, believe me."

Miriam continued rolling up her sleeve saying, "I lied. I just wanted a break from the coat."

Boone's lip quirked in his signature half smile. "Fair enough."

They stood side by side, Boone talking about the different varieties. Even with the lights, it was still dim in the black night, but they were able to pick a few and carry them over to a tall table where they sat across from each other on barstools. As she started to arrange the roses in a vase, Miriam resisted the urge to go find her coat. Even the warmth of the greenhouse couldn't completely banish the chill of the night.

Poking a stem into several areas trying to find the right spot, Miriam said, "Thank you for tolerating me in your greenhouse. I know this is where you go for a little quiet, and here I am never being quiet."

Boone sat back on his stool, crossing his arms over his chest. With a hint of a grin, he said, "Quiet isn't your thing, is it?"

Miriam, still focused on the flowers, absentmindedly said, "Talking is sort of my job, so no, quiet isn't my thing."

"And you're good at your job."

Miriam looked up from her task, saw teasing in Boone's eyes, and threw a short stem cutting at him. He dodged to the side and laughed.

Picking up another rose, Miriam was surprised when Boone's hand reached out and touched her arm, his fingers wrapping around her forearm. Freezing in mid-motion, Miriam looked up to his face. He wasn't laughing anymore, and his eyes were laser-focused on the roots of the olive tree that wrapped around Miriam's arm.

In almost a whisper, Boone said, "Huh. It's true. You really do have a tattoo."

Matching his tone, Miriam said, "I have a few. But what do you mean I really have them? Had you heard rumors or something?"

"Oh, it's what all the little old ladies talk about."

Miriam tilted her head in question.

Boone clarified, "I sometimes drive the bus to Friday night bingo for them."

"That is the least 'Boone' sounding activity I've ever heard of."

"I had a game of poker against Grandma go terribly wrong about a year ago."

Miriam breathed out a laugh mingled with an, "aah." Then her eyes lowered to where Boone's hand still held her arm gently in his grasp. Even in the cold, his fingers were warm. Miriam's fingers wouldn't melt butter at the moment.

Seeing her seeing him, Boone's hand retreated with more haste than was necessary. Bemused, he said, "It looks like roots. What's the rest of it?"

Without thought, Miriam unbuttoned the top buttons of her flannel shirt and lowered it to expose her shoulder and back. She spun around on the stool so that Boone would have a full view of the ink she had acquired during the year leading up to seminary. She and Lucy would spend long hours in the tattoo parlor, Lucy keeping her talking to distract Miriam from the pain. Miriam heard Boone's stool creaking as he stood, coming closer to see in the dim light.

Leaning her head to the opposite shoulder so that her hair wouldn't hide the top of the tree at the base of her neck, Miriam explained her tattoo. "It's an olive tree, a symbol of peace in the Bible. I got it right before I went to seminary. I'd become interested in religion and had been reading scripture and several of the mystics. Julian of Norwich was my favorite. It was all so beautiful and full of love and full of peace, but when I looked around me, the religion I saw in my community was judgmental, full of anger and fear. I wanted to change that. I guess that's why I went to seminary. Anyways, I got the olive tree to symbolize the peace I saw in God."

Miriam almost jumped in surprise when she felt the sandpapery fingertips of Boone's work-roughened hands touch the tops of the tree and slowly graze all the way down to the roots that had been visible below her sleeves. With fingers colder than right before she delivered a sermon, Miriam shakily unbuttoned one more button and lowered the shirt off of her other shoulder. Clutching the middle of the shirt in a fist over her breasts, Miriam secured it around her.

"Tell me about the birds," Boone said.

"They're doves flying towards the tree. Doves often symbolize the presence of God. It's a dove that lets Noah know there's land after the flood."

As Miriam tilted her head to the opposite side, granting Boone access to the dove grazing the base of her neck, his hand brushed curls from her neck. A shiver ran down the length of Miriam's body, a shiver born of freezing temperatures or days without regular heating or a sudden and overwhelming awareness of Boone's proximity. Who could say, exactly? Maybe it was awareness of the intimacy of their conversation, of all that she was exposing to his eyes and his hands. It was followed immediately by the realization that she wanted to allow the shirt to fall further. She wanted to face Boone and feel those perfectly worn fingers touch her face and her neck and more. She wanted more.

His voice husky, Boone said, "I have a tree tattoo, also."

Miriam turned to face him as he unbuttoned his shirt cuffs and pushed the sleeves sloppily up his arms, not taking care to roll them as Miriam had done. The skin above his auburn beard was flushed as if his pulse was also a rushing rapid. Turning his fists palm-side up, Boone placed his forearms together so that the two sides of a tree came together at the center, the junction of his arms marking a line of symmetry.

Miriam gasped at the stark beauty of the black drawing. Awed, she asked, "What kind of tree is it?"

"It's an American Chestnut. The East used to be full of these beasts. They were enormous, like the Redwoods. And then one day in the early 1900s, a blight came to America from a tree that was imported from China. Within a few years, all of the American Chestnuts, billions of them, just died."

Boone's exploration of her tattoos wordlessly granted Miriam permission to reach out to this lonely, ghostly tree. Running a finger over the lines of the trunk, she said, "That's tragic. It's like a national treasure I never knew existed. How had I never heard of them?"

"People don't talk about losses too big to understand. That's why people don't want to hear that the environment is suffering, that we're losing plant and animal species at astonishing rates. It creates a pain and sense of loss they can't easily quantify or understand."

"Why's it in two halves? Is that symbolic?"

"Nope. It just looks cool."

Miriam smirked even as her eyes continued to roam. Looking up, she saw the tip of something barely visible over his collar. Shrugging back into her shirt, Miriam pulled down on his collar. It was a bird wing, and she wanted to see the rest and to hear the story behind that bird. Moving her hands to his top button, Miriam asked, "May I?"

Boone nodded once, giving Miriam all the permission she needed. It took two buttons to reveal the whole bird.

"A passenger pigeon," Boone said.

This time, there was color in the haunting depiction of the bird. Miriam instinctively knew it, too, was extinct.

Barely above a whisper, Miriam said, "Are there more?"

***

In answer to Miriam's question, Boone unbuttoned his shirt and cast it aside. He couldn't allow Miriam to continue unbuttoning his shirt for him. He couldn't take the torture of seeing her frigid hands work their way down his shirt, untucking the hem from his pants. He was already breathing roughly trying to contain the heat she had stoked within him by simply undoing the first few buttons.

Over the preceding decade, Boone had slowly collected the tattoos that covered his torso and arms, but he'd rarely shown them to anyone. He'd never exposed himself so completely to someone else's scrutiny, but Miriam seemed mesmerized by the story his tattoos told. Boone had orchestrated this exhibit over the years he'd studied the earth, its ecosystems, its plants and animals, and all the horrifying damage humans had inflicted in their quest to conquer and tame.

As Boone stood bare from the waist up, Miriam studied the Marshallia Glandiflora that ran along the left edge of his abdomen. Her finger ran along the stem, stopping at the daisy-like flower on top. If Miriam had raised her eyes, she might have noticed Boone's jaw clenching. It took considerable effort to resist the urge to look down at her still unbuttoned shirt, its opening gaping wider as she leaned in for a better look.

On his date the previous week, Boone noticed Miriam's curves in the black sweater she'd worn at the restaurant. It seemed forever ago. He'd noticed her then and had wanted to stare at her instead of looking across the table at the comparably unimpressive @catsandcoffeegirl. And now, here Miriam was: no rigid white collar, no layers, her buttons undone.

"It's like entries in a flora and fauna book," Miriam whispered in fascination.

Boone could feel her warm breath moving over his abdomen as she studied each tattoo with only inches between them. "It's not just like it. Most are actual entries in books from the 1800s."

"Why did you pick these specific ones?"

"Because they're extinct. All of them are extinct."

Miriam's eyes darted up to his even as she stayed bent in front of him. After a moment's scrutiny, she looked back down at an ivory-billed woodpecker just beneath his left pectoral. Her hand reached out and stroked the picture of the bird. Slowly, she walked around his body, touching each individual entry in the colorful dirge that clothed Boone's body.

When she completed the full rotation, she stood upright and looked directly into his eyes. In the tone used at the crest of an epiphany, she said, "Huh."

"What?"

"I'd always classified your eyes as icy blue. In my mind, they were icy. But I was seeing them wrong. They have little specks. They're robin's egg blue. I don't know why I thought they were cold."

And then, she wasn't looking at his eyes anymore. Her gaze had lowered to his mouth, and Boone's eyes responded by also lowering to her lips - lips the same color as the Eden Climber roses he grew for their exceptionally soft pink blush. Boone realized with painful clarity that there had never been a woman he'd wanted to soak in like he did Miriam Howatch. He wanted to stare at her for hours. He wanted to be in her presence and hear the soundtrack of her musings and watch her mindlessly twirling her hair. He didn't want to read about the damn bats anymore. He wanted to read her expressions, her movements, her roaming eyes that now held a question Boone didn't know how to answer.

There were several ways he could respond. He could close the distance between them, stepping closer or leaning forward or pulling her to him. Her shirt was already falling open, inviting his hands to roam. Would she reciprocate, running her hands over his bare chest? From her shallow breathing and the part of her lips, he thought she might. He could feel adrenaline and desire charging the air between their bodies. A single touch was all it would take to toss a match on kerosene, and the heat would feel so damned good after days of ice and snow.

Or he could step back and pick up his discarded shirt. He could breathe in deeply so that his fingers would stop shaking long enough to manage the buttons. He could yawn and say it was time to call it a night.

Just as he dismissed the latter option, raising his hands to pull her towards him, he noticed that Miriam was shaking. Goosebumps ran down her forearms beneath her rolled sleeves, and her teeth made cartoonish chattering sounds. The spell broke, and a third option appeared.

Rubbing his hands up and down Miriam's arms, Boone said, "You're too cold. We've gone too long without coats. Let's get you in and I'll stoke the fire. We'll get the living room as warm as possible."

"This is ridiculous. I don't know what's wrong with me. It isn't even that cold in here."

"Just because I keep it above freezing doesn't mean it's toasty."

"Yes, but you'd think I'd be used to the cold after the week we've had, right?"

As she rambled, Miriam looked at her feet, her eyes downcast. Her hands shaking, she tried in vain to button her shirt. After a couple of failed attempts, Boone assumed the task, his fingers rarely cold even in the worst conditions. When he was finished, Miriam murmured a soft, "Thank you," as she turned around and grabbed her coat, giving Boone privacy to put on his shirt.

After shirts were buttoned and tucked in and coats were once again zipped to their necks, when all the tattoos were once again in hiding, Boone followed Miriam out of the greenhouse, stepping into the deep footprints she left in the path to the house.

***

As Miriam opened the door to the kitchen of the house, she was struck by the lack of warmth that met her. Walking into houses in the middle of winter was usually an embrace, the contrasting warmth engulfing a person. The absence of that warmth was a disorienting experience no matter how expected it was.

And Miriam was already disoriented. Her mind reeled with a rapid replay of scenes from the greenhouse. They'd unbuttoned shirts and shown bare skin. Boone had touched her, and she'd touched him. For Miriam, the touches had been caresses disguised as investigation. Boone's touches had felt the same.

Before her body betrayed her, before the chills had no longer been containable, she saw intention in Boone's eyes. He made a decision, and she knew in her bones that he had decided to step towards her, to close the small space that still separated their partially clad bodies. And she had wanted him to. She'd wanted to make the move towards him, too, but a thread of uncertainty kept her frozen in place. How could the same man who was so dismissive of her vocation, of the work that oriented her life, suddenly be attracted to her? Miriam was honest enough with herself to admit she desired him. But she also knew she wanted someone who wanted all of her.

How desperately she'd wanted him to take that step. Miriam had never burned for intimacy the way she had in their snow-covered glass house. The desire had been so overwhelming, that she suspected it was to blame for her shivering just as much as the cold.

As Boone followed behind her, he said, "I can heat some water for tea to help you warm up."

Miriam smiled but declined the offer. "I just want to cover up on the couch. Rubie and I made up our beds before she went upstairs. I'll get ready and be there in a minute."

The bathroom did nothing to help her shivering. The cold tile of the floor and the unforgiving frigid water had both assaulted her already cold body. Wearing flannel pajamas, more left-behinds from Travis, Miriam shuffled into the living room.

Boone had also changed and was already lying beneath his covers reading the same book he'd been working on all week. It occurred to Miriam that she had read three novels in that time. Maybe it was a dense, academic affair.

As she crawled into bed and shimmied down deep into the stack of covers, Miriam cursed her teeth for giving away her discomfort with persistent chattering. Boone's eyes flicked away from his book to glance in her direction, concern creasing his brow.

"You okay?"

"I'm fine, really. I just got chilled."

Boone's gaze returned to his book. She would like to read, as well, but she didn't want any skin outside of the covers, not even her hands to hold a book. Turning over, Miriam straightened her body along the entire length of the back of the couch. She hoped that by pressing against the barrier, she would soon banish the chills. Her arms wrapped around her body in an unsatisfactory hug. Nothing she did seemed to bring any additional warmth.

After about five minutes, Boone blew out the reading candle. Miriam forced herself to breathe deeply, hoping to combat her shivers with stubborn mind-over-matter.

Just as she was contemplating feigning the need to return to the bathroom so that Boone would have a chance to fall asleep without the background noise of her ridiculous chills, Miriam felt a touch of pressure on her arm.

"Miriam," Boone whispered, the sound gruff and uneven in the quiet night. "Miri, let me help."

She started to tell him no, that she would be fine, that she would stop shaking like a frightened kitten any moment now. But before she could, he had pulled back the covers and was lying behind her, his body cupping her body, no gaps or mismatched corners. He was tall and she was tall and they fit like the blocks in the Tetris game she'd played as a child in the nineties.

Boone's hands, warm enough they felt like he'd held them in front of the fireplace's flames just for the purpose of taking away her chills, wrapped around her arms, rubbing gently, the callouses scratching pleasantly. Miriam could feel puffs of warm air as he breathed against the back of her neck.

As she lay there receiving Boone's offering, it occurred to Miriam that she hadn't been taken care of in a very long time. She hadn't been touched, truly touched, in what felt like ages. And the friction of his rough hands started to stoke warmth that did far more than simply subside her shivers. She felt a burning deep within that spread out and infused every part of her body.

There was only one small gap of space that existed between their bodies. Sometime after first crawling behind her, Boone had moved his pelvis back a few inches, putting a small but telling distance between their most intimate regions. Miriam wanted to press back into him, to see what he would do and where that small act of interest would lead. But just as she began to move against the warm, hard body that held her own so gently, Boone's beard tickled her neck as he whispered, "Try to sleep."

"Alright," Miriam answered, the suggestive push of her body paused by his words. Boone was here in kindness to aid the shivering damsel in distress. This was an act of chivalry on his part, not an advance. After a while, Boone's hands stopped rubbing her arms, leaving only his thumbs moving in small, massaging circles. A few more minutes passed, and much to her surprise, Miriam fell asleep in Boone's embrace.

***

Rubie's eyes opened to the pitch black of a world without electricity. She always woke up a couple of times a night. Usually, a quick trip to the bathroom was all it took for her to fall back asleep. However, after rolling out of bed, pulling on her thickest house shoes, and walking to the bathroom, Rubie's stomach growled the tell-tale growl of hunger.

Late-night snacks were a common occurrence for Rubie. When Rupert had been alive, he often woke in the middle of the night only to find Rubie's side of the bed empty but for rumpled covers. He always knew to head to the kitchen where he'd find her with a warm glass of milk and a thick slice of buttered toast. Sometimes she'd fry them both up a few slices of bacon just for kicks before they returned to their bed for the rest of the night.

Never one to ignore a growling tummy, Rubie decided that it was a fine night for some buttered toast. With her cushioned house shoes, she was confident she could tip-toe past Boone and Miriam without waking anyone.

Walking down the steps, Rubie cursed the squeaky fifth stair. As she took the final step, she stood still at the base holding her breath, waiting to see if she'd disturbed anyone's rest. Looking over to the pallet where Boone had slept all week, Rubie was surprised to see the covers thrown to one side and the makeshift bedding abandoned. At first, she figured this meant she'd have company for her midnight snack.

But then Rubie's eyes scanned over to the couch, and there she saw the mound of covers was far too broad to accommodate only Miriam's slender frame. No, the slope of the covers was unmistakable as her grandson's broad shoulders. Rising onto her tippy toes, Rubie saw Miriam's characteristic curls just beyond Boone's beard.

If Rubie Rutledge had still been a young woman with the knees of a young woman, she would have jumped in place as she silently cheered the sight on her old, plaid sofa. As it was, her arthritic hands clenched into fists and she pumped them into the air in a mimed celebration. Deciding she wasn't that hungry after all, Rubie turned around and started back up the stairs taking special care on the fifth step to tread lightly.

Chapter 15

The sun was only suggesting it might rise when Boone extricated himself from the cozy cocoon in which he and Miriam had slept. To be strictly accurate, it was more where Miriam had slept. Boone had only managed to doze a few minutes here and there. Gingerly crossing the living room, Boone slipped on his boots and coat in the kitchen and headed out to the barn. The sun was shining, and the air had less bite to it. Boone felt in his bones that they were turning a corner. It would only be another day or two before temptation would be blessedly removed from his house.

As Boone went about feeding the animals, his mind remained on the sofa. The chills that had racked Miriam's body subsided soon after he crawled in beside her. He'd surprised himself when he pushed aside voices of warning and crossed the space separating their beds. In reality, he probably could have abandoned the job of warming her soon thereafter. The problem was that he hadn't wanted to let go.

Miriam's body fit perfectly against him. It had felt natural to hold her in his arms, as natural as it felt to care for his plants. Her curls were exactly as soft as he'd suspected, and they smelled even better than a Madame Alfred Carriere rose.

In fact, he'd spent much of the night staring at her curls wanting to reach up and spin one around his finger in just the way she did when she was deep in concentration. He'd wanted to, but he'd kept his body as still as the world of ice outside.

Boone knew that something had shifted between them just as he knew the weather was shifting. He and Miriam had formed a friendship over the past few days, but it wasn't simply a friendship. For Boone, there was an undercurrent of attraction that kept any space they shared pulsing with an energy he'd never experienced. There were times the previous evening in the greenhouse when they'd been running their hands over each other's bodies and sharing the stories behind their tattoos when he'd felt certain she noticed the energy, too. Her eyes had looked as shocked and captivated as he had felt when she unbuttoned her shirt and turned her beautiful, bare shoulders towards him.

And she didn't even need to be in the room for Boone to feel it. When they'd come in from the greenhouse, and she'd gone to the bathroom to prepare for the evening, Boone had imagined her changing clothes, had imagined the goosebumps that would cover her skin as she ran a cold wash rag over her body. When she was in the room, he couldn't take his eyes off of her, but when she left the room, he couldn't stop imagining her.

Whatever it was between them, it was inconvenient. Sure, she looked nice and approachable in flannel shirts and blue jeans, but the second the ice thawed and the roads cleared, she'd be back in a white dog-collar shirt preparing for another sermon. With a simple wardrobe change, she'd become as approachable as a bear. In a world filled with beautiful women, Boone was falling for the one he couldn't have, the one he couldn't allow himself to have. He couldn't be with someone whose entire existence was tangled in the web of religion. Period.

So Boone had kept distance between them even when every fiber of his being protested. As he held her on the couch, he'd kept his pelvis back several inches knowing that if he truly hugged each inch of her to him, he would lose all self-control in an instant, and she would've felt his desire in ways we wouldn't be able to deny. Instead, he'd kept that modicum of space and tried to concentrate on the least sensual topics possible. He'd spent a good amount of time enumerating the different varieties of manures.

Now, reliving the memory of the previous evening in the cold reality of the barn, Boone admitted how very close he'd come, on more than one occasion, to complicating their nascent friendship with kisses or touches or moments of eye contact that stretched into significance. He'd kept from crossing these lines only by steely self-resolve, but that was rapidly crumbling. As he ran his hand over a horse's mane, Boone recommitted himself to trying what his Grandmother had been begging him to try. He was going to find someone to date. As soon as electricity and internet access allowed, he was going to go on Matchables and revamp his profile so that it was a little more honest and a little less dream-man for the over-eighty crowd. Then, he was going to go on dates, as many dates as it took, until he found someone who would make him forget Mother Miriam Howatch.

When Boone left the barn and reentered the kitchen, Rubie stood at the stove carefully flipping eggs so their yolks remained intact. It wasn't fancy, but it was Boone's favorite breakfast, and no one could execute an over-easy quite like Rubie.

"Good morning, Grandma," Boone said, removing his snow-crusted boots before coming further into the kitchen.

Rubie interrupted a tune she'd been humming long enough to say, "Mornin', Boonie. Thank you for the flowers." She looked over her shoulder and beamed in his direction, looking like a woman who had either consumed far too much coffee or had recently found out she was about to become a grandmother.

"You're welcome," Boone said, smiling warily. "Miriam actually arranged them."

"Indeed? How very, intensely interesting."

Rubie resumed humming. She shimmied her shoulders as she seamlessly moved from humming to singing the words, "What a wonderful world." Boone knew that in her mind, she was singing along to Willie Nelson's version of the classic song. It would always be Willie Nelson's version.

Boone arched an eyebrow. "How much coffee have you had this morning?"

Before Rubie could answer, Miriam walked into the room. Her hair looked like she'd just rolled out of bed - probably because she'd just rolled out of bed - and Boone thought it suited her. Perhaps more than suited. He wanted his hands caught up in the curls, tousling them more. In fact, his whole body tensed with desire. Now that he knew how she felt to hold, he was having a much harder time convincing himself that he didn't really want to hold her.

Miriam said through a yawn, "Good morning, Louis."

This paused Rubie just long enough to say, "Oh, I'm being Willie."

"Obviously," Boone chimed in, his eyes refusing to look away from the person he'd spent his night holding. Deciding he should do something besides ogle their house guest, Boone started crossing the kitchen to the French press full of dark coffee. At the same time, Miriam headed in the opposite direction towards the pantry. When they met in the middle, both lowered their eyes, and Boone's lighter skin couldn't hide his blush. They each stepped first to one side and then the other, looking unfortunately similar to preteens stumbling through their first school dance. Finally, they both paused, looked up, and Boone pointed to his right. "I'll go this way."

During the awkward passing, the background score of the kitchen had ceased while Rubie watched the two young ones fail at simply walking past each other. Once Boone finally got around Miriam, he noticed his grandmother resuming the song with even more vigor than before. With sickening clarity, Boone knew that, somehow, his grandmother had seen him holding Miriam, likely during one of the brief periods when he'd slept. How would he convince her that under no circumstances were he and Mother Miriam ever going to be an item?

***

Even by Rubie Rutledge's standards, Miriam noticed the older woman being more eccentric than usual. She hummed loudly, and her arms swayed like a ballerina with each kitchen task she completed. To be honest, the theatrical movements were more like those of a student ballerina, one in the beginners class for girls barely out of toddlerhood. But regardless, Rubie was feeling the music today.

After Miriam and Boone each sat down with their cups of coffee to wait on the eggs Rubie was frying, Rubie switched to an energetic rendition of Dolly Parton's "Why'd You Come in Here Lookin' Like That?," her feet shuffling in a two-step as she crossed the kitchen. Placing plates of eggs in front of them, she stopped the song to say, "I ate before you each came in. I'm just going to head upstairs for a few more minutes of shut-eye."

Boone looked skeptically at the sprightly woman who had just danced across the kitchen in her floral housecoat and pink, puffy slippers. Expanding her wrinkled eyes into a pose reminiscent of one of the Precious Moments figurines nestled in gaps throughout the house's bookshelves, Rubie said, "It's hard getting old." Then, she pranced out of the kitchen to the more somber tune of Dolly's "I Will Always Love You."

Once she'd exited the kitchen, Boone and Miriam were left with only the faint crackle of the fireplace in the adjacent living room. Miriam said, "She's in rare form this morning."

Boone took his fork and broke the yolk of his egg. Growling under his breath, he said, "God help us all."

Miriam was exceptionally attuned to the emotions of people around her. It was a skill that helped in ministry but could make everyday life uncomfortable. This morning, Rubie was the very picture of contentment. Boone, on the other hand, looked to be wary and guarded, the transformation from the previous evening startling.

When Miriam's eyes had opened to sunlight streaking through the lace curtains in the living room, she'd immediately felt the absence of Boone. She'd woken several times throughout the night just enough to confirm that he was still there, still holding her, still breathing against her neck. Every time her eyes fluttered open, she'd felt amazed all over again at the newness of this intimacy from someone with so many barriers. In one evening, she'd examined his entire torso, realized the sentimental yet noble reasons behind each piece of art, and been held and caressed by him in return. Yet throughout the shockingly intimate evening, Boone had prevented any single part from becoming overtly sexual. Did he feel the same attraction for her that she felt for him?

Personally, Miriam felt no confusion. She knew exactly what she wanted. She wanted to pick up right where they'd left off the previous evening, but to take everything a step further. This time, instead of fingers running over inky lines, there would be lips and tongues. When she lay spooned against him, she would eliminate the space he'd so carefully guarded the previous evening. And she would take his bearded face in her hands and kiss him unabashedly.

The train of erotic thoughts running through her mind robbed Miriam of her appetite. Setting down her fork, her eggs began to grow cold in the already cold room. Taking the coffee instead, Miriam took a long sip, stealing a glance at Boone as he repeatedly stabbed his eggs.

Suddenly, his fork, too, clattered to the table. Looking directly into her eyes, Boone said, "I'm sorry about last night. It was inappropriate of me to crawl into bed with you like that. I should've just gotten you some extra blankets."

Miriam deflated, the remembrances of their intimate moments falling like beads from a broken necklace. Picking up her fork, Miriam cut a piece of egg, her eyes lowered. Then, she took a mental step away from the scene in which she sat. She saw a bruised man who clearly couldn't give unreservedly to another. She saw a woman, timidly posed across from him, slouching and ashamed.

At the sight, Miriam hardly recognized herself. She was a woman who had made her way in a man's profession. She didn't allow herself to be cowed, and she didn't let someone else's hangups dictate her own responses. But here she was, acting as if her feelings meant nothing unless he reciprocated them.

Straightening her shoulders and lifting her head, Miriam looked into Boone's robin's egg eyes and said, "Well, that's a ridiculous apology. We both know another blanket wouldn't have offered the same warmth as a human body. And besides, I liked it when you held me. I like when you touch me, and I like touching you. So, please, spare me the apology."

Boone responded only with widened eyes and a silent, partially opened mouth. Standing up, Miriam did something she rarely ever did: she left her plate of uneaten eggs for someone else to clean. Putting on boots and a coat in fluid, decisive motions, Miriam declared with the utmost dignity, "I'm going out to chat with the barn cats." She let the door slam behind her.

Chapter 16

After spending a day sorting scraps of fabric by color and arranging stacks according to the rainbow (good old Roy G. Biv), Miriam looked around the cold house for something else to distract her from the previous evening and disappointing morning. She and Boone had spent the day avoiding one another. Miriam was avoiding him because she was both mortified that she had so blatantly declared she liked him and also unwilling to take back her pronouncement. She imagined Boone was avoiding her because he was an emotionally stunted male who considered the morning's non-argument Exhibit A for why they should desist all touching and holding and tattoo exhibits.

Despite his captivating eyes and charming half-smiles and fascinating tattoo choices, Boone Rutledge was unavailable. This was a fact Miriam was determined to accept. It wasn't a wedding band or sexual orientation or the more common boundaries that one might assume. In fact, Miriam couldn't identify the barrier. She just knew that a barrier stood between them that was both intangible and impassable.

Not in the mood to read another novel filled with angst and sexual tension and passionate love scenes, Miriam wanted to hear Lucy's voice. When Miriam was disoriented or lonely, she reached out to Lucy, the oldest and truest of her friends, and suddenly, the world would feel a little more orderly, and she would feel a little more capable of handling the storms.

Sneaking across the hall from Rubie's room where she'd been sorting fabric, Miriam closed herself into Boone's room. Since it was the only room in the house not currently being used, they had closed its door to preserve the negligible amount of heat the fireplace sent upstairs for the bathroom. While the cold was uncomfortable, it practically guaranteed privacy.

Wrapping a throw around her shoulders, Miriam settled on the neatly made covers of Boone's bed and attempted to ignore the masculine, woodsy scent that lingered in his room. Taking her phone out, she turned it on. A call to Lucy was worth depleting her battery. Lucy - bless her - answered within two rings.

"Miriam? Miriam, is that you? I've been worried sick about you. How are you and Boone and Rubie doing out there? I can't believe you got stuck in the middle of nowhere in the worst ice storm in fifty years!"

When Lucy was stressed, she rambled. Miriam smiled at the evidence of her friend's concern. "If you'll inhale, I'll give you an update."

Lucy's laughter sailed across the phone, and Miriam felt a little of the tension releasing from her shoulders. What she needed was a girls' night with Lucy and Edith where no complicated, obtuse men were allowed.

Lucy said, "Seriously, how's snowmageddon going for you?"

"We're doing good. Rubie and I have completed a whole slew of little projects around the house. I fixed a few furniture repairs she needed, and we sorted all of her fabrics. Also, the very best part: she has this insane collection of romance novels from - I don't know - when did Harlequin romances become a thing?"

Lucy had her own impressive collection of Regency romances. She said, "I don't know when exactly they became a thing, but I do know I need to visit this house."

"I know, right? It's like having no choice but to eat double chocolate fudge brownies for three meals a day. I'm three-and-a-half novels into this week."

"It sounds like you've stayed busy, which doesn't surprise me at all. How's Boone doing?"

Miriam took a deep breath as she decided that the battery power loss could only be truly justified if she used the opportunity to confide in Lucy and get an outsider's perspective. She said, "Boone is complicated."

"That's an interesting adjective."

"We've been sleeping in the same room."

"Go on."

"Like, two feet - tops - separating us. Except for last night when there were no feet separating us because he got on the couch with me because I was really cold. It was just because I was really, painfully cold." The phone was silent, so Miriam added, "You know - body heat."

Miriam could see in her mind Lucy pushing her glasses further up her freckled nose as she processed the information. Finally, Lucy said, "How's that all working for you?"

"I got warmer."

Another pause was soon followed by the whispery tone Lucy and Miriam had always used in undergrad for the more salacious bits of gossip: "So you slept on the same sofa as Swooney Booney?"

Miriam groaned. "Let's take a moment to remember that Edith owns the full patent on that nickname. I did not invent nor do I condone the use of Swooney Booney."

"Noted," Lucy drawled slowly. She continued, "But that having been firmly established, have you found yourself swooning lately?"

Miriam thought of his fingers running along her shoulder as he examined her olive tree, their tips rough and hardened by working in the soil. She thought of his eyes, so unique and beautiful, focused on her. Really, how could she have helped herself? "Maybe a little bit."

Miriam heard Lucy sigh deeply as if gathering her thoughts. When she spoke, her words were slow to come and thoughtful in their delivery. "Miriam, you are one of the most confident women I know - you and Edith. When Forrest and I were getting together and then not getting together and then maybe getting together..."

"Yes, fun times," Miriam interjected with a fond smile.

"Yes, well, when that business was going on, I would either call you up or, when that wasn't convenient at the moment, I would visualize what you or Edith would do. Visualizing your response always made me a little wiser, a little stronger."

"And visualizing Edith?"

"Well, I'd curse more."

They both laughed, and it felt so good and uncomplicated to laugh with Lucy. But then, Miriam said, "I don't feel wise right now, Luce. I'm attracted to this guy a lot. Like a lot, a lot."

"So the 'little bit' comment might've been an understatement?"

"Maybe. I haven't felt this drawn to someone ever. But something is going on with him that I don't understand. He's not telling me something, and Rubie is being a good grandmother and not interfering, but dammit, now is the time to dish - and I know good and well that woman knows how to gossip."

Miriam's elbows rested on her knees, and her head lay in her hand shaking in perplexity as she spoke. She laughed talking about Rubie even as she knew the words were partially true. Rubie had always conspiratorially whispered gossip into Miriam's ear at church events. But where Boone was concerned, she was a model of discretion. It didn't surprise Miriam when she paused to ponder on it. When Rubie did gossip, it was never mean or callous. Really, gossip was too crass a word for what Rubie did. It was more that she reveled in the stories that were happening all around her, and she shared the stories with Miriam like she shared her paperback romances. But Boone was more than a good story to Rubie.

Lucy said, "Be careful, Miriam. In all the years I've known you, you've managed to never really get hurt by a guy. You've never been into someone enough to let them hurt you. If Boone has issues you don't understand, that could be dangerous for you. You could get your heart broken. But if he's really as great as he seems to be, he might be worth a little heartbreak. Only you can decide that."

Miriam wanted to groan at the ambiguity of Lucy's advice. She also wanted to give her a pat on the back for delivering what was ultimately the soundest advice possible. Maybe Lucy should have gone into ministry.

Regretfully, Miriam said, "My battery has lost another four percent. I'd better go."

"Sure thing. Let me know when you rejoin civilization."

Miriam chuckled. "Will do." And then, more soberly, she said, "Thank you, Lucy."

"You'll be careful?"

As her mind drifted to the moment she unbuttoned her shirt in the greenhouse, Miriam wasn't entirely sure she would be careful. Boone made her feel reckless. Lucy would worry, though, so sounding like the good soldier, Miriam said, "Yes, ma'am. I'll be careful."

When they each hung up, Miriam pulled the blanket around her shoulders more tightly. What she wanted to do was lie in a warm room and listen to music and replay each scene that had happened with Boone over the past week. Sure, he didn't like ministers, but why? She was missing something, and maybe if she did a mental rewind, she'd find the answers. Still holding the blanket tightly around her, Miriam headed downstairs with an idea. When she reached the bottom, she found Rubie also wrapped in a blanket reading a book in front of the fireplace.

Rubie looked and said, "Did you get all the sorting done?"

"Sure did. I love organizing stuff. Thanks for letting me take over your room for a bit."

"Are you kidding me? Thank you! It will make planning a quilt so much easier."

Miriam sat down by Rubie and said, "Rubie, I have a sort of strange question."

"Go on."

"I noticed you have a record player."

Rubie looked over her shoulder to the record player by the window. "Yes, Boone got that for me this Christmas. Our old one broke years ago, and mine and Rupert's collection of vinyls has been going to waste ever since. Boone bought that so we could enjoy that special sound you only get with old records."

Miriam smiled uncertainly. "Yes - well - feel free to say no to this. But I was just wondering if I could carry it out to the greenhouse. I know there is one outlet in there, and it's so nice and warm. I was craving a little music."

Rubie clapped her hands together. "What a marvelous idea, dear. Of course, you can do it."

"I don't want to disturb Boone. Do you know if he's out there right now?"

Rubie waved off her concern. "He's working on some big project in the barn this afternoon."

"Perfect." Miriam stood up to grab the player and leave, but then she paused. "Do you need help with dinner? That's coming up pretty soon."

Rubie reached out and patted her hand. "Miriam, you go get a little time with some music. It does a soul good. I'll make dinner, and you and Boone can do the clean up afterward. Sound good?"

"Thanks, Rubie." Miriam reached down and kissed the top of Rubie's frizzy hair before she headed out.

***

Boone stepped into the kitchen after an entire day of giving Miriam a wide berth. His eyes scanned the room and into the connecting living room before he stepped fully into the meager warmth provided by the oven and stove top.

"Hand me the butter, will you?" Rubie asked in the characteristic way questions were worded in Kentucky. It always left the distinct impression that the words had been shuffled like Scrabble tiles before being spoken.

"Yes, ma'am," Boone replied as he picked up the jadeite butter dish. He placed it on the counter next to the pan of grits Rubie was vigorously whisking.

"Where's Mother Miriam?"

Rubie picked up a salt shaker and shook it in rhythm to the whisking. "My, my. Aren't we formal? I thought after nearly a week under the same roof, you would have dropped the 'Mother.'"

Boone gave a beleaguered sigh. "Forget I asked."

Shaking a wooden spoon coated in grits, Rubie chided, "Don't you get grumpy with me, Boone Rutledge."

"What makes you say that? I'm not grumpy today."

Boone hadn't been particularly grumpy that day. He'd merely been avoiding humans, and when you were snowed in with only two other humans, it did get obvious. However, he hadn't been grumpy.

"Oh, I've seen you, young man," Rubie said, her voice raising as she warmed up to the argument. "You go cuddling that girl all night, and then you hold her at arm's length during the light of day. You don't know what you want, so you're trying to have it both ways. And when you're keeping your distance, you get all surly and lonely like some old Appalachian hermit."

Boone winced. Was he like an Appalachian hermit? If not, he'd say his odds of becoming one were improving daily. However, he had no interest in letting Rubie know she'd tapped a kernel of truth. "I have no idea what you're talking about. Yes, I held her last night, but that was only because she caught a chill in the greenhouse. And I'm not some lovesick boy sulking about. I'm simply a grown man in need of a shred of privacy. That's all."

"Humph," was the only reply Rubie offered. After a minute of tense silence, Boone started to leave the kitchen when Rubie said, "Boone, if you told her the full story, you might be surprised by her reaction. I think you'd find an ally, not another person judging or belittling or putting disclaimers on who God loves or doesn't love. You shouldn't live with that story so bottled up inside."

Boone worked his jaw, his whiskers moving as the muscle tensed. Finally, he spoke.

"I have you and Travis. I don't need some self-righteous religious zealot to help me work through past traumas. I'd say I'm doing pretty well on my own."

"Miriam doesn't have a self-righteous bone in her body, and you know it," Rubie snapped. Turning from the bubbling grits, Rubie looked into his fixed face, knowing she'd provided the section of the gene pool that resulted in his impressive stubborn streak. The spark of anger that flared so quickly in her was extinguished just as fast. Setting down the wooden spoon, she walked up to him, reached her hand to his bearded cheek, and patted the whiskers. Whispering, she said, "Oh, Boone. I'm not going to be around always, and Travis has Paul and whatever children they'll be raising soon. Take it from someone who had the very good fortune of spending decades with the man of my dreams. You deserve better than what you're settling for. And you will never find better until you let go of all this anger and fear and hurt you've held onto for so long. Trust me, son. Travis doesn't need you to hold onto it. He let it go long ago."

Boone was an intelligent man. He'd gone through undergrad, graduate school, and his Ph.D. program all with high grades, receiving special honors at each level. He was often the first man his colleagues consulted when they were struggling in their research. He'd been quick to learn new content when he and Forrest decided to create their hybrid course. But he could honestly say as he listened to his grandmother that he did not entirely understand what she meant. He knew the general sense of contentment he'd felt since moving back to Paducah was beginning to wane, that a restlessness had set in. He knew he hadn't immediately canceled Matchables when he heard about his account as he would have expected himself to do. He knew that despite being a big fan of solitude, he was beginning to feel twinges of loneliness at unexpected times. But he could not see what Miriam had to do with any of it.

Turning back to the stove, Rubie said, "Dinner will be ready in about twenty minutes. Go out to the greenhouse and let her know, okay?"

Boone walked back to the door, put on his cold, snow-encrusted shoes, and headed back out, the icy snow crunching with each step.

Chapter 17

The record player was as heavy as the Arc of the Covenant. Fortunately, determination for Miriam was like spinach to Popeye, and she was determined. She planned to turn on a song with the kind of familiarity and infectious rhythm that wouldn't allow her to remember how vulnerable she'd made herself. She would forget for a moment that he'd clearly exerted as much, if not more, effort than herself to avoid being in the same room that day. She would forget that so far, the snow didn't seem to be melting, and there was little hope for a quick, graceful exit.

As soon as she made it into the greenhouse, Miriam walked over to the outlet next to Boone's workstation. She gingerly set the player down on the table, plugged it in, and grabbed the Eagles album she'd found near the top of Rubie's stack. It was obviously a much-loved vinyl, its edges soft and worn from years of Rupert and Rubie pulling it out for what Miriam could only imagine had been very enthusiastic dance parties around the living room. Not for the first time, Miriam wished she'd met Rubie's other half before he passed.

Laying the needle carefully on the album, a shiver of excitement ran down her back at the initial crackling sound that preceded the first notes. Her father had kept his old records, as well, and he introduced Miriam to the Beatles and Carol King and Joni Mitchel all with the soft static of his player humming in the background.

Sitting on the same stool she'd used the previous evening as Boone examined her tattoos, Miriam crossed her arms on the table and laid her forehead down, the corduroy of Rupert's old coat pressing into her skin. She'd likely have tiny rows imprinted on her forehead from the fabric. Closing her eyes, she blocked out the space and the memories so fresh that, had they been cookies, their chocolate chips would still be gooey. With the same determination that brought her to the greenhouse, Miriam focused on the music and its tightrope walk that spanned both rock and country without completely giving in to either.

After a few songs, her favorite, "Take it Easy," started crackling out of the speaker. Standing up, she swayed to the music, spinning around with her eyes to the ceiling, the rows of windows still white with snow. Miriam jerked her head in the direction of the door when she heard its characteristic squeak. Not even an international spy could sneak into this greenhouse.

Boone stepped in, his eyes locked to hers the moment the door shut behind him. The music infused the place already so full of life with even more artistry as if the notes were gliding through the leaves and vines and blooms.

Miriam wasn't sure if it was the unusual sound of music in this quiet space or her presence, but Boone's looked astonished. He was fighting something within, fighting a feeling or an impulse. Miriam saw fear and anger and hurt, but she saw something else, too. Something new. Something she suspected answered so many of her questions.

***

The moment Boone walked into the greenhouse and saw Miriam in its center, looking up at the old windows with the same reverence he felt in the space, he was frozen by his want for her. The familiar music coming from the record player felt alien and exotic in this space that was always so silent, just as Miriam herself seemed like a new species of flora standing among his plants. She was content in his greenhouse in the same way each plant he brought into its windowed interior seemed to immediately thrive.

As she looked back at him with questions in her eyes, he slammed back into their morning conversation, the very one he'd run from all day with various contrived jobs in the barn. Without a preamble, he picked up the conversation exactly where they'd left it. Stepping towards her, Boone said in a voice trembling with raw honesty, "I like holding you, too."

"What?" Miriam said, the music too loud for Boone's low voice to carry.

Walking around the row of plants that separated them, Boone came to a standstill. Her brown eyes squinted, the question there only readable to those who knew her best. In the past week, Boone had become part of the circle who could read her expressions. Lifting his hands slowly, giving her time to step away, Boone repeated, "I said I like holding you, too."

Wrapping his arms around her, Boone pressed her against himself. Unlike the night before, he left no room between them, their bodies lining up with cosmic perfection. Miriam answered by embracing him, her arms firmly holding him with the same certainty she had bravely displayed that morning when he tried to dismiss whatever was forming between them. Boone felt overwhelmed with respect for her willingness to speak her truth even in the face of rejection.

Burying his face in the curve of her neck, Boone inhaled her soft, cottony scent. He suspected that even if she hadn't been stranded by ice and snow, she would still not be a woman who wore perfume. He hoped he was right. She was perfect as she was.

As her hands ran up and down his spine, Boone kissed the curve of her neck, climbing his way in slow, lingering kisses. She gasped in surprise but did not push him away. Instead, she pressed herself into him even more, her hands moving to his beard.

Finally, he reached her lips. Pulling away to look once more into her eyes, he waited for a sign that she wanted to stop now, but none came. Tilting his head, Boone leaned forward until their lips met.

Just as their bodies had fit, their lips seemed custom-made for each other. Reaching a hand behind her neck, Boone finally allowed himself to touch the curls at the base of her neck, the ones she played with as she was reading about schoolmarms and surly ranchers. Perhaps, if he had not been so surly, he could have tasted her sooner.

Groaning with pleasure and regrets and relief that she was finally in his arms, Boone deepened their kiss, his tongue finding her own and touching over and over in rhythms not synced with whatever Eagles song was now playing, but rhythms just as musical nonetheless.

Pulling away from her kisses, Boone said, "I want to touch you, but I'm afraid my hands will be cold."

She smiled thickly, looking half drunk on whatever was happening between them. "Boone, your hands are never cold. Don't you know that?"

Bending down to resume kissing her, Boone's hands quickly found what he was looking for as they passed the boundary of her shirttail. Wrapping around her back, Boone was shocked at the softness of her skin. He worried that his hands were too rough from years of digging around in the dirt, that he would mar her perfect skin. But just as he considered withdrawing, Miriam whispered into his ear, "Your hands drive me wild. Their roughness is so you. I loved you touching my tattoos last night."

It was all the encouragement Boone needed. As if of their own volition, his hands moved up and around, cupping her breast through her bra even as he cursed the cumbersome coats and winter clothing they were being forced to work around. He reached around her back searching for the clasp that would at least ease access, but froze at the sound of a scream outside the greenhouse.

"Boone! Boone! Help!"

Miriam and Boone looked at each other with alarm for only a moment before they rushed to exit the greenhouse. Opening the door into the darkening, twilight sky, they saw Rubie, halfway between the house and the greenhouse, lying flat on her back in the snow.

Chapter 18

Boone ran out of the greenhouse with Miriam on his heels. Halfway to the house, Rubie was sprawled in the snow wearing a knee-length, mauve puffer jacket and a knit hat in the colors of the rainbow, her frizzy hair sticking out beneath the edge of the hat. As they raced towards her, Boone skidded the last few feet. Kneeling in the snow, Boone swallowed his panic. "Grandma, what happened? Are you okay?"

Miriam knelt on her knees, too, the snow immediately soaking through the denim of her jeans. She briefly wondered when the snow had gotten so wet, the single-digit temps having kept it dry most of the week. Holding Rubie's hand, Miriam rubbed Rubie's icy fingers between her palms in a fruitless attempt to warm them.

Waving away both of their ministrations, Rubie said, "I'm fine. I'm fine. I was just coming out to get you two for dinner, and I took a little slip. That's all."

Leaning back on his heels, Boone's lips thinned with frustration. "What were you doing coming out here? I was getting Miriam for you." With each word he spoke, he came one step closer to yelling at the poor, beleaguered woman lying in the snow.

Never one to meekly stand by while her grandson chastised her, Rubie said, "Do you know what happens to grits when they get cold, Boone Rutledge? You were taking too damn long, so I decided to get the job done myself. We were five minutes from mealy hockey pucks, and now there is even less time to spare. Get me inside right now."

"The texture of grits is not our top priority right now, Grandma." Boone's voice rose with what sounded like irritation, but what Miriam suspected to be fear. Miriam knew just enough about the Rutledge family to know Boone and Rubie were mostly estranged from Boone's father and the rest of the family. The two of them with Travis composed a tight clan that was still mourning the loss of Rupert. Miriam heard white-knuckled anxiety and grit in each word Boone spoke.

Without asking permission, Miriam took over. "Rubie, listen to me. I need you to take a moment to feel each part of your body. Does any part hurt in particular?"

Rubie's eyes looked into Miriam's own, and what Miriam saw was an absence of fear but also the acknowledgment that she must submit to Miriam's questioning, that the situation could not be brushed off. After a moment, Rubie said, "My left ankle is smarting a bit."

"Okay. That's good." Miriam scooted down to Rubie's ankle to examine it more closely. Boone's eyes followed her, his silence a submission to Miriam taking charge. "Can you move it for me?"

Rubie answered with more movement than Miriam expected.

"That's good. You have a sprain, and it will swell up tonight, but nothing is broken. Now, I need you to roll over to your side."

Rubie obeyed, even though her movements were halting.

"And now, Boone and I are going to help you up."

Without any dialog or discussion, Boone and Miriam worked in unison intuiting what the other would do and intrinsically knowing how to contribute. Within a couple of minutes, Rubie was standing up, her arms linked with Boone and Miriam on each side. Slowly, they hobbled their way back into the house.

Once through the back door, Rubie said, "Alright, let me get everyone's drinks and we'll sit down to eat."

"No!" Miriam and Boone both called out in unison.

Fully intending to ignore them, Rubie took one step and proceeded to stumble. Thankfully, Boone acted quickly, catching her mid-fall. For a moment, the kitchen was silent as Miriam held her breath waiting for Boone to explode.

Finally, Rubie sheepishly said, "Y'all might have to get the drinks."

Boone's reserve shattered. "Grandma - so help me - I'm taking you upstairs where you will lay in bed with that foot propped up and rest whether you want to or not. We will bring you your food, and you will not argue with me. And I mean it."

"Goodness, child. You don't have to get so bent out of shape. Just make sure you hurry with all those plans of yours. A few more minutes and those grits won't be fit for the slop bucket."

Boone didn't say another word, but a muscle in his jaw twitched compulsively as he picked his grandmother up into his arms and, angling his body sideways, carried her up the narrow staircase to her room.

***

Miriam leaned back onto the pillow propped against Rubie's headboard. She'd be sleeping upstairs in Rubie's room to keep vigil on the wily patient. Boone was convinced that without a chaperone, Rubie might try climbing the rickety ladder into the attic or frolicking out to the barn to pet the cats.

Before sleep, though, first came cards. The two women sat parallel to one another, a stack of cards perched between them on a TV tray.

"Are you sure you want to subject yourself to a game of Canasta against me?" Rubie asked as she began passing the cards quickly between herself and Miriam. "I never lose."

Miriam smiled at the ominous tone of Rubie's voice. "I'm sure you don't, but it's always good for ministers to learn a little humility, right?"

The cards snapped like cicadas in summer as Rubie's arthritic hands dealt with surprising speed.

Rubie said, "Humility has never been my favorite fruit of the spirit. It's the same way I feel about bananas in an actual fruit bowl. They just don't get me excited to eat fruit like kiwis do."

"I personally find grapes to be lackluster."

"Yes, but without them, we wouldn't have wine."

"There is that." Miriam fanned out her cards and began arranging her hand. It was an abysmal deal. Rubie should have no problem living up to her boasts. It was just as well that her cards were lousy. Concentration was elusive with the events in the Greenhouse lingering in her mind.

"Miriam? You there, child?"

Miriam startled. "Sorry, Rubie. My mind isn't focusing like it should tonight."

"That's fine. I dealt, so you start the round."

Miriam picked up the first card on the stack and took a cursory glance.

Casually, Rubie said, "This snow had better thaw out soon. I'm almost out of my hemorrhoid cream."

Miriam schooled her face into the blankest expression she could manage and threw the card back into the discard pile. Then she realized she could have used the card after all.

"Damn it."

Rubie snorted. "Threw a card you needed, didn't you?"

Miriam scowled in response.

"I have that effect on people."

Rubie picked up the card Miriam had thrown.

Miriam said, "You don't even have hemorrhoids, do you?"

Placing the card neatly in her hand and discarding one that Miriam couldn't use, Rubie said, "Do you really want me to answer that question?"

Miriam growled in a way strikingly similar to Boone. Perhaps he'd developed that growl as a direct consequence of living with

Rubie. By the time she decided, yes, that was likely, her brain moved on to thinking about the very different kinds of sounds he'd made while kissing her. The ones that had been warm and deep and rumbly in the best way. Once again, Miriam threw the wrong card.

"Damn it to damnation."

Rubie cackled gleefully. "You'd better never say that at Altar Guild."

"Just make sure you never challenge me to a game of cards at Altar Guild, and my job should stay safe."

Laying down her cards before Miriam could get more than two in her hand to match, Rubie said, "You do seem distracted tonight."

Miriam drew another useless card and tossed it back to the discard pile. "I guess so."

"I used to get distracted, too. When Rupert would look at me like he wanted to rip my clothes off that very moment, I'd get mighty distracted."

Biting her lower lip, Miriam wondered if Rubie was sharing this information just for the heck of it, or if she and Boone had been that obvious tonight.

"Boone has always been the spittin' image of Rupert."

They'd been obvious.

Miriam said, "I did notice a resemblance in the photos around the house. The only difference is Rupert never seemed to be without a smile."

"Well, who wouldn't smile being married to me?" Rubie emphasized the question by laying down her last card and ending the hand before Miriam had laid down anything.

Miriam continued, "Of course, it isn't that Boone doesn't smile. His smiles are just measured, you know? It's sort of endearing."

Rubie smiled gently as she said, "Your deal."

Chapter 19

Boone stared unblinkingly at the flames. He was lying on his side, three quilts pulled all the way to his beard, but warmth evaded him. Perhaps, so many days without a fully heated home were starting to take a toll. Or maybe he'd become accustomed to Miriam's warmth the previous night. Regardless, he was cold.

The flames didn't remind him of Miriam in the greenhouse. There hadn't been flames of passion in her eyes or some burning passion exuding off of her. No, Miriam's warmth was more subtle, like the warmth that comes from the inside when drinking a cup of hot cocoa. He felt infused with her, not inflamed. This was no mere boyish infatuation.

It was a new sensation for Boone, one that left him confused. He had a few notches on his bedpost, a few passionate encounters or short affairs with sort-of girlfriends. But nothing had prepared Boone for what he'd felt opening the door to the greenhouse and seeing beautiful Miriam with her curly, brown hair and tall, slim figure standing in the middle of lush, green life.

Boone was the one who suggested Miriam sleep upstairs. It was to protect Rubie from herself. At this point, it wouldn't surprise

Boone if that woman decided to go for a joy ride on their horse, Chuck, to work out the achiness from her fall.

The added benefit to the new sleeping arrangement was that it gave Boone space to think. Boone had always been a person firmly rooted in his mind. Most of his living happened there, and it was only after much consideration that he ever acted on a thought. But when Miriam walked into a room, he lost his place. Suddenly, his mind would fog up, thoughts and words would flee, and he'd find himself doing things so unlike himself, like taking his shirt off to show some woman he barely knew all the, admittedly, strange tattoo choices he'd made over the years. Or like kissing an actual makes-her-living-in-a-pulpit minister.

Turning over to give his backside a turn facing the warmth of the fireplace, Boone stared morosely at the empty couch. He should have brought Miriam back in for the grits sooner. Then he'd have her sleeping across from him one more night. The snow was getting slushy. This could be their final evening with a house guest.

Still wide awake, Boone jerked when he heard the squeak of the fifth step, that handy fifth step. Miriam probably fell asleep hours ago, and Rubie would be taking a stroll for warm milk and cookies.

Flipping over, Boone said, "Grandma, you go right back upstairs this minute. If you need milk and cookies, I'll bring them up to you."

The figure kept walking, and when she got within range of the fire's dim light, Boone saw the silhouette of curls bouncing lightly with movement.

"I don't know about your grandma, but I'd take some milk and cookies. However, I'd rather you not bring them to me in bed."

***

The entire right side of Miriam's arm and leg were pressed against Boone as they sat on the sofa, her feet under her in an attempt to beat the cold. They'd arranged a king-sized, unzipped sleeping bag so that it was draped around each of their shoulders. Between the fireplace and the body heat their juncture was creating, Miriam was the warmest she'd been since the previous evening. Miriam felt an urge to be touching Boone constantly now, an urge that was satiated at the moment as they nestled beneath the heavy cover. When she left the cocoon, though, she knew it would only be a matter of minutes before she'd want to be back in this place, pressed against him.

Miriam was wearing plaid pajamas, probably a pair bought for Travis at Christmas who-knew-how-many years ago. They were green and red, and as far from the things sold at Kim's Secret off Exit 142 as could be imagined. At least, that was what Miriam figured. She'd never been in Kim's Secret. She'd never needed their merchandise.

Boone, too, wore plaid pajama pants, but his shirt was a thick waffle-knit with a henley collar, the buttons undone beneath his beard. Chest hair peaked over the V-shaped opening, and even this minuscule glimpse of what Miriam knew to be a broad chest made her avert her eyes like a fourteen-year-old girl at an end-of-school swim party.

Miriam had never considered herself shy, but everything felt different, foreign even, when she was with Boone.

Both Boone and Miriam cradled a cup of whole milk in their hands. Rubie claimed anything less than whole milk was one step up from dishwater. Rubie had been fighting the good fight against the low-fat diet fad since the eighties, and she wasn't planning to slow down anytime soon. Miriam dunked the vanilla sandwich cookie she and Boone had thieved from Rubie's junk-food bin (truly, a sizable specimen of Tupperware) into the rich, creamy milk, taking a moment of silence for all the years she'd been buying one percent simply because it was what she'd grown up on. Really, she hadn't realized.

"Whole milk is awesome. Why have I been depriving myself of this joy all these years?"

Boone used his index finger to fish out a piece of cookie that had broken off into his cup. "When I was growing up, Travis and I would spend as much time here as my parents would allow. My mom was always on some diet, and she only kept skim milk in the house, so I always thought milk was gross. Then, Grandma made me try it once, and of course, this is a whole other thing. I consumed a ridiculous amount of milk and cookies those summers, like a camel storing up for the desert."

"Would your mom not buy you some if you'd asked for it?" While Miriam's mother had always had one percent in the house, it was because no one in the family had ever objected. Miriam hadn't known better or she would have.

"Mom had ideas of right and wrong about almost everything in life. Still does, I guess. We don't really talk. Anyways, if she read somewhere that some food was bad for you, she cut it off for the whole family. Of course, that was before social media. I can only imagine the shit information she's using nowadays to make life choices."

Miriam almost spit out milk laughing. Shielding her mouth with a hand as she spoke, she said, "I spend a good amount of my job combating bullshit people have read on the internet. It's hard being a Baby Boomer these days."

"Huh. That sounds like a nightmare." Boone looked thoughtful as he digested this unexpected part of Miriam's occupation. "Anyways, I remember being hungry a lot as a kid. Until I'd get here. Grandma's like a bloodhound when it comes to other people's hunger. She can sniff it out immediately."

"Hmm." Miriam didn't want to embellish her response anymore, but the more she heard of Travis's mother, the more she did not care for the woman. Taking another bite of a soggy, milk-soaked cookie, she said, "Rubie offers me food constantly. And, I swear, she always has a jello salad on her."

Boone laughed, "Even in the middle of a once-in-a-century snowstorm, the woman has jello salad. Even when her grandson specifically says, 'Buy the practical food, Grandma. Purchase an apple, Grandma.'"

"She buys apples, Boone. She just mixes them with cool whip and marshmallows before she serves them." Miriam took another bite of cookie, calculating that she was one and a half cookies from a sick stomach. Pensively, she continued, "My favorite is the orange one."

"Your favorite what is orange?"

"Jello salad. I like the orange one. Every time I bite into one of those little canned mandarin oranges and the juice pops into my mouth, it reminds me of those addictive video games where you're shooting at little jewels that explode."

"That's what you think of when you eat jello salad?"

Miriam slurped her milk. "Only the orange one. I'm not that weird."

Boone was looking at her from the side of his blue eyes with one corner of his mouth quirked. Miriam's stomach did a short gallop like a horse pawing restlessly at the ground. His beard had felt so good brushing along her neck in the greenhouse.

She wasn't breathing nearly enough.

Finally, Boone broke the silence. "I prefer the pink kind."

"And I was starting to like you," Miriam said, shaking her head in disappointment.

Boone didn't seem to know how to respond. He finished the last bite of his cookies and set aside the empty cup. Miriam soon followed.

The fire crackled, but Miriam kept her eyes focused on a single piece of wood that looked like it would break off at any moment. When her eyes did look back to Boone, she focused on his collar and the light smattering of chest hairs. There were two freckles along his collarbone she'd not seen before. She looked up directly into Boone's eyes, the eyes she'd grown so fond of over the past week.

They were focused on her own neck. Actually, it was more on her hand that had been twirling the tight curls at the back of her neck. It was an old habit Miriam supposed most girls with curly hair developed. Lucy, who also had curly hair, did it. They used to joke about their mutual habit being better than some they could have. At least they didn't smoke a pack a day. With the sudden consciousness of what she'd been doing and of the attention it had garnered, Miriam's hand froze. Boone looked into her eyes, realizing he'd been caught.

He didn't look abashedly away as she'd expected him to do. Instead, he reached up and touched the curls. "I've been wanting to feel them all week. You play with your curls all the time."

"It used to drive my mother crazy. I guess I created a few rat's nests when I was younger."

"It sort of drives me crazy, too, but for very different reasons."

Miriam took the fingers that always twiddled with her curls and ran them over the coarse edges of Boone's beard. Then, she pulled his face down to hers and kissed him deeply, hoping he wasn't one of those men who needed to feel in charge, who always wanted to be the initiator.

Boone groaned deeply, the sound vibrating through her whole body and assuring her he did not mind her assertiveness. Emboldened, Miriam moved to straddle him. Immediately, Boone's kisses heated, his hands running all over her back and over her rear. She tried to keep quiet knowing they weren't alone in the small house, but a moan escaped as he caressed her. It felt so good to be touched, quenching a hunger only enough to make her realize she was famished and wanted far more.

Breaking away from his kiss to catch her breath, Miriam said, "These aren't the sexiest pajamas."

Boone laughed gruffly, leaning his forehead against her chest as he, too, breathed like he'd been running a race. "Trust me. You don't need lace. You make flannel look real good."

Miriam lifted his chin to look into his eyes. "You look real good, too, Boone Rutledge. I especially like this spot right here." Leaning down, Miriam kissed the patch of skin she'd been ogling earlier. Then, she made her way up to his ear, the tip of her tongue leaving a path along his neck. Boone practically vibrated beneath her, his fingers clutching her thighs as he made sounds that encouraged Miriam to never, ever stop.

Moving her hands down his firm abdomen, Miriam found the hem of his shirt. She pulled it up, over his head, and tossed it to the arm of the sofa. Then she set back to admire the works of art all over the finely tuned chest, the wings of the birds fluttering in the firelight.

Boone clenched his jaw as if he were clutching his last shred of self-control.

Wanting to break whatever reserve he clung to, Miriam unbuttoned the top button of her faded pajama top. His eyes darted to the movement, and he watched, engrossed, as her hands moved to the next button. And the next. When she reached the final button, she stopped, waiting to see what he would do, wanting to make sure he wanted this, too.

Suddenly, Boone's hands released her thighs, and he ran them within the shirt over her shoulders, pulling the shirt down her arms until it lay in a heap on top of his own. He paused, looking at her like she was a particularly rare and special plant in his greenhouse. Miriam fought the instinct to cover herself. It had been so long. The last man to see her like this had been the guilt-ridden boyfriend from seminary. She didn't want guilt or shame, and she didn't think Boone would try to serve either to her. So she remained still as he studied her.

"You are so..." His voice was husky, trailing off. "I want a better word than beautiful."

Miriam released the breath she was holding.

Boone drew her to him, gentle but confident in his movements. Miriam's breasts pressed against his chest, the sensation new and strange and absolutely delicious all at once. He took her mouth in a hungry kiss, his beard coarse and undeniably masculine against her own softness. Then his mouth lowered, kissing the satiny skin of her breast until he came to her nipple. Taking the tip into his mouth, he gently sucked until Miriam's back arched, and she moaned with pleasure she hadn't known possible. She pushed her hips into Boone, feeling his own desire through the layers of pajamas that now seemed thin and easy enough to discard.

Moving to the other side, Boone extended the pleasure, convincing Miriam that she could find completion with only this simple erotic act. Running her hands into his hair, the ends tangled around her fingers as she held his head to her.

He returned his kisses to her lips, his hands taking each breast and continuing to massage the tips as Miriam returned his kisses savagely, abandoning decorum.

Breaking the kiss, Boone said, "Miriam. Miri, we have to stop."

Bereft at the notion and adamantly opposed to the suggestion, Miriam spoke a single word: "Why?"

His breathing ragged, Boone took a moment to say, "You're a minister."

"I'm not a Catholic priest, Boone. I'm a grown woman who wants this. Who wants you."

Boone didn't need much convincing. His hand encircled the base of her neck as he pulled her back into a deep, hungry kiss. Moving with agility, Boone transitioned Miriam to the couch, laying next to her with their bare chests against each other. Working his hands down to the waistband of her pants, his movements jerky with pent-up desire, Boone lowered her pants until they were low enough that she could shimmy them the rest of the way off. Thoughts of shame or embarrassment were far from Miriam's mind as Boone's hands moved between her legs.

Inhaling in surprise and desire, Miriam reached down to Boone's waistband, tugging to take out one more barrier between them, but Boone stopped her.

"No, Miri," he whispered into her ear, his whiskers tickling. "Not now. Tonight, it's just you. Let me give this to you."

Miriam instinctively knew what he meant. Bringing her hands back up to his shoulders and neck, she held him as his fingers searched out the point that was pulsing with the need to be touched. When he found her center, he gently massaged her, finding she was ready for him. Sliding a finger into her, he slid out wet and began moving in rhythmic strokes over her.

Holding on too tightly, afraid she might leave finger-shaped bruises along his upper arms, Miriam's grip tightened as she kissed him deeply, her pelvis bucking against his hand in primitive, unorchestrated movements that she could not control. He seemed to know exactly what to do, when to slow down and let her soak in the pleasure, when to reach into her again to find more moisture, when to speed the thrusts to the beat her own body was setting.

Finally, Miriam buried her face into the curve of Boone's neck, letting his beard muffle the sounds of her pleasure as her entire body quaked in waves of release. She could not remember ever having felt pleasure so complete, and they hadn't even had sex.

Boone's arms wrapped around her as he pulled her to him. He kissed the curls at the top of her head caressingly, whispering, "Miri," in between harsh breaths and gentle kisses.

Little goosebumps ran down Miriam's arms as the heat of their lovemaking cooled, and Boone, so attentive to the conditions of anything in his care, pulled the sleeping bag over them. Content back within a cocoon of Boone's making, Miriam fought sleep, knowing she needed to return to Rubie.

As if he read her mind, Boone whispered, "Drift off for a bit. I'll wake you in a while to go back upstairs."

Knowing he would keep his word, Miriam sunk into sleep.

Chapter 20

The rising sun glinted off the snow and reflected into the house in streaks of light far more powerful than anything a light bulb would have provided. Lying on the side of the couch Miriam had recently vacated, Boone could still smell her scent in the divot where her head had lain. Stretching, Boone yawned so dramatically that he felt his jaw pop. It had been a long, sleepless night. He'd known that he wouldn't be able to sleep with so much desire pulsing through his veins, so he'd kept vigil while Miriam slept. Even after Miriam returned upstairs, sleep evaded him.

Desire wasn't the only thing keeping him awake. His mind was stumbling over the past week, over all the little moments that culminated in Miriam sleeping naked against him. Since her arrival on Valentine's Day, Boone felt he'd come to know Miriam. She was generous and gregarious and surprisingly bold. Confidence exuded from her, a confidence that must have been threatened many times as a woman in a male-dominated profession. In fact, she didn't exhibit the meekness and deference to men that had always characterized female virtue in the church of Boone's youth. It left him wondering why she hadn't pursued a career in law or business or anything else, really, where women with strong personalities tended to be found.

Deciding that putting off standing wasn't going to result in him feeling more rested, Boone rolled off the couch, threw on a pair of jeans and a fresh thermal shirt, and headed to the kitchen. He was both exhausted and buzzing with adrenaline as he prepared a breakfast tray for Rubie. It wasn't long before Boone was taking a sip of his second cup of black coffee, willing the brew to give him the energy he needed to keep Rubie resting. It would be a full-time job.

Pursing his lips in an attempt to suppress yet another yawn, Boone thought again about the source of his exhaustion. Really, his mind was singularly focused on Miriam, on Miri. After she'd fallen asleep in his arms, her bare chest pressed against his own, Boone had lain wide awake feeling her, feeling awed, frustrated, maybe a little fallen, and utterly bewildered at the way she strolled into his well-ordered, uneventful life and sparked chaos.

He'd made sure she found satisfaction while keeping himself from release, and his body protested for hours as she'd nuzzled against him and made little sleepy sounds he'd tried to memorize. Even in a haze of passion, Boone was cognizant of the melting snow and all of its ramifications. Once the ice melted, this little thing he and Miriam had cultivated in a dark land of snow and ice could never persevere. What had happened between them would melt into memory just like the sheet of ice on the roof above Boone's head, dissolving one drip at a time. Their values were too incompatible for any other outcome. So Boone had kept a boundary in place, one he hoped would give her comfort in the coming days and weeks as they parted ways.

Boone arranged a fried egg, overly dark toast (he never got it quite right), and two slices of bacon onto a Corelle plate wreathed in olive green flowers that they'd been eating on for as long as he could remember. Rubie's Corelle plates would survive a bombing squad, Boone was sure. He placed the plate on a tray, and in a moment of whimsy born of sheer exhaustion, he placed a rose he and Miriam had cut a few days ago in a narrow vase next to the glass of orange juice.

When he walked into the bedroom, Miriam and Rubie were already setting up in bed flipping through an old Trinity Episcopal directory and laughing at the hairstyles and facial hair choices from the early eighties.

"Deacon Troy had a mullet?" Miriam was laughing loudly while wiping a mirthful tear from the corner of her eyes.

"A permed mullet at that," Rubie said, gripping Miriam's arm as she bent over with laughter.

Boone had woken Miriam a couple of hours before sunrise so she'd have plenty of time to sneak back to Rubie's room undetected. When their eyes met, she didn't blush or avert her eyes or suddenly become completely absorbed in the pictures in front of her. Instead, she looked at him directly and smiled like they shared a particularly delicious secret. Which, Boone supposed, they did. But it wasn't the reaction he'd expected. He'd feared regret and words of condemnation and shame. She might have deemed him vulgar or sinful.

Miriam simply looked delighted.

"Good morning, Grandma." Nodding his head towards Miriam, he said, "Miri," and then, realizing that level of familiarity might give them away, awkwardly added, "-am. Miriam."

She grinned knowingly.

"How'd you sleep last night?" Boone directed his question to Rubie whose hair was a stunning display of frizzy bedhead. It stood on ends in all directions, and her housecoat sported a print of magenta flowers and lime-green vines on a particular shade of orange last popular in the 1970s. Boone suspected the local thrift store wouldn't be able to pay someone to take the dress if Rubie were ever to donate it. So it was a good thing she never would.

Rubie picked up a fork and said, "I slept fine. Everyone can rest assured that Rubie Rutledge rested like a particularly well-behaved, non-colicky newborn. So can I get up now?"

"Nope." Boone sat down as he concisely delivered the verdict, the mattress dipping dramatically where his weight landed. Deciding that the scowl she was giving demanded more from him, Boone added, "Give me one more day of rest, Grandma. For my peace of mind, okay? If you're still feeling well tomorrow, you'll have my blessing to ride roughshod once again."

Miriam pleaded, "Look how tired he looks, Rubie. Those bags under his eyes. I mean, really. It's the least you could do." A poorly concealed grin told Boone that Miriam knew good and well any bags he might have beneath his eyes were far more a result of her little visit and not from worrying over his spry grandmother.

"You're right, Mother Miriam. He looks awful."

Boone groaned.

Sighing, Rubie said with great magnanimity, "I'll stay in bed. For his sake."

"How good of you." Miriam winked at him even as she spoke to Rubie. Thankfully, Rubie was too engrossed in her bacon to notice. Hopefully, the breakfast would also distract her from the flush that rose on Boone's cheeks above his beard at each smile and covert communication Miriam flashed his way. Suddenly, he was regretting being such a damned saint the night before. After all, she was a grown woman. She didn't need him deciding what was best for her. And she'd wanted him. Boone knew this to his discontented core.

"I've got grading to do this morning, but I'm going to be in the greenhouse this afternoon. If you'd like to join me, Miriam. You know, just to get out for a minute. I mean, you don't have to, but if you want to…"

Boone circled around searching for an exit to this painfully awkward invitation when Rubie, her eyes darting between her grandson and her minister, said abruptly, "She'll head out during my nap after lunch. No need to watch me sleep, dear."

Rubie handed Miriam a slice of toast, undoubtedly because she, Rubie, thought it too dark. As Miriam took a bite that crunched loudly, she tilted her head towards Rubie and said around the mouthful, "What she said."

Boone stood up, the orange juice in Rubie's cup sloshing as the mattress returned to its equilibrium. Leaving the room, one side of Boone's mouth quirked in a smile, satisfied that he'd have more alone time with Miriam before the end of the day.

***

Miriam pulled a blanket snuggly to Rubie's chin as the woman snored the snore of a den of grizzly bears. She'd fallen asleep after a lunch of pimento cheese, crackers, and fruit that Miriam brought up for them to share.

There was no need for a midday nap for Miriam. Since her eyes opened that morning, she'd felt invigorated by the sunlight beaming through the house. Its glare through the window onto the mirror of Rubie's antique vanity had been like a perky, non-irritating alarm clock. Suddenly, the flowers of Rubie's wallpaper looked more springy, and Miriam felt that the snow might just melt after all. The thought was quickly followed by a twinge of melancholy at the thought of leaving the cozy existence she and Rubie and Boone had created for themselves over the past week. Surely, though, she and Boone would figure out a way to explore their budding relationship moving forward.

At the start of the day, Miriam had looked into a mirror to find her hair mussed and her cheeks rosy. To her own eyes, she looked like a woman who had spent the night with a man. She'd wondered if it would be obvious to Rubie. Would the upturn of Miriam's lips or the apparently permanent flush around her neck give her away?

Miriam had shrugged. If it did, oh well. She rather liked the idea of people knowing she and Boone meant something to each other.

However, as the day went by, Rubie seemed unaware of Miriam's blushes anytime the conversation turned to Boone. Or, at least, Rubie was doing a good job playing dumb.

Miriam gingerly walked down the stairs, taking special care to skip the fifth. She was eager to go to the greenhouse and be alone again with Boone. At some point, they should talk about what was forming between them. They should put words to it. But if Miriam were being completely honest with herself, she just wanted to kiss the guy.

When she turned the corner into the kitchen, she stumbled upon Boone. He was sitting at the table with a stack of papers and a red pen in one hand. When he looked up to her, he smiled. It was so simple, just a smile. But Miriam felt elated at the realization that Boone, so reserved and stingy with his smiles, was happy she'd walked into the room.

As her mind raced for the perfect, flirtatious greeting (his smiles now left her speechless), the house came alive with sounds that had become unfamiliar over the past silent week. The fridge began to whir, and the central heat kicked noisily into gear. Lights that seemed so unnecessary in the sunlit kitchen sparked to life, and the digital clocks on the coffee maker and microwave started flashing with 12:00.

Boone and Miriam were both momentarily astonished as they each looked around, taking in the noisy return to reality. When their eyes once again met, Boone was no longer smiling.

"Well, I guess that's that. If electricity is restored all the way out here, the roads are probably open, too. I can take you back whenever you're ready."

Miriam was stunned. She needed more time to transition. She'd come down with plans for an old-fashioned make-out session in the greenhouse between the rose bushes and the winter greens. She was going to flirt and tease and spend hours late into the night on a single, narrow, plaid sofa with the tall, broad, bearded man whose eyes had just shuttered from her.

Trying to maintain her composure, Miriam said, "I don't have to leave just yet. I'm not in a rush to get home or anything."

Boone looked down at the stack of ungraded papers before him, his pen drumming impatiently on the table.

"Unless you want me to leave."

Boone rubbed his forehead. "It's not that I want you to leave. It's just that this little interlude from normal life is over. It's back to having lights. And once you have lights, you have jobs and duties and..." He stood up and walked to the sink, looking out the window where drops of water fell rapidly from the roof's melting snow and ice.

"I'm not sure where you're going with this, Boone."

"I just don't see how we fit into each other's real lives."

Miriam thought about the shirt hanging on the towel hook in the bathroom, its white collar awkwardly agape on the hanger. She was ready to put it on, to be Mother Miriam again and throw herself into her work. But she still didn't see why that should stand in the way of her relationship with Boone.

"Boone, professionals with careers can still date. There's room for you in my life. And if there weren't room, I'd make it. I mean, I know you're not the biggest fan of ministers, but surely you've noticed I'm not that bad." Miriam smiled encouragingly, hoping the gentle tease was clear in her tone.

Boone looked as though he might smile if only it weren't so painful. "I don't know, Miri."

Encouraged by the use of her nickname, Miriam walked up to him, her toes within an inch of his own. "Come on, Boone. I basically threw myself at you last night."

"I wanted you, too."

With that, Boone's resolve crumbled. Taking Miriam roughly into his arms, he pressed his mouth against her with the force of a starving animal who didn't know when its next meal would come. Lifting her, he placed her on the counter so that her legs could wrap around him. With their faces level, their kisses deepened, robbing Miriam of breath and rationality and any thought of melting snow.

Miriam's hands, shaking with adrenaline and want, reached down to the leather belt Boone was never without. Clumsily, she started to pull the end from the belt loops.

Immediately, as if doused by cold water, Boone stepped back. "I can't. I can't do this. I can't have casual sex with a minister."

"Why does it have to be casual? I feel something for you, Boone. This is real to me."

"I can't. Not with you."

The words stung, like a child stepping barefoot on a dirt dauber on a summer day. She tried to form words, to question why not her, when three knocks on the front door further dissolved the insular world they'd occupied for their brief, icy interlude.

Boone walked to the door and opened it. Miriam couldn't see who was on the other side, but she could hear the man clearly.

"Good afternoon, sir. I'm Sheriff Deputy Smith. Just letting folks out here know the roads have been cleared."

Chapter 21

Boone's fists gripped the old truck's steering wheel as he followed Miriam's small car. It took a while to get her things gathered, and Rubie had insisted she eat with them one more night. Now, Boone was driving behind her in the dark to make sure she got home safely. She'd protested that it was unnecessary, but, really, it was the least he could do.

When Boone's grandfather passed away, Boone inherited his early-90's pickup truck. The interior smelled like sawdust and Copenhagen, scents forever linked to Rupert Rutledge. Normally, it was comforting to inhale the scent, but Boone hardly noticed as he focused on Miriam's tail lights.

The sun that had awoken Boone had shined brightly all day. Snow and ice were melting rapidly, and Boone was starting to see the amount of damage done around the farm. He'd be spending his summer cleaning up fallen trees and branches.

Now that they'd made it through the storm of the century, something even more ominous and likely more destructive loomed in his future. He'd spent the last week playing with fire, allowing the attraction between him and Miriam to grow until it was more than merely the elephant in the room. They'd now acted on the attraction. They now possessed knowledge of each other's bodies, memories of long nights spent together, certainty that they were, at the very least, compatible when the lights were out.

But the lights were glaringly on. As the snow melted and the road crews cleared the downed trees and the electricity restored all aspects of their lives, Miriam Howatch would return to her pulpit Trinity Episcopal Church. Boone thought of his parents' church, so comfortable writing off the humanity of a scared pubescent boy who didn't fit the cookie cutter they deemed appropriate.

Miriam loved her profession and the field she had chosen to study. He understood that. He felt the same sense of vocation about his own career and field of study. He could never be with someone who was openly hostile to his career, and he would not expect Miriam to be with someone who didn't support her own. She deserved someone who could stand by her as Mother Miriam, not just Miri.

After about ten minutes of slow but steady driving over slushy country roads, they reached Paducah proper where the streets were well-salted and had been for days. The rest of the drive was a breeze, and soon Boone was weaving through the church parking lot. Once they reached the small house on the back of the grounds, Boone parked next to Miriam's car.

As he got out of his vehicle, Miriam was already walking to her front door, digging inside her large bag for house keys. Without glancing his way, she said, "I'm all safe and sound now, Boone. You can go home."

"I want to check your pipes and make sure everything is okay."

She shrugged indifferently, walking into the house but leaving the door ajar for him.

It only took Boone a few minutes to check the house. Looking around for Miriam, he found her in a small room that looked to be her office.

Boone said, "Everything looks good. They must winterize the property pretty well."

Miriam was sitting on a swivel chair facing her computer. At his words, she spun around. Behind Miriam, the computer screen showed a mess of unopened messages she would need to catch up on. Boone supposed he'd find the same thing when he dared to log on to his computer. Her phone was also on the desk, a light blinking as it charged.

"Thanks for checking," she said.

Boone looked around the small room. The walls were covered in an eclectic but attractive mix of paintings and sketches, all in old, mismatched frames. The room was still frigid, the heater not yet having sufficient time to heat it, but Miriam had lit a candle that gave an allusion of warmth. There were figurines placed on the bookshelves among her sizable library, probably statues of saints. The church Boone had grown up in looked down on the idea of saints. They thought Episcopalians and Catholics were heretical with their little statues and candles and stained glass images. Of course, all the denominations thought the others were going to burn, right?

As his eyes moved around the room, they landed on a wooden coat rack. Askew on one hook was a hanger with a heavy, white robe. It was laden with a stole and gold cord. The entire thing looked so shocking in the office of a young, single woman, one to whom Boone was attracted even as he tried his hardest to deny the attraction.

"Boone, really, you can go now. I'm fine."

"I knew you were a minister, but that robe..." His words trailed off.

"Yes, Boone. This is what I do. It's who I am. But what are you trying to say?"

His fingers slid into his thick hair leaving it mussed in the front. "I don't know, Miri. You're right. I'll head on back to the farm."

***

As Boone turned around to leave, the nonchalance Miriam had been clinging to shattered. She'd never been the one who played it cool. She'd always been the person who openly and unashamedly pursued what she wanted, what she believed to be right. That was what she'd done when her family and friends and professors had all balked at her decision to enter seminary. It was what she did every time she was looked down on for being a woman in a man's job. Why couldn't she do it with love, too?

And she was in love with Boone. Suddenly and against her will, she knew without doubt that she was in love with the man who looked like he'd seen a ghost when he saw her work clothes. It was damned inconvenient, but not insurmountable. She wouldn't allow it to be insurmountable.

Maybe it was because she grew up with loving parents despite how very precocious she'd been. Maybe it was because she'd had the same best friend since her first day of college, and that friend had loved her through every little disagreement, every mistake, every poorly spoken word. Maybe it was because her faith taught her that she was loved and worthy of being loved. But Miriam Howatch didn't want to play games with Boone. She didn't want to sit around and see if he liked her, too. She didn't want to live in fear of his rejection. So she was going to do what she always did. She was going to be authentic and hope it was enough.

"Wait, Boone. Stop."

Boone's steps ceased, but he didn't turn around. She saw tension in his shoulders. He was fighting with himself. He was making a valiant effort. And while she very much hoped to help him win future battles he might face, she was determined he'd lose this particular one.

Walking up behind him, she put her hands on the taught muscles of his back. Impossibly, they tensed more.

"Look at me." Her voice shook. It was too quiet. With effort, she said more firmly, "Please."

Boone turned around, and she swallowed a lump in her throat that formed at the sight of his sad eyes.

Cupping his cheek in the palm of her hands, Miriam said, "Don't look so sad. I love you."

Boone's eyes shut as if from pain, even as he turned towards her hand, kissing her palm. Finally, he spoke.

"I'm so sorry, Miriam, but you and I both know we can't do casual. That whatever is going on between us is too much for that."

"I'm not asking for casual. I said I love you."

"Please, Miri. Please don't."

Miriam's confidence that she could break through this wall faltered. Panic rose in her chest as she wondered if she'd miscalculated just how tortuous the battle Boone fought was.

"Why can't we love each other? Who, what is keeping us from that?"

Boone stepped away, turning from her. He ended up right in front of her robe, staring at it as he spoke. "I've seen ministers' spouses, Miriam. They sit two pews behind the front and nod along to every word. I can't do that."

"Yeah, they also usually have a perm, sing Soprano, and have a quilted casserole carrier with their name embroidered on it. I, personally, was planning on breaking a few norms when I got married. But I don't care about that stuff. You know I don't."

"Miri. I just can't."

"Boone, we've reached the point where you have to tell me why. I know something happened. I know that you have some old wounds. But, Boone, you took me into your arms. You held me and touched me and made me feel like you cared for me."

"I do care for you."

"Then you owe me an explanation. I deserve to know what I'm up against."

Boone faced her, his cheeks pale. "Knowing won't change anything."

"Tell me anyway."

***

Boone hadn't told the story of what happened the summer before he left for college since he'd relayed it to his grandparents after driving Travis straight from their parents' house to the farm. Grandma had put Travis to bed upstairs ordering him to rest, and then she and Grandpa and Boone had sat around the kitchen table while he revealed each horrifying detail. It was the last time he'd spoken explicitly about the events that still haunted him.

Looking into Miriam's warm but pained eyes, he said, "You know I have a twin brother, Travis."

"Yes, Rubie talks about him all the time. She adores you both."

Boone nodded. "Well, when we were growing up, Travis was always different. He was different from me and everyone we knew. When we'd color the little coloring pages they had for kids to keep them from getting bored in church, mine would be colored in all these dark colors. Blues and browns and I'd flatten out the black crayon. But his would always be in the light colors with the funny-named crayons. Salmon, seaweed, you know what I mean. Even when he was really young, he could color better than me. My coloring was efficient, but his was pretty.

"As he got older, people started noticing he was different. I never cared. I loved my brother, and I didn't give a shit if he was different from the other boys. But the church my parents took us to started to get uncomfortable with him. Suddenly, every few weeks there was another sermon about abominations and men lying with men and...well, you get the drift."

Miriam sputtered. "For the record, that is a horrible interpretation of the Biblical text. The original passage..."

"Miriam."

She paused, pursing her lips together in an inner struggle to concede the stage. "Sorry. Go on."

"Of course, the minister didn't have to convince my parents. They'd started talking about how something evil was inside Travis when we were only eight or nine years old. When we'd come to Grandma and Grandpa's house over the summer, Travis would attach himself to Grandma's side. She'd fill him up with words of affirmation. Tell him how kind he was, how smart he was. It'd only take a day or two back home before I'd see all the life seep out of him.

"As we got into our teen years, everything became more volatile. Travis started sneaking out, and who could blame him? It was awful for him in that house. One night when we were sixteen, my Dad caught him making out with another boy from our neighborhood. Well, you can guess how that went down. Dad wasn't one to use his fists. I guess I can say that much for him. But his words could sure do a number. Travis came home completely broken. He was convinced he was going to hell, and he thought maybe Mom and

Dad were right. Maybe he had a choice. Maybe he could change himself.

"So within a few weeks, they enrolled Travis at a camp that was supposed to save lost boys. I tricked my parents into sending me."

"How?"

"I looked at another guy on my baseball team."

Miriam nodded her head slowly. "Resourceful."

"Yeah, well, I wasn't going to let them send him alone. The camp was awful, no surprise there. When they weren't shaming the boys to the point of self-loathing, they were convincing them that they could pray their way to liking girls. It was a toxic mix of invalidation and false hope.

"Of course, Travis knew before we left that it hadn't worked. That he was still just as gay as he'd been his whole life. The next year was agony. He had to bear the additional condemnation of my parents and our church at having remained lost when they'd all tried so damn hard to save him."

"I'm so sorry, Boone," Miriam cut in. Every sentence he spoke painted a worse picture of his childhood, a childhood she'd already imagined to be bleak.

Boone didn't pause for her regrets. Finally telling the story, he couldn't stop. "One day, the minister had us all stay late after the fifth-Sunday potluck. He wanted to talk with Mom and Dad and Travis. I had a bad feeling about it, but they refused to let me in. As soon as they shut that door, though, I put my ear up against it as flat as I could.

"The minister, Brother Paul," Boone spoke the name like it was poison. "He'd been hearing things about Travis and another boy in a neighboring town. I'd known something was going on. They were teenagers, and probably a little bit of first loves. I was glad Travis had found someone in that podunk place to love him, make him feel special. Anyway, I was the only person who saw it that way. My dad went off his rocker, yelling that it couldn't be true, that the camp was supposed to have cured him, but Travis said it was. He didn't try to lie or hide. He just came out with the truth.

"Brother Paul said Travis couldn't come anymore to church until he got himself changed." Boone's voice shifted into the harsh cadence of an angry, Southern preacher. Pausing, he resumed speaking in his own intentional style, "He gave my parents some pamphlet for yet another place that would convert Travis. This one used more 'hands-on' practices. A chill ran down my back when I heard those words. I couldn't imagine what they'd do to him there, and I wasn't sure I could trick Mom and Dad again into sending me.

"When Travis left the room, he looked white. Like a ghost. He wasn't crying. I think he was in too much shock to cry. He just kept looking at me, his eyes begging me to do something, anything. But, Miri, I didn't know what to do."

Miriam's eyes glistened with unshed tears. "Of course you didn't, Boone. You were only a boy."

"That night, I walked into our bathroom, and Travis was slumped over the sink with blood dripping from his wrist. He'd used one of our shaving razors."

Miriam gasped, her hands clenched in fists as she listened.

"Thankfully, his hands had been shaking so bad, he wasn't able to do a very good job of it. The doctors were able to stitch him back up, but my parents refused any psychiatric treatment for him. They didn't believe in such things. They loved to disparage the Catholics, but they were looking for nothing less than an exorcism, and mental health care wasn't going to cut it.

"I knew if Travis went back to my parents' house, the unseen wounds were going to kill him. When the hospital discharged him, I drove him straight from the hospital to Grandma and Grandpa's house. By that point, we were only a couple of months from graduating high school, and I think my parents were just as tired of us as we were of them. Initially, they put up a bit of a fight, but Grandma threatened to turn them into CPS. The threat of public scandal was enough to put them off. Since then, none of us have had much to do with them."

"That seems reasonable." Miriam's voice was quiet as if she was making sure she didn't say too much and stop the flow of Boone's story. But Boone was coming to the end.

"And I also haven't walked over a church's threshold since that day."

***

"I don't know what to say, Boone."

Speechlessness was a rare phenomenon for Miriam. After all, her occupation depended on her knowing what to say at the worst of times.

Bewildered muteness was quickly followed by shame. By comparison, her life had been easy. None of her experiences compared to Boone's story. Perhaps, that was why faith came naturally to her. Even her little drama in Bethel seemed trivial compared to what Boone and Travis had encountered: cold, hard hate disguised as piety.

And knowing Boone, the idea of him suffering through those experiences was even more devastating. After all, this was a guy who memorialized lost species all over his body. How insulting a faith must be to dismiss a segment of humanity. How did she convince him that what he encountered as a youth was not her faith? That while they both claimed to follow Christ, they were fundamentally unalike?

Boone spoke through the thick tangle of thoughts clouding her mind. "You don't have to say anything. We've all worked through it pretty well. Grandma got Travis into therapy, and then she and Grandpa supported him when he wanted to leave for New York City even though they missed him. They knew it'd be better for him there, that he'd face less discrimination."

"But how about you? Everything you said, the whole story - it was traumatic for you, too. Travis wasn't the only victim, Boone."

"I've found my way." Boone volunteered no details.

The room was silent. Miriam looked beyond Boone through the window. From this side of the house, she could see the bell tower standing stoically in the distance. She loved this place, and she loved her place within it. But she also loved Boone.

"So this," Miriam pointed to the coat rack with the robe, "and this," she pointed to her collar, "and that," her head leaned towards the church building. "It's all one giant deal breaker?" Miriam held her breath, hoping he would refute her question. Surely, he had noticed that the people in his story were not the same as her.

Boone's jaw muscles clenched. "You have a deal breaker and I have serious baggage. We're both better off walking away."

He started to turn, but Miriam reached out and grabbed his arm.

Through the threat of tears, Miriam said, "No. I don't throw my hands up that easily. What happened to you and Travis is awful, but it wasn't me. You know I would never do that to someone. You know that isn't what I believe or who I am."

Boone put his hand behind Miriam's neck and rested his forehead against her own. His eyes were clenched shut, a dam about to burst. "Miri, I've spent my whole childhood caged by the anger and hate of Christians. And I've spent most of my adult life trying to pick up the pieces."

Miriam cradled his face in her hands, wiping a tear with her thumb. "They aren't me, Boone. I don't even recognize their faith."

For a moment, she thought he was going to take her in his arms and let her curls soak up whatever tears he'd been holding in all these years. She thought she'd convinced him she was different. She thought she'd won.

Standing up straight and pulling away from her caress, Boone said, "I just can't."

He walked out the front door, a cold current of air running through the house as it shut.

Miriam stood staring at the spot he'd vacated, a faint outline of dust where his work boots had stood. How could his boots still be dirty after a week of trudging through snow and ice?

She'd thought her love articulated honestly and unashamedly would be enough. Love had always worked out well for her before. It had herded her parents towards acceptance when she'd chosen a profession they didn't understand. It had kept her cushioned in a small but solid circle of friends, a family of her choosing. But what she'd failed to appreciate was that Boone had grown up and lived with far less unconditional love.

Turning around, Miriam's phone lit up, and the nauseating sound of birds chirping filled the office. Walking over to her desk, Miriam yanked the charger from the phone and threw the phone against the wall, tears running down her face. Collapsing into her chair, Miriam leaned her head into her hands, her fingers tangling in her hair. She held in the scream that desperately wanted to escape. She wasn't ready to admit to herself how very hurt she'd allowed herself to be. Besides, screaming was for melodramatic soap opera scenes.

After a length of time passed that could have been five minutes or could have been an hour for all Miriam knew, the tears slowed. Through eyes burning from prolonged crying, she stared at her phone lying across the room face down, silent. She stood and walked to it, crouching down. When she picked it up, she saw that the screen was shattered.

Chapter 22

Several days passed after Boone's departure before Miriam acknowledged the grip of a deep, all-consuming fatigue. Trudging her way through the past few days felt like hiking without enough water. She'd always assumed that if her heart were ever broken, she'd have a reserve of strength to rely on. How naive.

How many times had she been complimented on her poise in difficult situations? But those situations were dramas set in someone else's story. Sitting next to a parishioner whose family member was being put on hospice. Comforting a young couple after a miscarriage. Holding the hand of a child who'd just lost a grandparent.

And she'd been present for so much worse. When she worked overseas, she'd seen children affected by war and poverty and famine. She had sat with them in that agony, ministered to them. She had felt energized in those situations, sure of her calling and confident in her ability to perform in even the most challenging of circumstances. Compassion fatigue had merely been a buzzword in public discourse, not a real, tangible experience in her life.

Yet, here she was with something as small and inconsequential as a failed romantic relationship, one that hadn't even made it off the ground, and Miriam was gutted.

The only credit she could give herself at the moment was that she'd persisted. It had been her week to preach, and somehow, she'd scrounged together a sermon, not one of her most inspiring but a sermon nonetheless, and she'd delivered it to a building full of people relieved to have made it through the storm and be back doing normal-life things. If she was going to give a sub-par sermon, it had been the week to do it.

Now, Miriam was officially done with her Sunday duties, the busiest day of the week for clergy. She'd changed out of her collar shirt and was wearing an oversized hooded sweatshirt with her seminary's logo across the chest and a pair of black leggings. Sitting in her house after eating a bowl of noodles lightly buttered and seasoned with salt and pepper, Miriam looked out her window to the bell tower. Grabbing her coat, she wrapped a scarf around her neck and headed out the door towards the church.

As she walked into the sanctuary, she breathed in the scent of melted wax. The dark outside made the stained glass windows dim, their colors muted and hauntingly beautiful. When she reached the center aisle, she bent a knee and genuflected towards the altar as she made the sign of the cross. Walking past several rows, she sat down in one of the dark, walnut pews. Pulling down the padded kneeler attached to the pew in front of her, Miriam took to her knees, her hands clasped, ready to have a prayer breathed on them.

But no words formed. Nothing came. Nothing except tears, streams of tears she wiped away on the sleeve of her sweatshirt.

Miriam's shoulders, shaking with sobs, stiffened immediately when she heard footsteps in the back of the church. When the space was this empty, the slightest sound echoed off the stone walls. Not wanting a parishioner to see her so distraught, Miriam moved to stand when a familiar voice stopped her.

"Hey, you. I've been meaning to get in touch."

Turning around, Miriam looked at Porter's friendly, familiar face. When he saw her puffy eyes and splotchy cheeks, the teasing smirk that was perpetual in his expression vanished. His eyebrows meeting in concern, he said, "Miriam, what's wrong?"

Much to her annoyance, Miriam immediately broke down again into unchecked sobs. She'd been avoiding phone calls from friends since arriving home, instead sending texts assuring them she was fine but drowning in work after being gone for a week. And it was partially true. She did have a long list of visits that needed to be made and classes and sermons that needed to be prepared. But mostly, she'd just been hiding from those sincere, loving looks of concern she knew would be pointed her way if she hinted at her current inner turmoil, the very look Porter had just demonstrated without her even saying a word.

The bench creaked and adjusted as he sat down beside her. Reaching a hand out, he patted her shoulder with the ease of someone trying to comfort an opossum. Offering comfort wasn't the domain of most English professors.

Clearly not knowing what to say, Porter spoke in a halting fashion that made Miriam, trained for such times, feel pity for the guy. "So, are you okay? I mean, obviously, you're not okay. Is there anything I can do? I can get you coffee. I mean, I don't know where to get coffee here - specifically - here at the church. But I've been known to make a mad dash to Starbucks in record time. It's the upside of my tendency towards reckless driving. I can also just sit here. If you don't feel like talking, I mean. If you don't feel like talking, I'll just sit here."

He was quiet for a moment while his hand continued to pat her shoulder with no discernible rhythm. Then he added, "Yes, ma'am. I'll just sit here and awkwardly pat your shoulder."

A laugh sputtered from Miriam, breaking through the crying in an ungraceful snort. Porter ceased his patting as she straightened her shoulders and took a deep, calming breath. It only caught once on the exhale. Moving back to sit on the pew, Miriam said, "I like a guy... No, I mean I love a guy, but he doesn't love me back, and it hurts like hell."

Porter slowly nodded his head once, whispering as he did, "Oh. Okay." After a pause, he said, "Not to be nosy, Miriam, but you might have to give me a few more details."

Taking a deep breath, Miriam began filling in the details: "As you know, I got stuck at the Rutledge's house over the storm when I went to deliver Miss Rubie her Valentine's basket. Well, while I was there, Boone..."

Miriam's words halted, but Porter was already parroting his nod from before. "Okay."

"Yes, well, Boone and I did…things."

Porter's head was continuing to do small nodding motions as he took in the information. "Of course, you don't have to answer this, but did you two…you know? Did you do the one really big thing?"

Miriam smiled again. She and Porter were suddenly as prudish as Victorian ladies. She answered in equally vague terms, "Not quite, but I had some seriously impure thoughts."

"Dear me. Not impure thoughts." He smirked, his normal, teasing self emerging from the awkwardness.

Defensively, Miriam said, "Yeah, well, if the ice hadn't melted for another day or two,…" She stopped, unsure how to finish the sentence. Where had they been heading? What would have happened had the real world not intruded for a little while longer?

Porter let the unfinished sentence hang in the air for several beats before he tentatively spoke again: "I know Boone pretty well, Miriam. He doesn't seem the sort to lead on a woman he doesn't actually care about."

"So you think I'm wrong?" Miriam's eyebrows were raised in challenge, and Porter immediately backtracked.

"No, no. That's not what I mean. I'm just saying, I bet the guy likes you if the two of you…did things."

Porter used the back of his hand to wipe sweat from his brow. It occurred to Miriam that talking with one's minister about said minister's love life was probably stressful, like going to the DMV office or the dentist. Feeling a little guilty for questioning him when he was clearly out of his depth, Miriam tried to be gentle as she told him he was wrong.

"I'm afraid it isn't that simple, Porter."

"What do you mean?"

"Has Boone ever told you and Forrest about his brother, Travis?" Miriam picked off a few piles that had formed on her old sweatshirt as she spoke.

"Sure. He has a brother in New York. They seem pretty close. I've also heard Rubie talk about him. In fact, she was saying the other day that her grandson and his partner were going to be moving closer to home soon."

"Exactly, her grandson and his partner. He's gay."

Porter looked confused at her. "Of course he is. I'm not tracking with you, Miriam. How is that connected to you and Boone."

Tossing her hair from a left part to a right part, Miriam said, "Well, it isn't my story to tell, but suffice it to say some dumbass minister from about twenty years ago used homophobic nonsense to torture Travis and - in doing so - Boone."

"That's tragic, Miriam," Porter said. "But I still don't see how it's connected to you."

Miriam looked at Porter as she explained. "When Boone and I were snowed in together, and the rest of the world seemed a million miles away, and I was dressed in flannel shirts and blue jeans, when that was the situation, you're right, Porter. Boone could and did care about me. And he acted on that connection. But when we had to come back into the real world and I put my collar back on and I walked back up into that pulpit," Miriam's voice caught. "I remind him too much of old traumas."

Porter placed his hand on her shoulder, but this time there were no awkward pats. "Miriam, doesn't he know that you're loving and accepting of all people regardless of their sexual identity? For goodness sake, you attended the Pride Parade last June wearing your rainbow stole."

Miriam shook her head. "One minister at a Pride Parade hardly erases centuries of invalidation and abuse."

"True," Porter agreed. "But it does show where that one minister stands. Where you stand. You can tell Boone about your work with the Pride group here in town and how you love and support every member of our youth group no matter how they identify and that we have several members of this church who are part of the LGBTQ community. He'll understand, and then you won't be sitting here on a pew crying your eyes out."

"But what has that really cost me? Plus, it would feel like bragging. Pointing out a few good things I've done. I don't know, Porter. It's unbecoming. And I think Boone would find it condescending. The fact is that Christians in general, and ministers in particular, remind Boone of the single worst moment of his life. When he looks at me in my collar, he is slammed back into that nightmare. I don't want to do that to him."

A silence settled on them that's length attested to just how comfortable their friendship had become over the years. Porter was the one to break it.

"You've given me solid advice so many times over the years. I want to return the favor, but I'm not sure I'm in any place to dole out love-life advice."

Miriam felt a pit form in her gut. Another one, actually, to accompany the pit that had persisted since Boone's story. "What do you mean?"

Porter didn't look at her, instead focusing on his hands. Hands that Miriam realized no longer sported a wedding band. "Charlotte left. I've been saying it's business trips, and it was business trips for years. But for the past few months, the business trips are her living somewhere else, and the times when she is home are the trips, so to speak."

This is what the old men meant when they said, *when it rains it pours*. Miriam felt drenched to her bones.

"Oh, Porter. What happened? What can I do?"

Porter smiled a joyless smile as he looked up at her. "I didn't tell you so that you could do something, Miriam. In fact, I'm not sure why I just poured out my problems on you when you clearly have enough of your own crap to deal with."

"Thanks for pointing that out."

"You just have that effect on people, I guess."

"The effect where you just find yourself telling me things?"

"Yeah, that effect."

"Not the first time someone has told me that." Miriam was now patting Porter's shoulder without being awkward at all.

He said, "I'm sorry I shared this while you're going through so much, Miriam."

"Don't apologize."

"And yet, I'm going to."

Miriam rolled her eyes, but even as she expressed annoyance in the most juvenile way possible, she felt an odd relief knowing that she was not alone in her pain and that she could still be present for others.

Porter continued, "All I want is for you to not share this for a little while longer. I'm not ready for everyone to know. Not yet, anyways. I'm still processing."

Miriam would forgo asking for more details until she sensed he was ready. "It's a deal. I know nothing."

"You should do that thing where you pretend to zip your lips and throw away the keys."

Shaking her head, she said, "There's something deeply comforting about knowing that even a life-altering heartbreak won't make Porter Finch grow up entirely."

Porter sucked on one side of his inner cheek, thinking. "So you're in love with a guy who has been seriously injured by someone of your occupation…"

"That's right."

"…and you can't switch careers."

"Out of the question. I'm way too old to be changing everything about myself for a guy."

"Of course."

Miriam nudged Porter with her elbow. "So what's the answer, dude?" She smiled a little hopelessly.

"I'm not sure, Miriam, but I will say between you falling for a guy who can't be around ministers and my wife leaving me, we've had some pretty shitty luck."

Now Miriam was nodding her head. "You can say that again."

They sat companionably for a moment longer until Miriam broke the silence. "Come on. Let's go. I'm heading over to your place to hang out with Lucy and Edith tonight." They arranged to meet in Lucy's garage apartment behind Porter's house.

As he stood up, Porter said, "Is lightning going to strike because I cursed in the church building."

"In my professional opinion, it's likely. I stubbed my toe on a pew a couple of weeks ago, and a four-letter word slipped out. Look where that got us."

Porter laughed. "So you, Mother Miriam, single-handedly caused the ice storm."

Miriam stood up, too, following behind him as they walked down the aisle. "Almost certainly."

***

Miriam climbed the stairs to the apartment above Porter's garage carrying a half-dozen cupcakes in various flavors that she'd picked up on her way. She eyed the Red Velvet. It was the only thing that could possibly ease her current funk.

Soon, Lucy would leave her long-time apartment to join Forrest in an actual house. The thought deepened Miriam's melancholy, not because she wasn't happy or supportive of Lucy and Forrest's relationship, but rather, because she'd built many fond memories in Lucy's little apartment.

Lucy had a knack for creating inviting, attractive spaces. When she'd moved in here, Porter gave Lucy free rein to redecorate. Miriam, with her trusty DIY videos on hand, had contributed regularly to the work, helping Lucy build bookshelves, restore old furniture, and, of course, paint or wallpaper every surface within sight. If Miriam and Lucy had known each other as children, they would have furnished and decorated a dollhouse with just as much enthusiasm and verve. When they undertook projects together, it always felt like play.

Miriam stood in front of the marigold yellow door at the top of the stairs listening. She could hear Edith's loud, carrying voice like a news broadcaster playing at high volume. Lucy, her tone soft as feather's next to Edith's aggressive manner, responded to something that sparked Edith's laughter.

The snowstorm had interrupted the normal flow of their weekly girls' nights, and they were set to reunite and catch up on all that had been happening over the past couple of weeks since Miriam's birthday. As of now, Lucy and Edith knew little of the emotional roller coaster Miriam had ridden since that evening. They would have questions about what a week alone with Swooney Boonie had been like. But they'd also want an update on Matchables and any prospects she might have. How was she to tell them her heart was booked? And that the object of her love had rejected her within days of their relationship first budding?

Knowing that her embarrassment would merely be her own, that they would not shame her or treat her like it was her fault, Miriam raised her hand to knock, opening the door as she did so.

"Hey Miri," Edith called out. "Welcome back from your own personal Call of the Wild."

Lucy shot Edith an odd glance Miriam couldn't quite place, but her face quickly returned to normal. "Yes, come in. Have a glass of wine. I have all the wine." As Lucy spoke, she poured three generous glasses.

"And I have all the cupcakes," Miriam said, holding up the polka-dotted take-out container.

Within half an hour, the three of them were sitting around Lucy's vintage Formica table twirling pasta doused in pesto. All three had piled thick shavings of Parmesan on top, and Miriam barely contained moans of pleasure with each bite. It turned out Edith could do more than grade papers and terrify undergraduates. She could also churn out a mean pesto.

Throughout the meal, they talked about wedding plans and campus politics and what they'd be planting over the coming weeks as spring approached. At first, Miriam only found it mildly suspicious that no one brought the snowstorm or Matchables or Boone Rutledge into the conversation. However, as the second hour of the evening rolled around without a single question about Miriam's adventure besides the brief reference when she had walked in the door, Miriam was going full-fledged conspiracy theorist.

After cleaning up from dinner, the friends migrated to the living area. Lit by candles and a lamp and still enveloped in the scent of basil, Miriam should have been unwinding nicely. Instead, her shoulders ached with tension as she gingerly pulled down the accordion wrapper on one side of her Red Velvet cupcake. She eyed Lucy and Edith, both of whom were definitely quieter than usual. Edith was sucking on a twirl of lemon that had garnished her Meyer's lemon cupcake while Lucy picked off and ate the individual sprinkles on her vanilla cupcake. Finally, Miriam broke the silence.

"So, have either of you spoken to Porter tonight?" Little time had passed between when she and Porter parted company and when she arrived at Lucy's door. But in their tight-knit group of friends that had proved on more than one occasion incapable of discretion within the confines of their circle, Miriam knew thirty minutes was plenty of time. While Porter would never betray Miriam's trust to the vast majority of people, she could hardly blame him for caving in to Lucy and Edith. They were formidable.

Both of Miriam's friends stopped picking at their cupcakes as they looked at her with eyes enlarged with feigned innocence.

"We may have seen him, right Lucy?" Edith answered, deferring the question to the friend in possession of the most tact.

"Maybe, as we were carrying the pesto ingredients up. Yes, I do believe he arrived home at the same time as us," Lucy agreed.

Miriam set down her cupcake. "And I don't suppose you two asked him about me, did you? Maybe how I've been doing? If he'd seen me since the storm? If he'd heard anything about my stay at the Rutledge's farm?"

Edith added, "Or if he'd heard exactly how much time you'd spent with Boone Rutledge?"

Lucy darted a disapproving glare across the coffee table. "Edith," she said with warning.

Rapping her fingers on the side table by the couch, Miriam said, "And did he say anything about Boone and me?"

Lucy said, "No, but he did sweat profusely."

Edith had officially run out of self-restraint. "So we figured that meant you two had done the dirty but maybe it didn't turn out that well because men are pigs."

"You deduced all that from Porter's sweat glands?" Miriam asked incredulously.

Lucy shrugged. "We've both worked in the same small office with Porter for a very long time."

Edith added, "So, yeah, we can read his sweat glands like we can read a well-crafted piece of literary criticism."

Miriam took a sizable bit out of her cupcake and chewed thoughtfully before speaking. She briefly contemplated that it was only a matter of time before the people around Porter figured out that his marriage had derailed, but she would respect his wish for a season of privacy. Both Edith and Lucy were faking intense interest in their cupcakes while still shooting side-eyes at each other that encapsulated silent reprimands from Lucy for Edith's indiscretions and Edith's own insistence that, really, someone had to say something.

Swallowing, Miriam said, "So, let me preface with a quick disclaimer: what I'm about to say will sound rash and not well thought out, but it's the absolute truth. I'm certain."

"Miri," Edith said in a voice oddly gentle for her, "you have our implicit trust. We aren't going to doubt or question you for a second. No disclaimers needed in this space."

Pulling on the drawstrings of her hooded sweatshirt, Miriam said, "In the week I spent at the Rutledge's farm, I fell in love with Boone, but when I told him, he rejected me." Miriam hadn't planned to end the sentence there. She was going to embellish the raw facts, telling them about her sadness and humiliation and the complexity of it all, but a lump rose in her throat that halted further explanation.

Edith, her meticulously plucked eyebrows scrunched together, said, "I know I said no questioning, and I really did mean it. At the time."

"Edith," Lucy drew out the name. "That time was all of ten seconds ago."

Edith held up her hands in not-quite surrender while rushing her next words. "I know. I know. Just let me have one not-even-a question so much as it's a suggestion. Miriam, couldn't it just be good old-fashioned lust? We've already established that the man is swoon-worthy."

Miriam thought about Edith's question disguised as a suggestion. It did need to be asked. The answer, though, came to her immediately and without doubt. "No, it's not just lust. Don't get me wrong - lust is there. But when I think of Boone, I don't just see the broad shoulders or the thick, just-wavy-enough hair or the gorgeous tattoos all over his torso and arms."

"All over? Really? You want to tell us more about that?" Edith asked.

"Not the time, Edith," Lucy said.

"It's not all those things," Miriam continued, her voice rising with conviction. "It's how much he cares. He isn't flippant about any of the things that matter. He feels and cares so deeply about Rubie and his brother and each plant in his care and birds - birds that haven't even existed in a century - and..."

Miriam could see in their confused eyes that she was off track, but she kept going. "And because he cares so much, he's vulnerable. That huge guy in his dirty boots and faded flannel and with his scratchy beard is walking around with a beat-up heart inside. Can you imagine carrying the pain of all those you love plus Chestnut trees?"

"Huh?"

Miriam didn't pause to clarify. "With all that goodness, all that devotion inside of him, how could I not fall in love with him? How?"

The room was quiet as Edith and Lucy processed Miriam's outpouring. Edith, unsurprisingly, spoke first.

"Yep. You're in love."

Lucy, with more gentleness, said, "What do you want from us, Miriam? Do you want to go through the story detail by detail and analyze the hell out of it? Do you want to sob into one of my throw pillows? Or should we eat chocolate and re-watch the episode where Luke and Lorelei finally kiss?"

Edith, always one to enjoy problem-solving, added, "Or we could rewatch the RBG documentary I bought when Forrest broke Lucy's heart. I find Ruth always helps a broken heart."

If there was only one thing Miriam had learned from working in a profession where she was expected to make other people feel better, it was that most times mourning couldn't be bypassed. Miriam had encountered many broken hearts in her years as Mother Miriam, but she had never been able to offer more than simply her presence. There were no shortcuts.

Looking into the eyes of her friends who wanted so desperately to ease her pain, Miriam said, "Your desire to help is the best offering possible. But I don't think there's a band-aid that is going to fix this. I think I'll have to wait this one out - to let the healing process happen at its own pace."

Before Miriam could pat herself on the shoulder for her own display of patient wisdom, Edith said, "Well fuck that."

Lucy's hand went to her forehead in disbelief as Miriam, grinning for the first time in a week, said, "Excuse me, Edith. Do you have a better idea?"

"Of course I do. You don't have to sit around passively waiting for some post-yoga vibe to fall on you. No, you may indeed have to wait for this broken heart of yours to heal, but in the meantime, at least grab life by the balls, Miri. We spent a wildly drunken and surprisingly productive evening setting you up a Matchables account. It's time to use it. Now."

Miriam let the words sink in. Edith's suggestion wasn't the slow-cured wisdom of a spiritual adviser or the informed advice of a therapist or even the pricey pep-talk of a life coach. Nevertheless, Miriam couldn't dismiss it entirely. It was just so thoroughly Edith, and Miriam knew that as rash as it might sound, it was born of love.

Running her fingers through her hair until they caught on curls that wouldn't untangle, Miriam said, "But, a date? I just told you I've fallen for someone. Wouldn't it make me shallow if I turn to someone else the second I feel rejected?"

"No."

Miriam was shocked to hear the abrupt answer come from Lucy. She was supposed to be the voice of reason, the one who tempered Edith's more impulsive tendencies.

Looking between Miriam's questioning eyes and Edith's decisive, set expression, Lucy said, "It's not shallow, Miriam. If anything, it's simply being honest with yourself. Instead of sitting around mooning over an unavailable guy, someone who has hurt you within a very short time, you're accepting that he's unattainable. You're moving forward. I'm not saying that the next guy will elicit the same feelings. But he could be a basic palette cleanser."

Seeing in Miriam's softening features that she was about to win the case, Edith added, "Come on, Miri. What have you got to lose except maybe that sad puppy-dog look you had when you walked in here tonight?"

Indeed, what did she have to lose?

Chapter 23

"Boone, suppertime!"

Rubie's voice carried through the house, causing Boone to lay down the red pen he'd been using to eviscerate a particularly bad research paper. Rubbing his eyes, Boone leaned back in the wooden chair he kept at the small desk in his bedroom. It complained loudly beneath his weight as he stretched his sore back. He'd spent too many damned hours hunched over papers this past week. A trip to the greenhouse after supper was in order.

The harsh, Arctic conditions of the previous week already seemed like another season. The highs had been in the fifties for a few days, and the sixties were only a few weeks away. Despite the promise of spring, Boone mostly stayed burrowed inside, buried in his work. If he set down the red pen for even a moment, there was no telling where his mind might roam.

When Boone walked into the kitchen, he saw Rubie dressed in muted colors. No costume jewelry accents. No scarves or lipstick. Her shoes were the most practical and most beige pair she owned.

Examining the spread she'd set out for their meal, Boone saw a small, loaf-pan-sized meatloaf with peas and carrots. No jello salad. No pink fluff. Nothing particularly processed or extra high in sodium and carbohydrates.

"You okay, Grandma?"

Rubie was pouring two tall glasses of whole milk. She neglected adding strawberry Nesquik to her own glass before setting down. Eighty-nine was an odd age to suddenly decide eating healthy had its merits.

"Of course I'm okay. Why would you be asking that?"

"Oh, it's nothing." Boone remained unconvinced. "Your ankle's feeling okay?"

"My ankle's fine. I'm fine. Now eat."

For the most part, Rubie seemed to have healed completely since the fall, but Boone still felt wary. She lifted the hand-smoothed, worn wooden spoon from the peas and served herself a few spoonfuls. For a while, dishes scraped across the table, and pleases and thank-yous were muttered as plates were filled. Then, they ate in silence, the only sound coming from the clatter of their silverware on plates.

For the first time in recent memory, Boone was the one to break the silence. "Supper's good, Grandma. Thank you."

She shrugged. "It tastes a little bland to me."

She'd been less generous than usual with the salt shaker, but the simple fare was still satisfying. A little concerned that her dampened mood was due to fatigue from the snowstorm and her fall, Boone said, "I'll make dinner tomorrow night when I get home from my afternoon class, okay?"

"Sure, dear."

A full week had passed since Boone walked out of Miriam's little house. He was back into his routine, plowing towards mid-terms with students who were lethargic after their unexpected break.

Back at home, the house was quiet. Each day, Rubie became a little more quiet, a little less herself. Now that he had all the quiet he'd always claimed to want, he yearned for the chatter of before. He wanted Rubie to badger him about his dating life. He wanted to hear her and Miriam in the distance chatting while they tackled some little chore together. He wanted to show someone the orchid that had just bloomed in the greenhouse, the one he'd bought sickly at a nursery for a few bucks and had nursed back to health.

Unable to bear his grandmother's sudden moroseness, Boone threw down his fork on the table and said, "It's too damn quiet."

Stunned, Rubie looked at him over her glass of plain milk. Setting it down gingerly, she said, "I agree."

Sounding more angry than he intended, Boone said, "Why aren't you talking? I know you and Hyacinth went out for lunch today. Surely you have some story to tell."

Rubie's lips pursed. "Do you really want to hear about my day?"

Sincerity softened Boone's tone. "Of course, I do."

"We did go to lunch. Our waitress was wearing a pride pen on her apron. Miss Hyacinth and I made her sit with us when she went on break, and we told her all about the lovely librarian."

Boone instantly regretted asking about her day. Unable to banish all judgment from his tone, Boone said, "Grandma, should you be getting involved in other people's personal lives?"

He tried to convey with his eyes that the answer was no. Rubie waved a dismissive hand before using the edge of her fork to cut another bite of meatloaf. Without looking at him, she said, "Boone, if there is one thing I know, it is that the people of your generation are terribly lonely. I read an article about it in TIME magazine in the lobby while I waited for my doctor's appointment the other day. The least I can do is try to help alleviate this loneliness by butting in now and then. After all, I'm too old for people to get too mad at me."

Boone wasn't so sure.

She continued, "Besides, at least it keeps me out of this house. I don't know if you've noticed, Boone, but the only reason it is too damned quiet is because we both grew accustomed to Mother Miriam. We both miss her."

"I do not…"

Before Boone could finish his protest, Rubie held up a hand that breached no argument. "Boone, don't insult me by assuming I didn't know what was happening beneath my own roof. You have a thing for Miriam, and it's clear she's crazy about you."

Boone's elbows came up on the table, his hands linked with his forehead resting on them as he stared down at his half-eaten plate. "Maybe you're right, Grandma. Maybe there was something between us. But there wasn't enough. There wasn't enough to overcome what stands between us."

People were supposed to outgrow the expression Rubie was currently directing towards Boone around the age of eighteen. The arrangement of her mouth and the roll of her eyes should have been conveying how lame parents can be. Rubie said, "What the hell does that mean? What, exactly, is standing between two able-bodied, unattached adults who clearly have the hots for one another?"

Boone stood up from the table and walked over to the sink, pausing to look out the kitchen window. From there, he could see into the front, window-lined face of the greenhouse. His mind, unbidden and disobedient, went to the image of the smooth lines of Miriam's shoulder with a smattering of birds flying across to the olive tree drawn over her delicate shoulder blade. His fingers tingled at the memory of the soft skin, of the goosebumps his touch had summoned.

Not turning around, Boone said to the window, "When Travis comes home, he will not find a member of the clergy in this house. Even if Miriam isn't like the ministers we grew up with, I won't allow nightmarish memories to haunt him every time he sees me."

A hand squeezed his shoulder. Tenderly, without any of the annoyance he'd heard in her voice only moments ago, Rubie said, "Oh, Boone. Travis doesn't want you to sacrifice happiness for him. He doesn't need you to protect him, either. He's stronger than you realize."

Wanting to dismiss the discussion while also making amends, Boone turned around and hugged Rubie, his cheek resting on the coarse bed of her unruly hair. Releasing her, Boone said, "You go read for a while. I'll clean up."

***

Boone's silence told Rubie clearer than words could that the discussion was over. No amount of reasoning would convince him he was wrong. No amount of assurance would make him believe Travis was safe.

As he released her and began cleaning the kitchen, Rubie walked into the livingroom and eyed the Avon romance she'd started the day before. It was particularly dramatic with the hero's life having now been threatened on at least three separate occasions; she was only a third of the way in. If she sat down and opened its pages, she'd be lost in the story for a while. But when she eventually closed it, she would still have a lonely, hurting grandson who was keeping the woman he loved at arm's length for the noblest and most misguided of reasons. How foolish of her to have thought hate of those old ministers was what fueled him. No, Boone was driven by fear. He'd always been trying to protect Travis.

Bypassing the novel, Rubie went to the staircase. Holding tightly to the handrail, she took one step at a time. Thankfully, her ankle was considerably better and less sore than it had been the days immediately following her fall.

When she reached her room, she sat down on the floral bedspread next to the pink phone she kept on the bedside table. Rupert always teased her about the rose-toned phone, which, of course, meant she could never replace it now. It was a reminder of the decades of playful banter that characterized their marriage.

Picking up the phone, Rubie's arthritic finger slowly and intentionally dialed one of the many numbers she'd memorized by heart. Young people these days didn't know any phone numbers.

They relied on their phones for their memory. She always made it a point to memorize the numbers of the people she truly loved.

The phone only rang one and a half times before it was answered.

"Grandma? How's my favorite lady?"

"I need you to come home, Travis."

Chapter 24

The music from the Friday evening live performance was too loud for meaningful conversation, and that was fine with Boone. Between the cacophony of guitars strumming folksy rock, the thick scent of frying onion rings, and the steady stream of alcohol being poured by the endearingly solicitous bartender, Boone felt adequately numbed to actual thoughts. He was all senses. Smelling, tasting, hearing. No thinking. No feeling.

"You might want to slow down after this one." The bartender winked as she said the words. She was petite, tattoos and piercings displayed in abundance with her short, pixie-cut hair and cropped top. Even in the haze of alcohol, he could see that her smile was flirtatious. She'd pour him another if he asked. She'd probably even be his designated driver if he asked - if he decided he didn't want to go back to the farm. He'd figure those details out later.

It was unusual for Boone to indulge in alcohol, but there had been a noticeable uptick in the weeks since the storm. It probably said something about choices he'd made and feelings he'd felt. Boone was particularly grateful for the burn as another gulp went down. Thoughts were overrated.

Really, he'd earned the blissful solitude of his barstool with empty stools on each side. The previous night, he'd taken another miserable, deflating stab at Matchables. Five minutes into his date with @bluegrassgirl, Boone knew there wouldn't be a second date. For one thing, she was too short, and her hair was too straight. Also, when their conversation lagged and inevitably turned to the weather, she'd said something trite like, *How shocked had he been at that freak ice storm so late in the winter?* Boone barely held back a sarcastic reply about this new thing called climate change. Then he felt guilty the remainder of the evening for what an asshole he was being in his brain to this reasonably nice woman.

Boone was eating a bite of the cheesecake slice she'd insisted on sharing with him when he realized the standard by which he was judging poor @bluegrassgirl. It was no longer Ella Jean from the class of 2001 Jefferson High as it had been for the past fifteen years or so. It was Mother Miriam Howatch, Assistant Rector of the Trinity Episcopal Church of Paducah, Kentucky. Tall, adventurous, intelligent Miriam who didn't need makeup or perfume or hair products to be captivating even if a bit unruly. It really wasn't fair.

"Well, that one went down fast." Pixie-cut bartender girl was back, somehow grinning while also pouting her lips. It was like looking at a sexy emoji. As his eyes swam over her, Boone decided her Matchables tag, if she were to ever join the platform, would be @tattoosandbrew. It was a decent tag. She'd get lots of ticks. Through his blurred musings, Boone realized she was once again talking to him. "Promise me you won't drive. You're too cute to get twisted around some tree."

Boone quirked his mouth into a one-sided grin. "I'll get an Uber. I'd already planned on it."

Crossing her arms and leaning across the bar, her small breast made the faintest line of cleavage Boone could just barely discern through the sheet of tattoos across her chest. Drawing his eyes up, he concentrated on her lips as she spoke so that he could read them over the sound of the band. "You don't have to get an Uber if you don't want to. I'm off in thirty minutes."

He couldn't hear her voice, but the message was clear enough.

"I appreciate the offer, but I'd better stick with Uber tonight."

She didn't look too hurt. Rejection was probably extremely rare for her. Refilling his glass, she said, "That's too bad. Are you sure?"

"No," Boone said with a laugh. She grinned in response. In a moment of unvarnished honesty perhaps caused by his alcoholic stupor, Boone said, "I'm sort of hung up on someone right now."

The bartender shrugged. "I'm fine with that."

Smiling ruefully, Boone said, "But I'm not."

"Well, come back when you get over her, okay?"

Boone watched as she walked to another customer. A stew of regret churned in his stomach, but he was too drunk to know the exact source of all the regrets. Rubbing his eyes in a futile attempt to clear his thoughts, Boone's gaze scanned the room. It was filled with people eating bar food while enjoying the music. Only the bar had loners not reveling in the company of friends or a lover.

Towards the back of the room, Boone's eyes landed on unmistakable, chocolatey brown curls. She was laughing. He could see it in the way her head was tilting to one shoulder. She always did that when she laughed.

The man sitting across from her was tall and skinny and looked as though he'd worked in an office since he was about five years old. Boone calculated him to be either an accountant or an estate lawyer or a therapist. A therapist felt the most right. He probably sat with his legs crossed for one hour at a time while people confided all their worst thoughts to him.

In between Miriam and the man laid a sad, wilted red carnation. Boone figured it was some kind of recognition ploy, and he was immediately incensed that the man had brought a red carnation. There were a million more interesting flowers he could have chosen for Miriam. She was not a carnation kind of woman.

The two interacted with some reserve - it was clearly a first date - but the man leaned in more than was necessary. He was attracted to Miriam. It was clear. The nameless, pale, willowy man was attracted to the woman who had only a short while ago confessed her love to Boone. And Boone had walked away. He'd walked away and stayed away. And now some schmuck was leaning towards her while saying something flirtatious or humorous or wildly interesting.

After a minute or so staring steadily at the back of Miriam's head, Boone began to wonder if he was about to spark that phenomenon where a person knows they're being stared at without any evidence other than the intangible feel of an unmoving gaze.

Any moment now, she'd glance over her shoulder suspiciously searching for the source of the raised hairs on the back of her neck. And what would she find but an inebriated Boone with dirt beneath his fingernails and a sprinkling of dust around his boots? Next to @accountingonyou or @foreverjung or @hashisshittogether, Boone looked like Pig-Pen from Charlie Brown.

Spinning around clumsily on the barstool, Boone hit his chest against the edge of the bar enough to make him gasp. Beneath the fog of alcohol, Boone knew he should call over the bartender and order a very strong and very black coffee to go. He should stumble to the bathroom and splash cold water on his face. He should pull out his phone then and there and book a drive. Then, he should pray to the very God who he'd refused to speak to for over half his life. He should pray for escape before his presence was noticed.

But when @tattoosandbrew walked up to his section of the bar, Boone pushed his empty glass toward her and asked for more.

***

He was nice. The man sitting across from Miriam was nice. He was also funny, and his gaze was appreciative without being creepy. Even if fireworks weren't exactly flying, he was clearly interested.

All of which resulted in a hefty helping of guilt as Miriam made an excuse to step away from the table. She'd told him she was going to the bathroom and then picking them up a drinks menu from the bar on her way back. It would buy her enough time to adequately chide herself while standing in the stall with a toilet she didn't need.

Miriam hadn't dated in a very long time, and she'd been intimidated by the whole Matchables idea from the beginning. But here she was on her first date in years with the first guy she'd really conversed with online, and he seemed remarkably perfect. He had a great personality, a nice, lean build, he was intelligent (a research librarian at the university), and - bonus - he made her laugh. Or at least, chuckle. So why were there no sparks? Why was she rebelling against her own good sense? Even as she tried to stay positive, a voice within made its presence known with a relentless negative commentary. His shoulders weren't broad enough. He looked a little too put together - would a wrinkle in his starched shirt have killed him? His smiles were too wide, too easy to come. She missed the challenge of eliciting a smile on the lips of a man less prone to them.

The reality was that Miriam's heart was as pinned down as a tent stake. It had made a choice divorced from reason or reality, and it seemed disinclined to change course.

After biding her time in the stall, Miriam stepped in front of the mirror for a quick adjustment. She'd replaced her normal high, white-collared shirt with a dusty mauve sweater. Its v-neck dipped just low enough to suggest cleavage without actually showing any. The lighter color complemented the dark chestnut of her hair, and Miriam knew she looked good. The hems of her blue jeans were caught on the edge of her ankle boots, so Miriam bent over to fix it before heading back into the dining room. She felt more prepared to embrace the evening, even if embracing in this situation meant trying to enjoy the company of a likable person with whom she would never be more than friends.

Leaving the bathroom, Miriam walked over to the bar for a drinks menu. Leaning against the bar over an empty stool, Miriam waited for the bartender with the pixie cut to notice her. Looking across, she saw the bartender pouring a glass while laughing. As the bartender pushed the glass across the bar, she squeezed the forearm of her customer, clearly at ease and friendly with him.

Then, just beyond the bartender's spiked hair, Miriam's eyes landed on unmistakable light blue eyes. Boone's hair was mussed, and the half-grin on his lips vanished the exact moment recognition dawned.

Without making a conscious decision to do so, Miriam walked slowly around the bar, Boone's eyes never leaving her. The bartender, realizing she'd lost his interest, left to go to another customer. Once they were face to face, Miriam didn't know what to say. The best she managed was a "Hello" while leaning close to his ear so he might hear over the music.

Suddenly, Miriam felt Boone's hand on her lower back as he leaned in to say, "You look beautiful tonight."

Even over the music, Miriam could hear a telling slur on the last word. He'd almost held it together. Dismissing his compliment, Miriam said, "You're drunk."

He leaned even closer, and Miriam worried what her date must be thinking, but she wasn't worried enough to pull away. Boone's voice said huskily, "Only tipsy. But - fun fact - I think you're beautiful even when I'm sober."

Stepping away from him, Miriam said, "Boone, I'm on a date."

"I know you're on a date. And might I say, he looks all wrong for you."

Miriam's arms crossed as she nearly shouted over the music, "And what, exactly, makes you an expert? How do you know who is right for me?"

"I'd say I'm quite the expert. After all, I'm your type, and that guy is nothing like me."

Miriam's jaw twitched with anger. She hadn't known she had a type until a few weeks ago when she saw him working everyday in the barn or the greenhouse, the muscles in his back flexing with each chore he attacked. She hadn't yet seen her date's back - certainly not while performing manual labor. But she feared she would find it lacking.

Stepping away from Boone, Miriam said in a manner she hoped came across as nonchalant, "I'm returning to my date. To the guy who actually wants to be here with me."

Turning around, Miriam walked back to the table, her hips swerving a tad too dramatically as she weaved through the tables. Even she wasn't above hoping for a memorable exit from a guy who had rejected her.

As she sat down, Miriam said, "Sorry about that. Saw an old friend at the bar. I was afraid it would be rude to not say hello."

Her date waved a dismissive hand. "I understand. No problem."

But even as he spoke the words, Miriam saw a hint of discomfort on his face. The guilt from earlier flared anew. She really did need to be a better date.

Soon, their food came out, and pleasant conversation ensued over plates of burgers with fries stacked so high they fell off the edges onto the table. They were just far enough from the band to be able to speak without yelling. There was no natural way for Miriam to turn and see if Boone was still at the bar, but just when she thought she couldn't stand to not check for a moment longer, her date said, "I don't mean to point out anything awkward, but your friend has been staring at us for a solid half hour now."

Finally granted an excuse to turn around, Miriam saw that Boone was indeed staring, his hand around an empty shot glass. Taking her napkin off of her lap as she turned back, Miriam tossed it onto the table despite her meal only being half eaten. Hoping to ease the tension that Boone's glare had added to an otherwise pleasant first date, Miriam suggested, "Maybe he just really likes taxidermy."

The wall behind them was full of hunting trophies, most notable of which was a wild boar that did little for Miriam's appetite.

Smiling ruefully, her date said, "I'm pretty sure he's staring at you."

Feeling guilty for the tarnished date, Miriam looked straight into his eyes as she said, "We have a history. A brief but turbulent history."

"Aah."

Miriam turned again to see if Boone had developed some tact in the past minute. He was standing up, looking unsteady as he took his thick, canvas work coat off the back of the stool and began shrugging into it. Miriam turned back at the sound of her date's voice.

"Well, I don't think your friend is in any condition to drive. How about you go see to that, and if you ever decide you want a second date, you give me a call." As he spoke, he wrote his phone number on a coaster. "And next time, we'll go out of town for dinner."

Miriam took the coaster from his proffered hand, grinning at his final words. "Thank you," she said, but she did not add words of assurance or commitment.

After saying goodbyes, Miriam rushed to the back exit of the bar where she'd seen Boone leave. After all, she couldn't allow Miss Rubie's grandson to get in an accident even if he was being insufferable.

***

Boone leaned heavily against the door of his truck as he pulled up the app for a ride. The screen swam in front of him, and he cursed the foolery that had landed him intoxicated in a parking lot trying to find a ride. Just as the booking was confirmed, his phone was taken from his hand. Looking up, Boone saw Miriam, her curls back-lit by the security light, holding out a hand.

"Give me your keys, also."

"I wasn't going to drive. I was booking a ride."

Miriam glanced at the still-lit screen of his phone. Satisfied, she handed it back to him and said, "That isn't necessary. I'll give you a ride."

Boone neglected to tell her he'd already pressed the confirmation button.

She said, "Is Rubie healing okay from the fall?"

Boone was momentarily sobered by the change in subject. "Her ankle's fine. You'd never know she took a fall." He contemplated telling her how much Rubie missed her, but instead, he asked, "Where's your date?"

"That's irrelevant. But since you asked, it turns out, having you smolder in his general direction for the bulk of the evening made him cut and run."

"Wuss." Boone knew his tone of self-satisfaction would infuriate Miriam.

"No, Boone," Miriam said with fury rising in her voice. Stabbing his shoulder with a finger, she said, "You don't get to insult my date. Not after you made the entire evening - which, by the way, was my first date in a very long time - not after you made it intolerable."

Boone didn't resist her anger or her assault on his shoulder. He felt indignant, too. Her first date in how long? Men were so stupid to let a woman like that go unnoticed. Leaning back even more heavily on his truck, he adjusted his stance so that she was directly between his widely spaced boots. Perhaps it was the rage coming off of her, but she heated the entire front of his body.

Using the last shred of willpower the alcohol hadn't yet stripped from him, Boone kept his hands in his pockets as he quietly said, "I'm sorry, Miri. It's just," his words trailed off, the thick fog of alcohol skewing the path that might atone for the jackass he'd been. Trying again, he continued, "It's just, a red carnation? He's a red carnation guy. You deserve better than a red carnation."

Laughing bitterly, Miriam said, "Not everyone has a collection of rare roses growing in their backyard year-round, Boone. That's hardly a fair critique."

"And he's too skinny and too starched. He's too uptight for you."

He was right, of course. Even drunk, Boone knew the conclusion Miriam would reach after a few more dates with the guy. Even if he was right, though, the steely expression on Miriam's face told Boone he should have kept the assessment to himself. That he knew the relationship was doomed before she'd figured it out was the bitterest insult.

"How dare you," Miriam seethed, speaking words surprisingly dramatic for someone normally so nuanced. "How dare you assume you know me after one week in each other's company. One week, Boone. It hardly makes you an expert."

"It was no ordinary week, and you know it." They were the first words he'd uttered that evening that weren't slurred. They sounded exceedingly sober.

Taking a step back to put some distance between herself and the look of hunger in Boone's eyes, Miriam said thickly through emotion that had materialized out of nowhere, "You didn't want me, Boone. You gave a hard pass."

How unimaginable that the all-consuming passion he'd experienced since she walked into their house that February afternoon was somehow completely unknown to her. Defensive, Boone said, "I never said I didn't want you."

Before Miriam could know what was happening, Boone switched positions with her, the steel of the old pick-up truck cold as his gloveless hands gripped the rim of the truck bed on each side of Miriam. His elbows were straight, giving her space to duck away. He wouldn't stop her, but he didn't need to. She stood still, her chest rising and falling in deep, ragged breaths. The sight robbed Boone of further speech.

It was Miriam - blessed, beautiful Miriam - who finally closed the gap between them. Taking Boone's bearded cheeks into her tender hands, she pulled his lips to her own. Boone's resolve snapped like a taught fence wire being cut in two. His hands wrapped around her back. He sought to cushion her against the truck even as he pressed with his entire, needy body. The kiss deepened in aggressive, hungry strokes as they made up for the weeks apart.

The sounds Miriam made, the sighs of pleasure, were achingly familiar to Boone. Yes, he remembered this. He remembered her sound, her smell, her taste. He'd been starved for this.

Miriam's hands slid down his face and neck into his coat, her arms wrapping around his waist so they shared the same heat. So enticed by the sight of her without a high, white collar, Boone's kisses trailed down the edge of her neck, his tongue dipping into the crevices at her collarbone. She sucked in air, moaning in pleasure. He tasted perfume and pushed the thought aside that she had applied that perfume while preparing for a date with another man. Making his way back up to her lips, Boone reminded himself that only he had actually tasted her, that no one else had pressed her against a truck in the parking lot.

But before Boone could become too self-satisfied, the sound of gravel beneath wheels caused both him and Miriam to jerk apart, Miriam turning quickly so that the approaching vehicle wouldn't see her flushed face or the ruddy spots along her neck where Boone's beard had rubbed her raw.

The car pulled up to Boone, the driver rolling down his window. A young, college-aged man said, "You the one needing a ride?"

Still breathing like he'd just run a marathon, Boone said, "Yeah, that was me."

Turning regretfully to Miriam, he saw that she was still turned in the opposite direction, her eyes staring blankly into the dirty bed of his pick-up. Putting a hand at the base of her back, Boone said, "Miri?" He wasn't sure what he was asking.

Without looking at him, Miriam said, "Get home safe, Boone."

Boone watched her walk away and get into her car before he took his seat for the ride back to the farm.

***

Miriam's hands shook as she searched in her purse for keys. No matter how hard she tried to keep her purse organized, her keys were always mysteriously lost the moment she stepped into a parking lot. Grasping repeatedly, she finally felt the jab of cold metal.

Once seated safely inside her car, Miriam rested her forehead on the steering wheel, trying to process the swirl of emotions rushing past her. If emotions were paint, she would be a Jackson Pollock.

Miriam wanted to drive out to the farm and finish what they had started beneath the harsh light of the security lamp post. He wanted her, and even if her love wasn't reciprocated, there was something there worth exploring. She was tired of celibacy imposed mostly by the social awkwardness of her collar and title. Boone presented an alarmingly attractive solution to this problem. He also came with a very real possibility of heartbreak. After all, Miriam's heart had already been smarting for weeks over his first rejection. Could she take a second round?

Regardless of what she was willing to risk, Miriam couldn't follow him tonight. Yes, he was plenty willing. But what if that willingness was alcohol-induced? She'd hardly be better than a frat boy with roofies if she drove to the farm tonight. And by the time he slept it off, she doubted he'd even remember their embrace against that old, yellow truck.

So Miriam turned in the opposite direction away from the roads that led to farms and toward the old center of town. Within five minutes of weaving down the narrow streets of downtown Paducah, an area once strolled by Ulysses Grant as he waited to invade the South, Miriam saw the bell tower of Trinity Episcopal Church reaching above the tree line. There, she, too, would bide her time.

Chapter 25

Boone had been working in the greenhouse all morning, giving him the best view of the driveway. Even with clear visibility, he dropped the sheers and craned his neck each time he heard a sound outside. The car should've arrived ten minutes ago. Not terribly late, but Boone was anxious for Travis to arrive. He hoped his brother's presence would offer a distraction from thinking about long cold nights and dark parking lots and disappointed brown eyes.

Several weeks had passed since Boone made a fool of himself in front of Miriam. He'd not imbibed a drop of alcohol since, turning instead to an aggressively sober stance, a condition that was not doing any favors for his mood. Boone noticed students giving him a wide berth on campus, and Rubie had smacked him on the back of the head with a crocheted hot pad more times than he cared to remember. Rubie wasn't a violent woman, but she wasn't afraid to make a point, either.

However, Boone had gone twenty-four days without giving the evil eye to some unsuspecting stranger, ruining perfectly nice dates, or passionately kissing an off-limits woman in a bar parking lot. All in all, he felt sobriety was working out well for him.

Finally, another distant sound that caught Boone's attention proved to be the crunch of gravel beneath the tires of a rental car. He walked out of the greenhouse, not even noticing the mud puddles along the path. Spring rains were steady and drenching at this time of year, leaving Boone's boots in even worse condition than normal.

The Audi pulled up within a few feet of where Boone stood. A grin tugged at one side of his mouth as he looked at the shiny, steel-gray rental car parked next to the mud-caked junker he drove. There could not have been an image more emblematic of the differences between Boone and his twin brother.

Walking to the driver's side, Boone pulled open the door, hearing Malcolm Gladwell's voice, a favorite road trip companion for both of the Rutledge brothers. Travis, rummaging in a bag on the passenger seat, found his phone and paused Gladwell's clipped cadence. Turning to Boone, his face broke into a full smile, his eyes hinting at wrinkles that were not as far in the future as they used to be. He said, "You interrupted my book."

"Sorry," Boone said insincerely.

Stepping out of his car, Travis embraced Boone in a tight hug with plenty of masculine back-patting done by both parties. Stepping away from each other, Travis's eyes scanned the path between the driveway and the kitchen door.

"There is no way I'm going to get from here to there without caking these leather shoes in mud, is there?"

"Not a chance in hell, brother," Boone replied, giving his brother's back one more heavy-handed pat. "Not a chance in hell. But don't worry, we still have your Wranglers and flannel shirts. In fact, they were recently washed, so they should be fresh for you."

Travis, who'd just executed a maneuver close to tip-toeing on his way to the trunk, said, "You didn't have to wash them for me."

Boone shrugged. "We sort of did. Someone else borrowed them."

Travis looked surprised as he said, "Really? Who?"

An image of Miriam in the fitted jeans flashed through Boone's mind. He grumbled, "It's a long story, let's get your stuff in. How much did you pack anyways?" The trunk had several bags packed Tetris style.

Before the brothers could gather all the luggage, the kitchen door swung open, its doorknob thudding hard against the siding. In the doorway, Rubie stood in a quilted magenta housecoat over a green mu-mu, arthritic socks rolling down on her left ankle, and pink house shoes that looked remarkably like a child's stuffy. Possibly bunnies.

Despite not being too far from her grandsons, Rubie shouted as though she were delivering a life-saving message from across the span of the Grand Canyon: "There's my other baby boy. We've been waiting for you for at least 10 minutes. Road work, I suppose. Anyways, you two get in here. I have a feast worthy of a Saturday morning cooking show. If one of you two would teach me how to use social media, I'd probably become famous just with my food pictures."

"God help us if she ever learns to use social media," Boone whispered to his brother.

Rubie, proving once again that hearing was the least of her problems, said, "I'll just ask my lesbian librarian how it's done." Travis's eyes shot to Boone in question even as Rubie continued, "And I can't come out there to greet you, Travis, because I have on these fuzzy slippers Hyacinth and I found at that discount store over in Fulton, and I'll be damned before I let them get muddy."

With that, and without apparently needing to inhale long enough for Travis to return her greeting, Rubie slammed the door shut and returned to the kitchen.

Their eyes meeting over the roof of the car, Travis said, "I see age isn't slowing her down."

Boone simply responded with a laugh as he carried in the tan-plaid luggage, the sound of his brother's fine leather shoes squelching through the mud following behind him.

***

Boone would categorize his state of fullness following Rubie's feast as Thanksgiving Day full. Rubie had decided to make all the things she assumed Travis's fancy city life deprived him of. Dishes of beans, turnip greens, cornbread, Kentucky cured ham, and, of course, jello salad vied for space on the small kitchen table, the rims of the plates and bowls butting up against one another. Boone had thought of Miriam each time he'd bitten into mandarin orange slices in the jello salad, his attention called back to the meal more than once by Rubie or Travis repeating his name with escalating bafflement. After dinner, they settled in front of the fireplace with slices of buttermilk pie and cups of coffee.

Sitting on the couch fully satiated, Travis declared, "From now on, I'm wearing elastic waist pants. Paul is just going to have to get used to it."

Boone, a toothpick perched out of one corner of his mouth, said, "You are moving to Kentucky, so that seems reasonable."

Rubie with her feet propped on the ottoman responded, "I can't wait to fatten up that man. Paul is far too skinny."

Paul always jogged around the perimeter of the property when he came to visit. It was going to take substantial amounts of lard for Rubie to accomplish her goal.

Travis said, "As soon as he returns from his conference, I'll let him know your intentions, Grandma. He'll be thrilled."

Boone chuckled at the flat tone of Travis's voice. Through his laughter, he said, "I still can't believe you're moving back."

"Believe it, brother. I flew down to check out a condo in downtown Louisville that Paul fell in love with from the online pictures. Our realtor didn't think it would last on the market, so I rushed down without him. On the drive here, I got the call that our offer was accepted."

Rubie clapped her hands gleefully. "Congratulations, son. Imagine. A condo. It sounds so sophisticated."

"That's great news," Boone said.

The three talked for another hour or so as the flames died out in the fireplace. They discussed the holidays they would now spend together, the guest room that had Rubie's name on it, and the life he and Paul planned to build in Louisville. Finally, everyone agreed the dishes could wait until the morning.

Both brothers groaned against their straining waistbands as they moved around the bedroom getting ready to lie down in their respective twin beds. Normally when Travis visited, he and Paul would rent a room at a favorite Bed and Breakfast in Paducah. Since it was just Travis, he was staying in their old room, the two brothers in parallel twin beds in exactly the way they'd spent their childhood and adolescent summers.

"With you and Paul moving closer, I've got to start working on an addition. We could easily build a little guest suite off the east side of the house."

"I'd sort of miss Miss Hattie's B and B. I mean, if it was good enough for the prostitutes who serviced Grant's troops, it's good enough for me and Paul."

Throwing back the covers of his bed, Boone said, "Our house's history might not be as colorful, but Grandma did once make love to Grandpa on our front porch as she likes to tell anyone who dares to mention the house's charming architecture. So there's that."

Travis groaned, this time not from the side effects of gluttony, and rolled onto his bed. "We know far, far too much about our grandparents' sex life."

"Yes, we do, Travis. Yes, we do."

On the last word, Boone turned off the overhead light, leaving only the lamp shaped like a baseball glove on the table between their beds. As he laid down, the bed springs wailed in what Boone felt to be a particularly judgmental fashion. He hadn't eaten that much.

Travis laid on his back with his hands behind his head, looking relaxed and satisfied. Boone's mind briefly jumped to the image of his brother on another twin-size bed, his body curled in on itself in misery and insecurity.

"You do realize you sleep in a room that looks like it's for a twelve-year-old, right?"

Travis's words brought Boone back to the moment, to the lightness and ease of the evening. He said, "Yep. I'm aware. I just haven't had time to do anything about it yet, and even if I did have time, I wouldn't know what to do."

"Paul and I will come down for a reno weekend. It will be like one of those shows where they makeover a room, except we won't put tacky homemade craft projects on the wall or expect you to cry at the end."

Boone shrugged. "Sounds like a solid plan to me. I especially like the part where you don't expect me to be emotive. I wish the rest of the world would get that memo."

Travis turned his head sharply in Boone's direction. "Uh-oh. Is Boonie having girl problems?"

"No," he lied.

"Yeah, right. You should've been gay like me. It's easier."

Boone laughed while shaking his head. Travis's nonchalant joke about how easy his life had been as a gay man felt like a little deposit, one more sign Boone would file away to remind himself that Travis really was okay, that his life really had turned out for good.

Travis, turning to his side, said, "You getting laid, brother?"

Boone groaned at the blunt question. He rubbed his eyes and face forcefully, as he said, "I can't say it's a regular occurrence these days."

"I heard about your minister."

"She's not my anything."

Boone's voice had come out with more edge than he intended. Travis's eyebrows lifted as he responded, "I can tell. Your cheeks aren't turning the same color as one of your fancy heirloom tomatoes or anything. Nope, you look completely unaffected by the mention of her."

"Have you always been this big of an ass?"

Travis grinned. "Nope. But Paul says I'm getting impish with age. Speaking of which, can you believe I ended up with someone who uses the word 'impish' in normal conversation?"

Boone twisted the corner of his sheet around his finger as his mouth quirked. "I actually can believe it. You've come a long way from rural Kentucky. I always knew, though, that you would. That you wouldn't stay here. I knew you were meant for something a little grander."

"That's bullshit."

Boone jerked his head towards Travis, surprised at the words, but Travis was smiling fondly at him. In a soft, low voice, Travis said, "You never knew I'd make it out. The reality is you were terrified I wouldn't, at least not alive. Sometimes, I think you're still holding your breath."

Boone lay in silence. After a moment, he said in his own low, gruff whisper, "Maybe, but I always knew you would thrive if you ever did get out. I'm so very glad you got out." Then, in a louder, less serious tone, he said, "Plus, I wanted to have this room to myself, so it's extra good you didn't stick around."

Travis threw a pillow at Boone's head as they both laughed.

From across the hall, they heard Rubie's voice calling, "You boys settle down. It's way past your bedtime."

Travis, who had always enjoyed teasing his grandmother as much as she enjoyed stirring things up, yelled back, "You're one to talk, old lady."

Rubie called back, "I love you, too. Good night."

After calling back their own love-you's and goodnight's, Boone settled in to fall asleep when Travis's voice once again floated across the divide between their beds.

"Have you bothered to stalk her online? Because there are definitely pictures of her at a pride parade with a rainbow stole."

Boone thought about Miriam, so eager to help others, to make the world a little better. It was challenging for him to not dismiss her enthusiasm as naivety coupled with religious fervor - a combination he'd seen turn dangerous many times throughout his life.

He answered, "You know I don't do social media. And, besides, nothing is going to change the fact that she's a minister."

It was quiet long enough that Boone figured Travis had given up on trying to persuade him. Just when he was certain Travis was asleep, Travis said, "I know that for all those years, Boone, it was you and me against the world. It felt like the only people on our side were Grandma and Grandpa, and Mom and Dad kept them at arm's length most of the time. I know that during those times, my enemies were yours because that is the kind of brother you were and still are. But Boone, she's not our enemy."

A tree branch scratched against their window as springtime winds made the old house's walls creak. So quiet Boone could barely hear him over the house's chattering, Travis said one more time, "She's not our enemy."

Boone was still awake long after Travis had fallen peacefully asleep, his breathing in rhythm with the creaking of the house.

Chapter 26

Miriam sat in her office typing numbers into a spreadsheet she would present later at a committee meeting. After hitting *enter* on the final figure, she leaned back in her chair and shut her eyes. She hated the way staring at a screen made her eyes feel. It was one of many reasons why she was always the first to volunteer for the more hands-on tasks.

The office smelled like the oils she used for blessings, and the only sound was the periodic whistle of wind through the windows. It was a blustery spring day.

Suddenly, Miriam heard a quiet knock at the door accompanied by an even quieter whisper from the church secretary: "Mother Miriam, I'm sorry to wake you, but there's someone to see you."

Miriam blushed at the notion that she'd been sleeping on the job. Straitening her spine, she said, "Thank you for the message, Paula. I'm not asleep, though. I was just resting my eyes after staring at this computer for too long. Just send him or her in."

"It's a him, but he already walked over to the sanctuary. He wanted to look around, and I took the liberty of telling him you'd meet him there."

Miriam was glad for the excuse to put distance between her computer and herself. Crossing the arch-lined walkway that connected the church offices to the sanctuary, the wind almost lifted her off the path's stones. As she entered the back of the church, it was colder than it had been in the courtyard. The stone walls were holding tightly to winter.

Despite walking into the church countless times, Miriam still loved the initial moment when she opened the doors to step inside. The multi-colored lights from the stained glass, the cool openness, the heady scent of wine and bread that always seemed to linger long after the Eucharist had been put away.

As Miriam walked into the nave, she saw a man standing in a center aisle looking up at one of the many stained glass windows that lined the walls just below where the ceiling began its dramatic vaulting. Miriam knew each window like a child knows the illustrations of their most beloved picture book. Without following his eyes, she knew he was looking at a colorful rendition of Ruth kneeling in a field of felled wheat.

"I've always found it amazing," Miriam said, "that the artist could capture an expression of hope in a face made of glass."

The man didn't startle at the sound of her voice. He seemed completely at ease.

Turning his face to peer at Miriam, his features were softly lit by shades of gold from sun beams shining through Ruth's wheat. The image was so beatific, Miriam almost giggled. He must have been in on the jokl, because as soon as his eyes landed on Miriam, his face broke into a full, broad smile. Miriam's breath caught. She'd seen this smile before, only it had never spread so wide.

Everything about the visitor standing in front of her sparked a sense of recognition. His height, his auburn hair, his fair-colored eyes. However, his hair was cut short and styled meticulously, and while his eyes were light, they had more green than blue to them. And his clothes were not those of an agriculture professor. He wore slacks and a button-up without so much as a hint of plaid. And his shoes were clean. There was no dust anywhere near him.

"Good afternoon, Mother Miriam."

His voice was deep, but it lacked the gruffness she was accustomed to.

"You seem to know who I am," Miriam said. "And I suspect I know who you are, too."

He tilted his head as if waiting for her best guess.

"Travis Rutledge. You must be Travis Rutledge."

"What gave me away?"

"Your face."

Travis laughed loudly, the sound creating an echo through the cavernous church.

When his laughter died down, he said, "We aren't identical, but Grandma always said we were close enough."

Miriam couldn't take her eyes off Travis. She supposed she'd been starving for the sight of Boone, and as Rubie said, Travis was close enough. But she was curious why the brother of her not-a-boyfriend had arrived at her place of employment. "I'm thrilled to meet you, but what brings you here to Trinity?"

"Three things, actually. First, we had leftovers from the feast Grandma prepared to welcome me home last night, and she insisted I bring you some. Specifically, the leftover jello salad. She said it's your favorite flavor, and Boone and I don't appreciate it enough."

The transparent tupperware container Travis passed to Miriam showed an orange not found in nature. Miriam gently chuckled as she accepted the proffered gift. "Thank you. A person really shouldn't be a minister in these parts if they aren't willing to eat some jello salad. It's part of the gig."

Miriam looked up from the container, waiting for the other reasons he'd come.

"Second, I wanted to thank the woman who helped my grandmother through a once-in-a-century ice storm."

Miriam, suddenly feeling a rare surge of bashfulness, said, "I didn't really do anything."

"You kept her from driving Boone absolutely batty."

The joke immediately put her back at ease. She'd only been in Travis's presence for a few minutes, but she could already tell he was an easy person to be around. "Okay, I'll take credit on that one point. I acted as a buffer. And I ate all the pink fluff before it went bad."

"It's not really a salad if it doesn't have Eagle Brand Milk in it."

"Really, I think Rubie and Boone did more for me than I did for them. If I'd been here, I just would have frozen all by myself. But it was nice out on the farm. Rubie and I spent time doing little projects, and Boone taught me all sorts of things in the greenhouse. I mean, I doubt I have miraculously sprouted a green thumb, but

I might keep a succulent alive now. And then there's that library of your grandmother's."

Travis nodded his head knowingly. "Boone and I learned about the birds and the bees by covertly checking out books from that library. It was quite the education."

Miriam laughed. "There are worse ways to lose your innocence, I'm sure." After a moment, she said, "That makes two. Wasn't there a third reason you came?"

"Actually, Boone and I are throwing a little birthday party for Grandma Sunday evening, and we wanted you to join us."

Miriam thought of the memories that would crystalize into razor-sharp focus the minute she stepped into the colorful house or passed the foggy windows of the greenhouse or sat for a moment on that blasted plaid sofa where Boone had touched her in ways she'd almost forgotten she could be touched. But despite the painful reminders of what she'd lost before she even truly experienced it, how could she disappoint Miss Rubie? "Of course. That sounds lovely."

"Wonderful," Travis said, rubbing his hands together, obviously satisfied that he'd completed his task for the day.

Miriam said, "Would you like a tour of the building and grounds?"

"I would love that, but I promised Grandma I'd pick up this grocery list and get it back to her in time for her to cook yet another feast that will ensure I no longer fit into my pants by the time I return home."

At his words, they both sauntered to the door. Miriam said, "It has been about six weeks since the storm, and I'm just now feeling comfortable in my pants."

"I'm coming with Grandma this Sunday. Maybe we could do a tour then?"

Miriam was completely sincere as she said, "I'd enjoy that."

"Maybe I'll drag Boone's ass here with me."

Miriam laughed at the mischievous glint in Travis's eyes. "Good luck with that."

As they approached the double red doors at the front entrance to the church, words came forth from Miriam that she hadn't planned or meant to say. "Travis, I'm sorry."

He turned around with a questioning expression. "Sorry?"

What was she trying to say? She wished she could run to her study and prepare the next few sentences before delivering them. It was reckless for a minister to step into a pulpit unprepared; it was asking to either say the wrong thing or to say the right thing the wrong way. This was no sermon, but she'd been reckless to call out to Travis unprepared. However, she couldn't leave such loaded words hanging in the air.

"I'm sorry you were treated with so much hate by people who claim the same faith as me. I don't see my Jesus in them. I wish I could take all that pain away. I would never...I just would never treat a kid that way."

Travis changed course, walking up to Miriam and taking one of her hands in his own. "I haven't known you long, but I know my grandma, and that's enough. I already know your heart. And Boone does, too. He's just scared. Give him time."

Miriam felt reassuring pressure as Travis squeezed her hand, and then he was gone, wind rushing around Miriam as the door blew shut.

CHAPTER 27

In a little over twelve hours, Miriam would be slowly making her way down the aisle in the opening processional for Sunday morning. As always, Miss Rubie would be there in a colorful ensemble complete with costume jewelry and hair at six different angles, but this week, she might also have Travis next to her. The odds of Boone also attending were remote enough to keep Miriam's mind at ease. Blessedly.

Miriam was relieved it wasn't her Sunday to deliver the sermon. She would be busy as the celebrant, leading the many readings, prayers, and calls and responses. But Miriam wouldn't need to fear disappointing Miss Rubie with a sub-par performance the week she finally had a grandson with her.

Since Travis's visit, Miriam continued the same activity that had consumed her since the storm: she tried, and failed, to forget Boone. To forget his touch, his feel, his poetically tragic tattoos, his damned greenhouse, and his entire existence. Travis, with his soulful eyes and assurances that Boone would come around, had not helped her overall life goal of forgetting Boone. She couldn't sustain her anger, though. In the brief time Travis was in her presence, he'd charmed her. And of course, he advocated for Boone. They were brothers, brothers who appeared by all indications to share a deep and meaningful bond.

So, in an attempt to put out of mind Boone and church and the butterflies accumulating in her stomach, Miriam had utilized Matchables in scheduling another first date for Saturday evening. Maybe she would meet a man so fascinating and handsome and polished yet charmingly winsome, he would push away all thought of large, uncouth, gruff men with dirty boots.

Now, as she sat in front of a man whose body fat index had to be less than one percent and who had arrived at their date in joggers, Miriam felt pangs of guilt for what she was about to do to @joggingismylife. Really, though, she was exhausted just from the first fifteen minutes of conversation during which he'd delivered a curiously intense explanation of training routines for marathons.

When she'd gone to the bathroom a few minutes earlier, Miriam texted a quick SOS to Lucy. Within thirty seconds after returning to their table, her phone rang. Lucy was nothing if not reliable.

When Miriam answered, Lucy's bored voice said, "Miriam, this is Lucy, your friend. I need you to come immediately. It's an emergency. I think my appendix is rupturing."

Miriam clearly needed to talk with Lucy about coming up with more believable excuses. Reaching within herself for all the old acting tips from her high school production of *Crimes of the Heart*, Miriam said in an accent that sounded far more Southern than her usual style of speech, "Oh, dear, that does sound serious. If you need me, of course, I'll come. I'll leave right away."

"Oh yes. Very serious. You must come." Lucy sounded like she was either engrossed in a movie or a really juicy romance novel. Either way, she was barely giving Miriam an ounce of her attention.

Miriam hung up and immediately began apologizing for abandoning him so soon on their first date. It took a fair amount of convincing to dissuade him from escorting her out to her car. Thankfully, the waiter brought out the first part of their order just as she was standing up, and she insisted that @joggingismylife stay and not allow the kale smoothie shots he'd chosen as their appetizer to go to waste. As she walked to the door, she sighed in relief that she wouldn't need to choke down the smoothie. There was no way that guy would ever bring himself to pretend jello salad was a side dish, so it was safe to say they weren't suited.

Walking outside, Miriam was struck by the memory of ardent embraces beneath the harsh glow of security lights. There was nothing sexy about a parking lot until there was.

Getting into her car, Miriam drove home with the classic country station blaring. Johnny Cash was sounding exceptionally blue tonight, and Miriam drowned her melancholy in his crooning, moody lyrics.

Once home, she walked into her house, a place without any persons suffering from acute appendicitis. Walking past the cross she was gifted by her parents at graduation from seminary, a token that likely encapsulated everything they knew about Miriam's faith, Miriam crossed herself, asking forgiveness for the white lie that had liberated her from what promised to be a boring, if healthy, evening.

Walking to the kitchen, she opened the fridge door. Immediately, she felt chilled as she stared into the near-empty refrigerator - chilled like one might feel in a greenhouse during a particularly vicious winter storm. Miriam's eyes searched for something, anything to eat. Her date had lifted judgmental eyebrows when she'd mentioned the hamburger on the menu looking good.

In the middle of the second shelf, isolated from the few condiments and leftovers sprinkled throughout, Miriam's eyes landed on the container of jello salad Travis had brought to church. Mixed by Miss Rubie's hands, served at a meal of welcome and reunion, likely pushed around noncommittally by Boone's fork. Shutting the door, she decided she wasn't hungry after all.

***

Boone draped an armful of leis onto the pegs of a hat rack for guests to grab the following evening. Looking over his shoulder, he saw Travis bending over to plug in a neon sign with the word "Broadway" written in cursive.

Boone said, "I didn't know we added Broadway to the list of themes for this party."

Standing up straight, Travis replied, "It's her favorite thing to do when she comes to visit me and Paul in the city."

Boone looked around the living room. There was hardly a surface left ungarnished. As his eyes traveled over the eclectic mix, he tried to identify the various themes. "So I now understand the nod to Broadway, and the Hawaiian elements are obviously from her and Grandpa's fiftieth wedding anniversary trip. But the tie-dye shirts?"

"From her brief stint as a hippie."

"And the Hello Kitty faces?"

Travis shrugged. "When I took her to the party store, they spoke to her. Not sure what they said, but they spoke to her."

His eyes scanning the crazy quilt of party themes around him, Boone said, "It looks like a manic five-year-old went shopping at a party supply store."

Smiling broadly with satisfaction, Travis said, "Yes, it does. It couldn't be more perfect."

"It really couldn't."

Walking over to the sofa that was draped in tie-dye shirts, Boone sat heavily, rubbing his forehead as he took a deep breath. Travis joined him.

"What has you stressed?"

Looking up, Boone's eyes widened as he tried to articulate an answer. He hadn't noticed he was stressed, but there was tension in his neck and a pit in his stomach that must've snuck up on him. He'd felt this way for a while now, and if he pinpointed a starting point, it was sometime around the evening he walked out of Miriam's house with tears streaming down his cheeks in the frigid February air. He said, "Just work stuff."

"Bullshit."

Boone's forehead wrinkled. "You sure have been quick to call out bullshit since you arrived."

"Yeah, well, you're not being honest with yourself about much of anything, and it's my job as your brother, twin brother no less, to make sure you do. Which leads me to this: I met your minister."

Boone's hand fell to the couch cushion. "How many times do I have to say she isn't my anything."

"Not sure, but I'm pretty sure no matter how many times you say it, it won't make it true."

"Is she my girlfriend?"

"Nope."

"Is she my fiance?"

"Not that either."

"And unless I'm the most forgetful man this side of the Mississippi, I'm quite certain she sure as hell isn't my wife."

"Obviously."

"So, elucidate me. What is she to me?"

A pleading tone escaped Boone that broke Travis's heart. The spunk he'd been sparing with deflated as he said softly, "She's the woman you've fallen for, Boone. She's the one you want."

"Did Grandma call you?"

Travis smiled a half-smile startlingly similar to Boone's. "Of course she did." After a beat of silence, Travis continued, "But am I wrong Boone? Am I wrong about Mother Miriam?"

"No."

The front door swung open just as Boone heard tires skid out of the driveway. He and Travis turned around to the sight of Rubie lugging in large plastic bags with the words "Party Town" printed across each one. "I was telling Hyacinth about our little trip to the party store, Travis, and before I knew it, we were back there to get a few more things. I found Union Jack bunting to commemorate all the Regency romances I've read over the years."

"Naturally," Boone said as he stood to take the bags from Rubie.

Travis said, "We'll hang it over the paper accordion pineapples."

As the brothers resumed their work, Travis shot Boone a look that said, "I heard your confession and I'm not likely to forget," while Boone's eyebrow raised to say, "Believe me. I know."

Chapter 28

The Kentucky landscape flew past Boone's window. He was driving twenty miles over the speed limit in an attempt to not arrive late. Being late made a person more conspicuous. His goal was to blend in, to be unremarkable.

Travis and Rubie left a good twenty minutes before him. Neither guilt-tripped him about not going, nor had an explicit invitation been extended. But Travis's eyebrows sure rose high as he announced his intentions to join their grandmother for worship. With them, he broadcast his wish that Boone would cease being a horse's ass and come with them. Travis inherited his subtlety from Rubie.

After they vacated the farm, Boone did what he always did when he wasn't sure what else to do. He walked out to the greenhouse.

Once in the warm interior, Boone's eyes wandered around the premises, each spot reminding him of a different shared moment with Miriam. Where they'd talked about rose varieties. Where she'd stood while he told her about building the structure with his grandfather. Where they'd stood as they examined each other's bodies like sculptures in an art gallery.

Then, his eyes landed on the record player. He'd forgotten to take it back in. Walking over, he placed the needle carefully on the first song, and all over again, the Eagles were crooning "Take it Easy" into the airy openness of the greenhouse.

Travis was right, of course. Boone wanted her. Over two months had passed, but the wanting hadn't waned. It hadn't let up. It had merely accumulated into a bad temper and a sore neck. Perhaps, just this once, he could take a step back from protecting Travis and instead trust that very brother, the brother who'd never let him down, nor had he ever wanted anything but the best for Boone.

Checking his watch, Boone saw that the service would be starting in less than ten minutes. If he drove faster than was prudent, he might be able to sneak in, sit in the back, and at least lay eyes on her. It wouldn't be enough, but it would be something.

But before he left, he had one thing he needed to do. Pulling out his phone, Boone opened the God-forsaken Matchables app and scrolled until he found Miriam's profile, still unresponded to. Scrolling to the bottom of her page, he clicked on the "nest" without hesitation. Hearts and birds exploded across the screen with the words, "Nesting Notification Sent." It was the first time the Matchables app hadn't left him with a sense of dread.

Racing out of the greenhouse, Boone failed to notice a mud puddle several feet from the door. By the time he noticed, both feet were two inches deep in muck. It felt like he was being pulled into quicksand as he strained to liberate himself. Each boot made a sickening suctioning noise as he yanked free and resumed running to his truck.

By the time he arrived at Trinity Episcopal Church, Boone was shocked that he was only five minutes past the official start time posted on the sign. Grandma Rubie was clearly leaving well before when it was necessary. That woman did like to chatter.

As he walked to the large red doors at the entrance, Boone tried to discreetly rub off as much mud as possible along the concrete curbside. It was hopeless. It would take him weeks to walk off the caked-on mess.

Even from outside, Boone felt the vibration of the organ.

Boone was still focused on his boots when he opened the door, stepped in, and let the doors shut behind him. Immediately, the smell of burning candles greeted him. When he looked up, he realized he was in a room full of people lined up waiting for he wasn't sure what. There was a wide variety of robes in the room, a shocking amount considering it was the twenty-first century and no one was graduating.

Suddenly, the front of the line started moving and allowing more space to expand between the people, like a child pulling on a slinky. Boone's eyes landed on Miriam before he realized he'd been looking for her. She was at the back, apparently one of the last to walk down the aisle in the procession.

A white robe hung to her feet, the toes of her shoes barely visible beneath its hem. Something purple, a fabric of about 5 inches in width, draped over her shoulders. Boone didn't know what it was called, but he could guess its name would be Latin and anachronistic.

Miriam noticed him a few beats after he first saw her, allowing him a moment to acclimate to his Miri looking very much like Mother Miriam. But when she did see him, her eyes warmed in a way that was distinctly Miri. He saw the person he'd held through the night, the one who'd worked by his side in the greenhouse.

But for the first time since they met, these two aspects of Miriam did not clash for Boone. He understood that she was a rich, complex person and that she could be both faithful and passionate. She was not an acolyte of the purity culture he'd been raised in. She was not dressed in her white robe to lord her own goodness over others or to cast shame upon them. Miriam was exactly what she presented herself as being. She was a person full of love who was trying to use her gifts to serve a purpose bigger than herself. It was admirable, really.

As it came time for the final rows to begin walking, Miriam came closer to where Boone stood. Smiling softly, she whispered, "Hello, Boone."

He answered with a simple nod of the head, and then gesturing towards her robe, Boone said, "It suits you."

***

As Miriam took in the sight of Boone in boots that were obscenely muddy even for him, her mind offered up the least helpful monologue in the history of Christendom: *Oh shit. Oh shit. Oh shit. Oh shit.* It was not a small mercy that the words stayed internal.

Unfortunately, twenty minutes earlier, Father David called to inform her he was violently throwing up. His grandson had given him a stomach bug. That kid had always been a brat.

So, with very little notice - microscopic levels, really - Miriam would be delivering the sermon that Third Sunday in Lent.

Thankfully, she'd preached on one of the week's liturgical texts back in seminary, so Miriam dusted off the old print-out that still had a letter "A" circled on the top. She hadn't felt overly stressed. After all, it was just another Sunday, and an A-sermon was certainly good enough for Miss Rubie and her charming grandson.

It would do. Or it would have done if only the other grandson (the less charming one) hadn't just walked into the building.

Boone was going to hear her preach, watch her perform the occupation that stood between them, with a sermon that wasn't nearly good enough. It was an A, not an A-plus. And it wasn't going to come close to atoning for a childhood's worth of shaming and hate from his parents' church. It wasn't starter material for a theological masterpiece or a treatise on past sins of the church. It was none of the things Miriam would have liked her first sermon in front of Boone to be.

And to top off her mortification, for the first time in her ministerial career, Miriam was suddenly painfully aware of just how unflattering clerical garb was. Such vanity - and at the worst possible moment.

The line began moving before Miriam could compose a response to Boone's sparse statement that her robe suited her. It was a shapeless number in fabric one might expect to find as living room curtains in a very old person's house. With nothing more charming than a blank stare, Miriam began walking slowly down the aisle, pulled along like an unwilling participant in a game of tug-of-war by the tide of choir members who led the procession. As she progressed, the heads of the congregants bowed reverently at the cross. Miriam's lips moved soundlessly to the words of the hymn, making her think of the lip-syncing battles she and Lucy sometimes watched on YouTube. Unfortunately, her lip-syncing wasn't a fun party game. No, Miriam appeared to be incapable of making an audible sound, a situation that did not bode well for the sermon.

As she came to the fifth row from the front, Miss Rubie's standard spot so long as some unwitting visitor didn't get to church first, Miriam saw Boone squeezing past the people sitting on the outer edge of the pew as he made his way to sit by Travis and Rubie. He whispered apologies with the worry line on his forehead especially prominent. Miriam noticed one of the ladies Boone passed dusting off her black pants. For the briefest moment, she felt an absurd urge to laugh, and sound escaped her lips in a noise that resembled a squeaky tire more than singing.

Once stationed at her normal spot - the bench situated behind the pulpit - the service went by in a blur of standing, sitting, and kneeling. Miriam had never realized just how aerobic an Episcopalian service was until this morning when nothing but movement seemed to register; words didn't hold meaning, songs were flat and lifeless, scripture readings made as much sense as if they were read in a foreign language.

But while her brain was in a fog, her body, graciously, did as was expected. Stand, sit, kneel. Stand, sit, kneel.

Then, an elbow poked into Miriam's rib. The choir member next to her raised his eyebrows towards the pulpit. It was time. It was time to give a sub-par sermon in front of the one person who mattered most. She didn't know when he'd become that one person or how he'd maintained that singular position over weeks of intentional separation, but it was pointless to deny. All he had to do was walk into the building, and here she was, unable to think of anything or anyone else. His presence consumed her.

Climbing into the pulpit, Miriam tested the functionality of her vocal cords by saying, "Good morning." Relief flooded her when the words came forth without some pubescent crack.

Once assured she could speak, Miriam should have looked to her sermon. The manuscript would carry her through. If this morning were on a navigation app, delivering the sermon in front of her was the most direct route, free from road blockages, and with the earliest possible arrival time. She should have read the damn sermon.

But her eyes, her traitorous, curious, hungry eyes, had scanned the crowd. They'd scanned the crowd and landed predictably on the thick, unruly hair and pale eyes and full beard that Miriam knew to be pleasantly scratchy when skimming across her neck.

He'd been looking at her, too. Of course, he had. She, after all, was the show. Everyone's expectant eyes were on her, waiting for her to deliver a sermon that would hopefully be brief enough for them to miss the worst of the lunch rush at their favorite restaurants.

And since his eyes were conveniently focused in her direction, their gazes locked for just a moment. It would be dramatic to say it was as though no one else was in the room. But it was true that despite the roomful of eyes on her, Miriam felt seen only by Boone. At least she did until he looked away, his gaze ducking to the back of the pew in front of his own.

In that one motion, in the quick, subtle aversion of his eyes, Miriam saw his discomfort at being in that place, surrounded by those people. Yet, he'd come and was sitting next to his beloved, gay brother who had a million reasons to never trust Miriam or anyone adjacent to her. But he, Travis, had also come. His shoulders were relaxed where Boone's were rigid, and his face was lax - almost bored - where Boone's was timid. Miriam was at once humbled by Travis's grace and pained by Boone's fear. She saw in Boone just how much damage the church had done over the years, and she saw in Travis the peace that comes after forgiveness.

The organist cleared her throat, causing Miriam to startle to attention. Clearly, she'd entered awkward-silence territory. Running her fingers briefly over the sermon, Miriam flipped the paper over, the unprinted back showing nothing more than a smattering of coffee stains, probably from the professor who'd graded it. Then, she began to speak.

"I was going to get up here this morning and deliver a sermon that is technically a very solid sermon. Really, some A-level work. Not A-plus, granted. But a solid-A sermon."

Boone's eyes remained locked in a downward direction. Miriam continued.

"The sermon I prepared wasn't particularly different or revelatory compared to most sermons, which is natural, I guess. No minister can deliver an unforgettable, revolutionary sermon every week or even most weeks, despite the fact that most of us like to believe we're changing the world every time we open our mouths.

"We'd all be exhausted by constant revolution, wouldn't we? We don't come to church to be challenged. We come to be affirmed, to have comforting words spoken to us in a format that is rhetorically cohesive and pleasing. If you're a regular, these fifteen-minute spans of rhetoric become part of the rhythm of your life. You come every Sunday and you do the standing and sitting and kneeling and praying, and then you sit while one of us gets up here in these robes that the only other place you ever see are period pieces or horror films. And we get up here, and we tell you in a structured piece of writing what your faith can do for you. And then you go about your week.

"But the thing I can't get off my mind this morning is the unfortunate reality that despite this rhythm, some people haven't been shaped into better humans - that throughout the history of Christianity, certainly the history of Christianity in this country, people have gone through these motions while spending the rest of their week treating people they don't understand - people who look differently than them or sound differently than them or worship differently than them or love differently than them - treating those people with hate. There have been so many people to hate, it is no wonder we've had so little energy left for love."

Boone's position shifted. His head was still postured down, but his gaze was once again on her, covertly looking from the top of his eyes.

Miriam was no longer trying to parcel her gazes evenly across her audience. She was squarely focused on the fifth pew from the front. "We've done some awful shit in the name of this faith, haven't we?"

The air in the room seemed to momentarily lesson in quantity as the whole body gasped, but no one stormed out. Not one old lady took up a fan, and no one dared to whisper to their neighbor. The dramatic vaulted ceiling only held silence.

"Choosing love in this world can feel like trying to reverse a powerful tide using nothing but your hands. Perhaps, the best we can hope for is that when we treat others with love and respect and dignity, we apply a little salve to these wounds, like some ancient, mysterious poultice mixed by the wrinkled hands of an old witch doctor we don't understand. The scars will always remain, but scars don't negate the authentic healing that occurs when those who were rejected and reviled are suddenly welcomed and loved in our community.

"After years in seminary followed by years of ministry in places haunted by horrific crimes against humanity followed by years here in the States seeing the less obvious but just as life-altering damage our churches have inflicted, all I know is this: God is love, and I am made in his image, and, therefore, I must love. All we can do is try -

through that loving that is at the core of who we are as beings made in the image of a loving God - try to be part of the redemption that comes after all the ugliness."

It could have been a trick of the colored morning light beaming through the stained-glass windows, but Miriam thought she saw a glimmer of moisture in Boone's upturned eyes. Around a lump that had lodged itself into her throat, Miriam finished, "We must try."

Then, after a sermon that had been eight minutes at best and would likely not have merited even a B for its form or exegesis, Miriam stepped down from the pulpit and took her seat.

The members of Trinity Episcopal Church would win the lunch rush today.

***

The hem of Miriam's robe swayed with each step as she took Travis on a tour of the church. Boone stayed several feet behind, watching them talk animatedly.

There seemed to be endless details to marvel over. Every carved piece of wood. Every woven tapestry. Every blasted pane of stained-glass. Much to Boone's surprise, he had found out from listening to Travis and Miriam's conversation that his brother attended a church in New York City with remarkably similar architecture. They were comparing notes on the two buildings, each suddenly experts on religious art and Gothic architecture.

Boone didn't know why he was feeling slightly irritated with their dialog. Irritated wasn't even the right word. He was just restless. He felt like a kid who'd just guzzled a Mountain Dew and was then told to sit quietly for a standardized test.

The problem was that his mind was spinning between his reaction to seeing Miriam again after weeks apart and the distinct feeling that every word she'd spoken in that pulpit had been meant for him and him alone. The other hundred and fifty people had merely been eavesdropping on a conversation for two.

"You know, Travis, weddings are remarkably beautiful in this building."

Miriam's words jolted Boone out of his reverie.

Travis nodded slowly. "I can definitely imagine it. Paul and I haven't settled on anything yet, but I might take some pictures to show him."

Which meant another twenty minutes of Travis and Miriam discussing the "character" of the building and the details that merited a picture. Boone was certain no detail had been left undocumented by the time they walked out the front door into the cool spring day.

The ornamental pear trees were in full bloom, making the outside of the church building as magnificent as the interior. After ushering them out, Miriam paused and said, "I guess I'll tell you all goodbye, now, but I'll see you this evening for the party."

Boone wanted desperately to stall her, to figure out a way to get one more moment alone. If he could, he might sort out the energy coursing through him, the adrenaline that wouldn't let him relax. He hadn't slept well in weeks.

Had she looked at her phone since he'd pushed the nesting button? No Matchables notifications were on his phone of either rejection or mutual nesting. So maybe she'd been too busy to look at her phone. Or maybe she was too nice to out-right reject him, so she was opting to ignore the app.

As Rubie and Travis told her goodbye, Miriam looked to Boone with insecurity shadowing her features. Boone felt a jab of guilt that whatever was between them had created a dynamic where an otherwise secure, confident woman felt unsure in his presence. He'd done so many things wrong. He'd held sins against her that were not her own, and he'd pushed her away when she'd offered nothing but her love.

Travis and Rubie resumed walking to their truck, but Boone and Miriam were still planted in their spots, looking at one another. Finally, Miriam averted her eyes as she said, "I've been wanting to talk with you, Boone. I just wanted to say I'm sorry."

Boone tried to think of a single thing she should be sorry about. Nothing came to mind.

"What are you talking about? You've done nothing wrong. I've been the ass." His eyes darted to the building, unsure if such language was permitted on church grounds. Miriam, as always, seemed unfazed.

"I focused on myself, Boone. On what I wanted, and my…" Her voice trailed off, and then she finished weakly, "…my desire."

Boone felt his breathing become more shallow. Her desires were his favorite thing. Why was she apologizing, dammit?

"Anyways, I fear I ignored your wants, your past experiences, and how they shaped you. I didn't listen when you told me you couldn't give me more. I'm ashamed of how I failed you."

"Miriam, you didn't..."

"No," Miriam interrupted Boone. "Let me finish. I've been practicing this for long enough. I just want to say that what happened over the snowstorm, well, it was a beautiful, once-in-a-lifetime moment for me. An unexpected adventure here in our precious corner of Kentucky. I'm so glad I got to experience it with you, but now I'm ready to move forward as friends. If you'll have my friendship, that is."

"No." The word flew out of Boone's mouth before he could even fully consider her proposal. Friendship. That wasn't enough. It wasn't near enough. But before Boone could explain, before he could tell her he wanted more, the red door opened behind Miriam, and an older woman in pearls stepped out.

"Mother Miriam, it's time for the Outreach Committee meeting."

Miriam's eyes closed and her face registered a grimace so brief Boone was certain only he noticed. "Of course, Doris. I forgot we'd moved it to after church today. I'll be right there."

Miriam and Boone stared at each other meaningfully, each feeling the weight of what remained unspoken, but Doris wasn't going anywhere without Miriam. Boone tried to construct some code that would tell Miriam he wasn't finished with this conversation, but before his mind, which seemed as mired in mud as his boots, could compose a response, Miriam said, "It was lovely having you and Travis here this morning. I'll see you at the party later tonight."

And with that she was gone, taking Doris and any hope Boone had of getting out of the friend zone into which he'd just been relegated. After all, everyone knew that there was a time limit on these things. It was like those crime shows where everyone rushed to solve the case in the first twenty-four hours or it was destined to run cold.

Turning around, Boone started towards his truck, a clump of dry dirt falling off his right boot as he walked down the sidewalk. Halfway there, he came to Travis's fancy rental with the windows rolled down and his brother and grandmother each sticking their heads out of the front windows like dogs on a joy ride.

"You haven't left yet?" Boone asked them.

"Nope," Rubie said. "We were watching the show."

"Yes," Travis embellished. "Looks like you didn't get a rose."

Boone looked at him questioningly.

Rubie said, "Really, Boone. How do you not get a Bachelor's reference in this day and age?"

"I don't know, Grandma. I'm apparently not as with it as you are."

"Clearly," she said.

"Would you like some advice, brother?"

Boone scrutinized Travis, trying to decide if advice was worth anything at this point. Perhaps, instead of advice, he just needed a good hard drink. He responded, "Not particularly."

"Too bad," Travis said. "Here it is. You two clearly have a thing for each other. I mean, she just delivered an entire sermon while looking longingly at you, which might be the most weirdly romantic thing I've ever witnessed."

"It has definitely never happened on *The Bachelor*," Rubie interjected.

"Is that how we measure romantic gestures?" Boone asked.

Travis, looking uncomfortable after craning his neck out his window for so long, ignored the question and continued, "The point is that there is something there, and if you don't at least try, you're going to regret it for a very long time. Call me crazy, Boone, but I think she might be your Paul."

"Or Rupert," Rubie added, her eyes glistening and a tuft of hair blowing wildly despite there not seeming to be a breeze.

"But she just told me she wants to be friends," Boone said, starting to feel ridiculous standing in front of a car and having such an intense conversation with two people sticking out of each side.

"That's better than saying she wanted to forget your existence and hopes you rot in a gutter somewhere."

"Once again, Grandma, I am left wondering where you get your ruler for measuring the state of relationships," Boone said, exasperated.

Smiling, Rubie said, "Let's just say I've read a lot of very dramatic books and watched a lot of reality TV. We live in wonderful times, don't we?"

Boone looked to Travis. "Just friends, Travis. That's what she said. Just friends. I think it's too late. I think I have to let this one go."

"Damn it, Boone," Travis said, hitting the door of his car in frustration. "This is coming from the guy who basically kidnapped me from my own parents and refused to go near a church for almost twenty years. You've never been one to throw in the towel. You are easily the most stubborn person I've ever known. So, why are you giving up so easily now?"

Boone, at a loss for words, sputtered a few indecipherable sounds that finished weakly with, "But she's in a meeting."

"And she'll never get out?" Travis's voice hit a new register of annoyance.

"Jackass," Boone responded, but one side of his mouth had tilted upward.

Rubie, looking mischievous even for herself, said, "Go interrupt that meeting. That would really get under Doris's skin, the old biddy. I've never liked her since the time she told me I should try reduced-fat butter."

"She sounds like a real bitch," Travis said, his eyes focused on Boone, and his face lit with a smile declaring victory for this argument.

Boone looked back to his unruly, unladylike, fiercely loving grandmother. Rubie said, "Go get her, Boonie."

"But the party?"

Travis and Rubie simultaneously yelled "We've got it" and "It's already ready."

With this, Travis turned on the car, signaling that all was finalized. "See you later, Boone."

Waving, Rubie added, "And bring my favorite girl with you, will you?"

Boone watched the car drive away, then he headed back to the church. Five minutes later, wandering the church's corridors, he wished he'd paid more attention on the tour.

Chapter 29

Miriam didn't realize she was tapping her pen until a hand shot out and grabbed her own, stilling the nervous motion. Miriam looked around at the irritated glances directed her way. The meeting was taking place in one of the small libraries housed in the education wing at Trinity. The walls were lined in worn, earth-toned books, and Miriam sat at a heavy, round, oak table encircled by a half-dozen formidable women all north of seventy years old.

"I'm so sorry," she said. "Where were we again?"

The meeting resumed, but Miriam wasn't finding it any easier to pay attention. She was replaying in her mind practically every word she'd spoken throughout the morning. What had she been thinking going off script for her sermon? Had she simply embarrassed herself in front of the church? She'd sought some kind of resolution Boone probably didn't need or want. He likely moved on weeks ago, but she was still hopelessly affected by his very presence in a crowd.

"What do you think, Mother Miriam?"

Miriam's eyes shot to Mrs. Smith. She thought that Boone had looked charmingly disheveled that morning, but that was hardly the answer to Mrs. Smith's question.

Just as she was about to ask Mrs. Smith to repeat the question, the door to the meeting room cracked ajar. Boone leaned in, scanning the room until his eyes landed on Miriam.

His hair was standing on end, achingly reminiscent of his grandmother's inability to maintain tidy hair. His cheeks were flushed above his beard as if he'd been running through the hallway. When he stepped into the room, Miriam saw that, of course, his boots were still filthy.

"Can we help you, young man?" Mrs. Broadbank questioned beneath a hat worthy of the Kentucky Derby.

Before Boone could form an answer, Mrs. Smith, never one to mince words, asked, "Who are you?"

"Why, it's Rubie Rutledge's grandson," Miss Hyacinth said.

"Of course," Mrs. Smith said. "The hair."

Boone's expression transformed from deer-in-headlights to offended.

Mrs. Broadbank said, "He might be Rubie's, but that doesn't answer the question of what he's doing here."

Boone gulped, moistening a parched mouth so sound could be manufactured. "I was looking for Miri." Seeing only blank stares, he clarified, "Mother Miriam."

It did not escape Miriam's notice that he used her nickname. It also didn't escape her notice that every eye was turned to her face, a face that was no doubt blushing.

"And what do you want with Mother Miriam?" Doris asked rather brazenly. Miriam suspected Doris was put out with having her meeting interrupted, especially by a man in flannel and work boots.

"I want," Boone started, but his words shorted out like a programming glitch. His eyes focused on Miriam, and she read there his frustration at his own failure to arrange words into coherent patterns.

"You want what, young man?"

Miriam didn't know who called out the question. At this point, every aged voice in the room sounded about the same. But Miriam waited. She wanted him to answer the question.

"Miri, I want to not be your friend."

"Well, that is an odd thing to announce," Mrs. Broadbank scoffed.

Doris said, "Yes, Miss Rubie is a bit eccentric, but she isn't rude."

"Amen," several women confirmed in murmurs.

Boone shook his head in frustration. "That isn't what I meant. Miriam, can we talk in private, please? Can I speak with you not here? Not in this room?"

Miriam thought about his resistance to being with her specifically because of her occupation, her calling. And while, rationally, she knew he was merely asking her to step out of the room for a quick word, it all felt more consequential, like if she stepped out now, she might step away from other, bigger things later.

"I'm sorry, Boone, but this is my place. We have an agenda and a purpose, and I can't leave just now."

"Okay," Boone said, his voice tentative in thought. "I'll wait, then."

He pulled a chair back, the scrape of the legs sounding deafening in the small meeting room. Most eyes were directed in shock at Boone, but Doris's were squarely placed on Miriam, her eyebrows raised as if asking what Miriam planned to do about this situation. Miriam planned to finish the meeting.

Taking a deep breath, Miriam said, "So, I believe we were talking about summer childcare for working families in the surrounding neighborhood. Who would like to be in charge of the job postings?"

***

Boone didn't have a game plan for what to do next. He tried to roughly follow the meeting, but his eyes kept landing and staying on Miriam. She'd taken off her robes and was just wearing a tab-collared shirt and black pants. But what she was wearing wasn't what he focused on. Instead, he kept staring at the tail of a tattooed bird that just barely peaked out from beneath her rolled-up sleeves. He knew exactly where it was flying. He stared at Miriam's brown eyes and how they focused on each speaker, making each person feel they were being heard. He stared at the springy curls of her bobbed haircut, and thought about how tangled his fingers could get within those ringlets if given time to explore.

Then he'd felt disapproving eyes glaring at him - several sets, actually - and his eyes studiously diverted to his hands clasped in his lap to keep him from thumping nervously on the table.

Finally, the meeting was adjourned, and everyone cleared out of the room except Boone and Miriam. She didn't even acknowledge he was there, instead shuffling papers and stuffing them into a leather bag.

Boone said, "Can we talk now?"

Miriam's movements stopped for only a second before she resumed her activity. If he didn't know better, he would swear she was as nervous as him.

"Actually," she said, each syllable pronounced too precisely, "I'm walking over to my house, but you're welcome to tag along."

Boone jumped at the opportunity to talk with her while walking. Maybe if they were moving side-by-side, not facing each other across a room, he'd be able to articulate the mess of thoughts and feelings scrambled in his mind.

As he stood up and headed to the door, they each reached it at the same moment. Boone stepped back, extending his arm graciously to let her pass. She took up his offer without even a thank you.

"Miriam, are you angry about something?"

Boone followed a couple of steps behind, but everything about her gait and posture was tightly wound.

Without looking back or stalling her rapid steps through the labyrinth of hallways, Miriam asked, "What gave you that impression, Dr. Rutledge?"

It was the first time she'd ever not used his first name, and it did not bode well for this conversation. He replied, "Oh, I don't know. Just...," he sputtered, "you. Everything. I'm not known for being socially aware, but you aren't exactly hard to read right now."

Miriam pushed through an exit door that led into the back of the church grounds. Boone wasn't sure where they were, but the door lacked the customary red paint of most entrance doors in Episcopal churches. It was a discreet wood, and where it ejected them didn't have a paved walkway, but rather stepping stones paced so that most would need to take wide steps. They did not slow down Miriam with her naturally long gait or Boone with his height.

Miriam cast back a glance as she said, "Well, I'm sorry if I'm not swooning at the sight of you, Boone, but you've spent weeks avoiding me and acting like nothing that has happened between us mattered in the slightest, and then you show up at my place of work, the very place of work you say is the reason you can't be with me, and you act like I should drop everything for you. Do you know how hard I've worked to get to a place where I can even suggest we be friends, Boone? Do you have any idea what that cost me?"

Her arms flew up in the air with frustration as she posed her question. Boone wanted to reach out and pull her around, make her stop and look at him, but she'd sped up her steps until she was several stones ahead.

"I think I have some idea, Miriam. These last months have been hard on me, too." He tried to think of how to tell her he'd been missing her every moment since she'd left the farmhouse. What he ended up saying was, "The farm is too damned quiet."

This, blessedly, stopped her hurried steps a few paces from her front door. Turning around, she said in bafflement, "I thought you liked quiet."

Boone, his voice equally strained, said, "I thought I did, too."

Before he could elaborate, she turned around, walked up the steps, and stormed into her little cottage without pausing to pull out a key.

"The door wasn't locked?" Boone seriously considered a brief lecture on safety practices, especially with a single woman, but Miriam cut him off, yelling from inside the house, "Don't go there, Boone."

The door was left ajar, and Boone stood on the porch contemplating his next move. He really shouldn't enter without an invitation. But leaving the door open was an implied invitation, wasn't it? Tentatively, he placed one muddy boot over the threshold.

Miriam darted around the small living room moving objects without anything seeming to get tidier.

"Can I help you?" Boone asked.

Miriam, glaring for a brief but chilling moment in his direction, snapped, "You can close the door. The house is drafty enough as it is. But no, you can not help with the manic and generally non-productive cleaning I do when I'm angry."

Looking around for something to do as Miriam resumed her activity, Boone noticed her phone sitting on the entryway table. She'd likely been without her phone since early that morning. A spiderweb of cracks spread out from one corner. Running a finger along the screen, Boone asked, "What happened to your phone?"

Rearranging throw pillows that were already neat enough, Miriam said, "We had a disagreement."

"You should look at it."

"Why?"

Boone picked it up, holding it out to her. "Just look at it. Please. But be careful to not cut your finger on that screen."

Miriam rolled her eyes at the warning, but she took the phone and unlocked the screen.

Immediately, the particular pattern of tweets that always accompanied a nesting notification filled the room. Her face stayed expressionless, and she placed the phone on the arm of the couch without any response.

"Wait, where are you going?" Boone's question landed flat as Miriam stomped down the hallway with no indication that she'd heard him.

Leaving the living room, Boone followed. Despite being more than a little intimidated by her anger, he felt a pull. After weeks of missing her, they were under the same roof. She was a gravitational force pulling him down a narrow hall into a doorway she'd disappeared through.

When he stepped into the room, he immediately knew it was her bedroom. It was unfussy with layers of neutrals punctuated by reds and wooden accents. It felt classic without being intimidating. He knew instantly that any space they created together would be a warm and comfortable place to be, and he was surprised by the notion. But maybe he shouldn't be surprised. After all, it wasn't so difficult to imagine living with someone he'd already been snowed in with.

Miriam was nowhere to be seen, but Boone could hear her rustling movements behind a door he assumed to be the closet. Deciding it might be easier to speak with her if she wasn't staring at him with those angry eyes, he said, "Miriam, you know all that stuff you said about us just agreeing it was a special week and we'll now be friends and all?"

She sounded distracted as she replied, "Yes. What about it?"

"I don't like that plan. And I can't help but notice you did not pass on me just now on Matchables."

Miriam's head peaked out of the closet, followed closely behind by the rest of her. She clutched a few clothing items in her hands and walked to the bathroom without taking her eyes off him. She really had mastered the glare, hadn't she?

Boone tried to keep from sounding bruised as he said, "Do you have a response to that?"

"I didn't select the nesting option, either." The bathroom door slammed behind her.

Boone walked over to the shut door, and leaned his forehead against the cold, hard wood. If he was going to convince her to trust him, he was going to need to say more, to flesh out his normal terse statements with some actual emotions and substance.

***

The bathroom was barely bigger than a closet, the hexagon tile of the floor only covering a few square feet. On one side, there was a pedestal sink and an old toilet that was original to the house and comically short, making Miriam feel like Alice in Wonderland every time she went to the bathroom. On the other side was a stall shower with a glass door where Miriam had draped the dress she planned to wear to Rubie's birthday party. The party was still several hours away, but she'd been at a loss for what to do to keep up her flurry of activity. If she dressed now, she could go to Lucy's house for the afternoon to rehash whatever was transpiring between her and Boone at this very moment. She'd leave for the party from there after her therapy session.

She was unbuttoning her collar shirt when Boone's voice came through the door so clearly, she knew he must be standing within inches of her. There was no mistaking a single word of what he said.

"I love you, Miri."

Her hands paused on the last button, and her jaw clenched in an effort to keep emotions from flooding her. With steely resolve, she continued undressing.

Boone's voice once again filled the tiny bathroom. "I don't know what I was so afraid of."

Not pausing in her activity, Miriam said, "That I'd turn out to be a homophobic, pious, hypocritical bitch, I imagine?"

Boone laughed softly, and Miriam could see in her mind the left side of his mouth lifted. She knew it was the left side.

"Yes, I guess that's what I was afraid of."

Miriam stepped into a red, knee-length dress with a deep v-neck that was a million miles from her normal Sunday attire. The skirt was pleated, offering a charmingly prim contrast to the almost sexy top. It was certainly over-dressing for the occasion, but the occasion was Miss Rubie's birthday, so being inappropriate was in the spirit of things.

Boone said, "But I'm a scientist, Miri, and I've collected all the evidence."

Miriam hesitated. Despite her tireless effort to not be pulled back into a place where he could hurt her, her hand raised to the door, her palm resting at the exact spot where she sensed his voice.

He continued, "Grandma loves you, and that woman can detect hypocrisy like a bloodhound on the hunt. Travis spent all of five minutes with you before he issued his stamp of approval. Forrest and the whole English department love you. Even your history in ministry is a million miles from what I grew up with. You've actually helped people, sacrificed for others, been willing to take stands when most would only think about keeping their job."

Miriam stayed silent, her breathing too quiet to be heard through the old, solid-wood door. After a brief moment of silence, Boone said, "Good grief, Miriam, I just loved hearing you talk this morning. What you said was beautiful, but just your voice was enough. I've missed hearing your voice."

Miriam, her head now resting next to her hand on the door, replied, "It wasn't my best sermon. If I'd known you were going to be there, I would've..." Miriam wasn't sure how to finish the sentence.

"Don't, Miri. Don't act like you need to change a thing for me, not even a single word."

A tear threatened to spill, but Miriam shut her eyes tightly. Pushing past the tightness she felt in her throat, Miriam said, "I won't give up my faith or my vocation for you, Boone. It hurts like hell not being with you, but I won't do it."

"I'll never ask you to, Miri. I give you my word. I'll never ask you to."

Miriam's hand slid to the brass knob, and she turned it slowly, giving Boone plenty of time to step back. Once the door opened, Miriam stared at Boone's startling blue eyes and his lumberjack attire and his burly beard and his perpetually dirty boots. His hair stood up at the front as if he, too, had been leaning against the door to be closer to her. It was the same Boone, but he now existed in a different reality, one where their love was possible. It felt as though she'd walked through the wardrobe to a different dimension entirely.

"You look beautiful."

Miriam looked down, remembering that she was dressed in a way he must find remarkable given her normal attire. She explained, "I thought I'd go ahead and dress for the party. I was considering spending the afternoon at Lucy's so I could over-analyze every single moment of this day. And you. I was planning on over-analyzing you."

"Surely we can think of something more entertaining to do than analyze a brute like me."

Miriam could think of no response. But her back was cold, so she turned around. "Could you zip it for me?"

The back of the dress had a zipper that was tricky to do on her own. Normally, she'd put on a jacket and drive to Lucy's for the final zip-up. Being single usually wasn't too tiresome, but then there were zippers.

The air vacated the room as she felt Boone's eyes on her bare back. It was a long zipper that went all the way to her waist. He took a step, closing the space between them. When he spoke, his voice sounded dry.

"I could zip it for you." Miriam inhaled as she felt his fingertips slide down her spine. He continued, "Or I could not zip it. I'll leave it up to you."

Miriam breathed roughly as she tried to think through the options. There were only two, really. Zip the dress up, or don't zip it. It shouldn't be hard to decipher the right answer. Shaking her head to clear a parade of not particularly helpful thoughts running through her mind, Miriam decided to - just this once - focus on what she felt, to do exactly what felt right.

"I don't really need to get dressed yet. I suppose the zipper could wait."

With those simple words, everything shifted. Suddenly, Boone's lips were on Miriam's neck. She felt grateful for a bob cut if only because it gave him more freedom to languidly run his lips down the curve of her neck, his whiskers sending shivers down her spine.

Then his hands joined in, spreading the opening of her dress wider as he slid each hand around the sides of her waist. His fingers were warm despite the fact he'd just been out in the chilly, early spring air. Miriam melted backward into him, leaning her body against his as she arched her neck to give him better access to the space just beneath her ear.

Suddenly, she was turning in his arms so they were facing. His blue eyes, usually so cool, were the blue at the center of a flame. Hands trembling, Miriam began unbuttoning Boone's plaid shirt. She loved that she already knew what waited beneath - each tattoo memorializing something beautiful, something lost. She already knew Boone, but she was about to know him in a new way, a way that would enrich the bond they had built on those cold February nights.

As if inspired by her boldness, Boone, too, started pulling down on Miriam's dress. She paused her own work just long enough to shrug off the dress, leaving a red pool of pleated chiffon around her feet.

Once her dress came off, everything else effortlessly fell to the wayside. The next thing she knew, they were falling into bed together, a bed she didn't have time to make that morning after receiving the phone call that she'd be preaching. Normally, she despised an unmade bed, but in this instance, an unmade bed was convenient.

Boone was slow and methodical in his lovemaking. He worked his way down with attentive, firm kisses until he reached her breast. Then he stopped as if in wonder of the rather small breast Miriam had always felt insecure about, but the insecurities fell away as Boone looked up at Miriam, quirked his perfect half smile, and then took her nipple into his mouth, his tongue making circles that made Miriam dig her fingers into his shoulder. He paid the other breast equal attention, making Miriam doubt if she could wait any longer for him.

Finally, he returned to her mouth, and Miriam, gaining some control, rolled him onto his back and straddled him. She couldn't believe the intimacy of the moment, nothing separating them. She was pressed firmly against him, and he was ready for her. Lifting her hips, Miriam barely had to reposition for Boone to slide into her.

It had been so long, and yet everything came so naturally. Boone held her hips in his firm but loving grasp, moving her perfectly in rhythm with his own thrusts. Within moments, the pace accelerated, and Miriam felt herself coming to a precipice. Just as a tingling sensation started spreading from her center to her limbs, Boone pressed deep into her, his breathing rough and jagged as he, too, released into her. As her orgasm released, sending shock waves of pleasure through her body, Boone thrust deeper with each pulse of her center, and Miriam wondered how he already knew exactly what to do when she reached her climax.

Eventually, Miriam rolled off of Boone and laid by his side with her head resting on his shoulder. She let his chest lift and lower her with his deep, slow breathing. The minutes passed, and Miriam hoped Boone's slower pace in life would always help her embrace moments instead of always rushing toward the future.

But before Miriam could explore that thought, another hit her like a train: she'd just had sex without any sort of protection for the first time in her life. Lifting her head, she said with more stress in her voice than she'd intended, "Boone, we forgot a condom. I mean, I'm on the pill and all, but still."

For a fraction of a second, she saw shock cross Boone's face, but it was quickly followed by a smile - a full smile. Looking down at her, Boone said, "Miriam, it'll be fine. Because you're going to marry me. Probably pretty soon."

"Really?"

"Yes, at that big fancy church of yours. I heard someone say it makes for a beautiful wedding."

That big fancy church did make for a beautiful wedding, but Miriam wasn't going to concede too quickly. "Is that so, Boone Rutledge?"

He yawned, acting nothing like a nervous lover asking a girl to marry him. As fanciful as it was, Miriam imagined all the years of Rubie and Rupert's love sliding down to Boone and herself, as if they were the natural heirs of that iron-clad, secure, but infatuating love.

Miriam felt Boone's contentment seep into her, and her eyes became heavy. Before she completely succumbed to sleep, Miriam said, "So when you said you wouldn't do casual sex with me, you meant it."

Boone's arms squeezed more tightly around her. Sleepily, he said, "Never with you. It could never be casual with you."

Chapter 30

"Do I look overly tousled?"

Boone and Miriam stood on the front porch of the farmhouse about to walk in, but Miriam stopped his hand before it turned the door knob. She hadn't looked this nervous stepping into the pulpit to speak to a roomful of people. Her cheeks were flushed just as they'd been in the greenhouse that cold evening when they'd shown each other their tattoos. Boone said, "You look absolutely lovely."

"That isn't what I asked, Boone." Her expression could not have been more serious. "I asked if I look like I just tumbled out of bed after an afternoon of unrelenting sex."

"Oh, is that what you asked?" Boone's face was not as lopsided as normal when he smiled down on Miriam who did, in fact, look a little tousled. "Here, just let me…" He tried to smooth down a few stray curls, but really, her hair always looked a little tousled. "There, all better."

Miriam glared skeptically.

Once again, Boone's hand was stopped before he reached the door knob.

"Yes?"

"There's just one more thing I need to do."

Boone watched as Miriam fished her phone out of her purse.

He said, "Miri, you can text from inside."

"Just wait." She didn't look at him as her thumbs scurried about her screen.

Boone jumped when rabid tweets emanated from his back pocket. Pulling his phone out, Boone looked at the screen. "It says my nesting request has been accepted."

Miriam's eyes widened. "Really? Is she a cutie?"

Boone snaked his fingers through Miriam's hair as he pulled her in for a kiss. He meant for it to be a relatively chaste kiss, but his tongue slipped into her mouth and his other hand kneaded her ass through the thin fabric of her dress, pulling her flush against him.

When they finally came up for air a few minutes later, Miriam said, "I'm tousled again, aren't I?"

Boone merely winked in response as he opened the door, this time without Miriam stopping him.

When they walked into the farmhouse, there was still a half hour to go before guests arrived. Travis had texted Boone several times throughout the afternoon assuring him that all was under control and that he, Boone, should stay exactly where he was, each text ending with a row of winking-face emojis.

Boone would normally have insisted on bearing equal parts of the responsibility, but he'd been intoxicated. Even if Travis had texted that a tornado had gone through the house destroying every last accordion pineapple and Hello Kitty balloon, Boone didn't think he could have pried himself from Miriam's company. After all, she had been as eager as he was to make up for the weeks since the snowstorm, and they'd built up quite a bit of sexual tension that needed to be released, apparently in the span of a single afternoon.

As they walked through the house, Boone could hear Grandma and Travis talking in the kitchen. Boone knew he had a goofy grin on his face, but there was nothing that could be done about it. He'd spent hours with a mostly unclothed Miriam, and he was too giddy with disbelief and relief to control his facial muscles.

When they turned the corner into the kitchen, Travis and Grandma both paused their conversation. Each stared unabashedly at the new couple with their own goofy grins making Boone think of bobble-heads on a dashboard.

Finally, Travis broke the silence: "Look who's here."

Rubie, grinning conspiratorially at Travis, said, "I see our guests are arriving. But of course, you two aren't guests."

Boone, placing an arm around Miriam's back and squeezing her shoulder, said, "I'd prefer Miriam not be considered a guest. In fact, she made a pretty good roomie, wouldn't you agree, Grandma?"

"It was sure nice having another woman around here."

"Well, I think you might get to see Miriam more often. Grandma, Miriam and I have something we need to tell you."

"If it isn't that the two of you have finally hooked up, I don't care."

Sighing, Boone said, "I was going to word it more tastefully, Grandma."

Travis looked to be enjoying the exchange far too much. "But where would the fun be in that?"

Rubie, practically rubbing her hands together in excitement, said, "If you want me to be tasteful, you should hide your business better. I'm going to have to pick up a cigarette again just from sitting in your afterglow."

"Is it that obvious?" Miriam said, and then she hit Boone on his upper arm. "I told you."

Boone, massaging his arm, said, "It's just Grandma. She can spot an afterglow a mile away because of all those seasons of *The Bachelor* she's watched."

Rubie dismissed her grandson's explanation with a wave of her hand. "No, Boone, it's just that I've truly loved before. Rupert and I were very sexual, you know."

"We know," Travis and Boone said in unison, and Boone went from rubbing his arm to massaging his temples.

Miriam, however, seemed to be affected in the opposite way by Rubie's bluntness. Somehow not paralyzed in discomfort as Boone found himself to be, Miriam laughed and said, "If we remind you in any way of Rupert and yourself, I'd say we're off to a promising start."

And just like that, the awkwardness of initial love, of those moments when family and friends first see their loved ones transformed by infatuation, evaporated. Miriam walked to Rubie and gave her a warm hug. Boone sat next to his brother as Travis slapped his shoulder roughly, beaming with satisfaction at his and Rubie's accomplished mission.

"Well, Rubie," Miriam said. "The decorations look amazing. They are truly you."

Rubie replied, "We were shooting for whimsically chaotic."

"Like I said. Truly you."

***

When the doorbell rang announcing the first guests, Travis stood to welcome the early arrivals only to have Rubie pause him with a hand. Looking around the circle at her grandsons and Miriam, Rubie said, "Before we let them in, I do need something from you three. Tonight, there will be two single, older gentlemen here: Albert and Freddy. Albert is the one with enough nose hair to sweep a chimney, and Freddy has age spots in the shape of a turtle on his left cheek. Both of them are under the impression that they are my boyfriend, and neither knows of the other's existence. I just need y'all to be dears and keep them separate, okay? Okay, let's go."

With that, she dismissed them to greet the guests.

"This should be fun," Travis said in a voice as dry as Death Valley.

Boone looked at Miriam with a pained expression, but she simply laughed as she assured Boone and Travis that all would be fine. And with that, she went to greet guests, perfectly comfortable in the whirlwind that spun around Rubie Rutledge.

"Boone, my brother..." Travis started.

"Yes?"

"I think you've done the impossible."

"And what would that be?"

"I think you've found a person who can be in Grandma's orbit without being driven to insanity."

Boone huffed a small exhale of epiphany. "I think you're right. I didn't even realize until this very moment that was a requirement I had. I definitely didn't put it on my Matchables profile. 'Needs to be comfortable around eccentric old women who often find themselves in pickles of their own creation.'"

"That would've attracted the ladies."

Boone and Travis were standing to the side, content to let Miriam and Rubie greet the influx of guests coming through the doors. Leaning towards his brother, Boone whispered, "Thanks for giving us the afternoon."

Travis waved a hand. "Of course. But you and Miriam do owe me and Paul a date night once the babies arrive."

"Babies?" Boone wasn't sure he had heard his brother correctly.

"Babies. Yes, babies. We have a surrogate, and twins will be arriving four to five months after we move to Louisville."

Boone felt a lump forming in his throat. He looked away quickly, unable to stare at Travis's sincere, joyful eyes without tearing up. Swallowing hard, Boone said, "I think we can handle that. Babies can't be that much harder to keep alive than roses, right?"

"Boone, that's as sound of logic as I've ever heard."

***

Miriam stood in a corner sipping a cup of cloying, neon pink punch while people-watching. It was normally in her nature to be amid the socializing, but she was taking a moment to herself to revel in this singularly remarkable day.

While sitting in the kitchen earlier chatting with Boone, Travis, and Rubie, Miriam had felt part of a family in a way that was unfamiliar. Between having nomadic parents, no siblings, and a career that kept her on the move up until a few years ago, she'd been living life untethered. But surrounded by jadeite dishes and gingham curtains and the Rutledge trio, Miriam knew she was home.

While she could have sat there all evening basking in the company of this newfound family, there was a party to attend. And it was fun. The evening was filled with people eager to celebrate the most eccentric and entertaining of their acquaintances. Rubie kept everyone's plates full, their cheeks sore from laughter, and, somehow, Albert and Freddy were still unaware of the other's existence.

Miriam couldn't quite believe the events that had transpired over the course of the day. It would appear Boone was as crazy about her as she was about him. Apparently, he wanted to marry her. She'd gone from a slow-burning gloom to utter contentment in a matter of moments. Basking in their newfound joy, Miriam didn't notice Porter approaching until he was a foot away smiling at her knowingly.

Porter said, "Given the looks I've seen darting between you and Boone this evening, I'm going to assume you are no longer just thinking impure thoughts."

"Seeing as how I'm the minister, I probably shouldn't get all confessional on you." Miriam couldn't keep a smile from her lips or a blush from rising into her cheeks. She might as well have told him precisely how many times she and Boone had done the deed that very afternoon.

"I knew it." Porter pumped a fist like he'd just won a bet on the Super Bowl. "I knew he had feelings for you. I told you, didn't I?"

Miriam laughed gently as she said, "Yes, Porter. You get all the points."

Sobering, Porter said, "Miri, do me a favor, will you?"

"Sure, Porter. Anything for you."

"Let yourself enjoy this. Take time to build it. Take a second to not put every human in a five-mile radius before yourself. No guilt."

It took a moment for Miriam to reply. "Consider me absolved." She continued, "But are you taking care of yourself Porter? Are you ready to let people in so we can all be there for you?"

For a brief moment, a cloud passed over Porter's face. It looked unnatural given Porter's typically jolly demeanor. "I'm getting there, I think."

Miriam wanted to ask more, but a church member arrived taking her attention before she had the chance.

***

Several times throughout the evening, Boone and Miriam lost each other in the hubbub of people. Miriam didn't know how Rubie knew such a diverse group of people from so many walks of life and different ages, but she also wasn't surprised. A personality as big as Rubie's was bound to pick up a wide array of friends over ninety years. Standing in a group who'd gathered around the fireplace, Miriam turned slowly in a circle looking for Boone over the head of the crowd. He was the tallest there by several inches. Finally, she spotted him coming into the living room from the kitchen.

His eyes brightened at the sight of her, and Miriam was surprised when he wrapped his arms around her despite the throng of people around them. Unable to conceal her feelings on her face that had always been easy to read, Miriam conceded to not even trying. She kissed Boone, not overly passionately, but gently, relishing the feel of his whiskers.

"I see Matchables worked."

Boone and Miriam broke off the kiss abruptly, both looking for the source of this observation. Their gazes each landed on Miss Hyacinth, dressed in a floral and ruffled party dress that likely dated from the Eighties, and a rather petite woman with a pixie cut who looked positively giddy. Miss Hyacinth's companion gave a little wave and said, "Hello. I'm Krista."

Boone nodded his head in recognition. "Oh. The librarian?"

Clearing up the misconception, Miriam said, "We didn't meet on Matchables."

Krista asked, "Well, how did you end up together?"

Miriam thought back over the past couple of months, over the dozens of small moments that had pushed her more and more in love with the burly, slightly muddy man next to her. "It's a long story, but it involves the usual things. Mutual friends, late-night bar encounters, a historic ice storm, seemingly insurmountable differences, and a good deal of jello salad."

Boone, whose arm was still wrapped around Miriam's waist, said, "Yes. That's about the sum of it."

After Miss Hyacinth and Krista moved along, Miriam whispered into Boone's ear, "We can cancel our Matchables accounts later tonight."

"Too bad we can't have a burning ceremony for online profiles."

***

Miriam wrapped Rupert's corduroy coat around her red dress. It was instantly familiar, like the first sip of a pumpkin spice latte at the beginning of fall. Yes, this is what it feels like to be in the Rutledge home.

Stepping out the kitchen door, she started towards the greenhouse. Everything was all cleaned up from the party, and Boone had excused himself to go water plants a few minutes earlier. As soon as Miriam was done putting Saran wrap on the last plate of leftovers, she asked Rubie for the use of Rupert's coat and left to go to her favorite place on the farm.

As soon as she walked into the cozy interior, Boone looked at her with hunger her body instantly responded to. Within seconds, they were in each other's arms, kissing hungrily as Boone's hands worked their way beneath her skirts, running along her thighs.

Breaking away from the kiss, Miriam said breathlessly, "Boone, it's been five hours."

He just growled as he worked his way to her cleavage, taking advantage of the dress's neckline.

Ten minutes later, Miriam was panting while leaning against Boone on a workbench for which that they'd found a new use.

Boone's smile was that of a fully satiated man. "Well, that was a first for this old greenhouse."

"I don't know, Boone. Rupert and Rubie probably didn't leave many spots on this farm undefiled."

The smile temporarily left Boone's face. "Can we not think about that right now?"

Miriam laid her head back on his shoulder. If she was quiet enough, she would swear she could hear the plants grow. It was Boone who broke the silence in his low, gravelly whisper.

"So after that big church wedding..."

"Yes?"

"Afterwards, we'll invite everyone out to the farm, and we'll have a reception outside around the greenhouse. That way, Grandpa will be there."

"Rupert is always welcomed."

Miriam craned her neck, staring at Boone and trying to calculate how serious he was. His honest eyes said it all. He was deadly serious.

Miriam said, "And instead of wedding cake, we'll have Rubie's jello salads - every flavor."

"Vats of jello salad. She'll be thrilled."

Miriam laid her head back down, enjoying the feel of his chest hair against her ear. "Alright. You had me at big-fancy-church-wedding, but the jello salad clinches the deal."

It was quite some time before Boone and Miriam returned to the house with all the plants watered.

Chapter 31

Miriam sat at the head of a large conference table in one of the church's classrooms. People were still mingling, waiting until five minutes or so after the class was supposed to start. It was never a good idea to start on time. The stragglers would be offended.

For several months, Miriam had been researching the history and theology of environmentalism. So far, the class looked to have a solid turnout, which boded well for discussion. Rubie was seated in the center, keeping several people around her, including Porter, laughing.

Miriam hadn't told Boone about the class starting. Their relationship was just beginning, and she didn't want him to feel pressured to interact with her career more than he was comfortable.

Just as she stood to call the class to order, the door opened for one final straggler. In walked Boone, dressed in his customary flannel and blue jeans with mud-caked boots. He must have just come from the university's fields where he taught students to cultivate the land in hands-on classes.

Miriam tried to keep surprise from her expression, but she'd never had much of a poker face. Boone, sheepish anytime he was the center of attention, waved his hand as he mumbled a greeting. Miriam glanced at Rubie and Porter to see if they were as surprised as she was. Rubie looked like the personification of the hashtag "#knewit." Porter was darting his eyes between Boone and Miriam while grinning.

Mrs. Broadbank, who apparently remembered Boone from the last time he'd barged into a meeting, said, "I hope you aren't here to unfriend our Mother Miriam again. Young people are supposed to take care of that sort of messy business online these days."

Boone, paling, said, "No, no, no. I just wanted to..." Miriam smiled at his lack of eloquence. It was endearing how befuddled he became in a roomful of mostly older women. "I just...Miri...Mother Miriam that is. I'm sorry to pull you away for even a minute, but can I talk with you in the hall?"

After the last few weeks, Miriam felt secure granting that request without fear of larger implications. Looking at the room, she said, "I'll be right back."

In the hallway, Boone's hands immediately touched her arms, rubbing her forearms as if he was warming them up. They rarely were in one another's proximity without touching.

"Yes, Boone Rutledge?"

"I'm here. At a Bible study." He sounded truly shocked.

"I see that. How did you know this was going on?"

"Rubie announced it loudly multiple times over the past few days. She's never seemed so eager for me to know her schedule.

In fact, normally she keeps her schedule secret because she says I have judgey eyebrows when she has dates with her poor, clueless boyfriends."

Miriam gasped in mock indignation. "Judgey eyebrows, Boone? Shame on you."

He just half-smiled. "But in all seriousness, I'm here. And I'm not going to say I'm not still angry with God, but your version of him doesn't seem so bad. And if the Bible advocates for the environment like you say it does, I guess we're on the same team, right?"

Miriam's hands cupped his face as she looked seriously into his eyes. "I've never doubted for a single moment that you were one of the good guys whether or not you've been on a church pew for the past two decades."

He rested his forehead against her own. "I know we haven't prepared, so I'll just sit and listen to you. I like doing that. You can pull me in whenever you want."

Miriam took his hand, squeezing. "That sounds perfect."

Turning, she opened the door and led Boone into the classroom. As soon as they walked in, the murmur of conversation died and everyone looked at Boone with an undercurrent of distrust. After all, he'd once dumped their beloved Mother Miriam in an altar guild meeting.

As Boone scanned the room for a seat, Rubie patted the chair next to her. "Boonie, there's an open spot next to me."

Boone couldn't completely suppress a smile as - in a tone that lacked true annoyance - he said, "Oh, goodie."

Epilogue

Six Months Later

As the chilly fall breeze blew through PSU rattling the brightly colored leaves of the trees, Miriam missed the warmth of her robes. The location could not have been more fitting. Hart Building, where the English Department was housed and where Lucy and Forrest's love had grown slowly over years of working side by side, stood as the backdrop for the altar. Nestled between the arcane campus buildings and thick rows of trees, no sun could get through to warm the hundred or so guests who'd witnessed the vows. It was the first wedding in a while Miriam had attended but not officiated. The thin, eggplant satin of the bridesmaid dress didn't offer much protection from the cooler temperatures of October.

Edith walked towards Miriam in a matching dress, her arms hugged tightly around her waist. She said, "It's colder than the stares students give me when I pass back their graded papers."

Miriam said, "You'd never know it looking at Lucy."

The two bridesmaids huddled close for warmth as they looked in unison towards the bride. Lucy, wearing an elegant, three-quarter-sleeved bridal gown, seemed completely unaffected by the chill.

She practically glowed as she mingled with the wedding guests. Miriam watched her friend, contentment warming her from within almost enough to combat the chill.

Many of the wedding guests, Miriam included, took more ownership of the wedding than was fair. But the couple's romance had been preceded by years of friendship, and their circle of friends had rooted for them long before Lucy and Forrest even considered the possibility.

Miriam smiled as Porter, walked up to her and Edith. His three children, all of whom had participated in the wedding, were happily basking in the attention of the various grandparent-aged guests.

Porter said, "Well, it took a decade, but we finally got them married."

"Hell, yeah, we did," Edith said robustly.

"That had more Kentucky accent to it than I've ever heard from you," Miriam said.

"It sneaks up on me when I get excited. Or in this case, triumphant."

Laughing, Miriam said, "Surely they would've figured out they were meant for each other without us."

"Not a chance," Porter insisted. "If it weren't for us, they'd be spending this very evening editing one of Forrest's papers while making moon eyes at each other and blushing."

"I almost felt embarrassed for them back then," Edith said, but her coy smile belied the words.

"Regardless," Miriam said, coming to Lucy's defense, "We haven't spent a whole decade trying to get those two together."

Porter said, "But it felt like it."

Thinking back to the years of Lucy pining over Forrest and unable to sustain any kind of meaningful romantic relationship, Miriam did have to agree. There had been some long stretches in there.

Miriam could see Boone across the crowd standing several inches above most. He and Porter had been the groomsmen, and Miriam now knew that Boone in a black suit was quite a sight to behold. It had been difficult to focus when she'd first spied him across campus arriving with the men. His shoes were even clean.

Prying her eyes from Boone, Miriam returned her attention to Porter.

"Porter, are you alright?"

"I'm fine."

"No, you're not," Edith said, her characteristic bluntness on full display. "You haven't been alright in a while. I still can't believe it took you so long to tell us."

Porter said, "I didn't want to burden you all."

"I could've been helping with the kids last spring," Edith said. Despite being voted the most terrifying professor on PSU's campus three years in a row, Edith loved kids.

Miriam felt relief when Porter had finally confided in the group several months ago, but the support he received from his friends couldn't entirely erase the fact that divorce sucks. He'd always been the most relaxed, the one quickest to grab on to an adventure, the one least likely to stress over a stack of grading or some little drama at church. But even he didn't get to skip out of mourning the end of his marriage.

Miriam thought about the past week's festivities. Bachelor and bachelorette parties. The rehearsal. The rehearsal dinner. One toast after another raised in honor of two people committing their lives to each other in marriage. Miriam asked, "Has this been torture? Being completely surrounded by love and marriage and romance?"

Edith added, "And cartoon hearts floating out of Forrest and Lucy's eyes? And Boone and Miriam's eyes, also, come to think of it?"

Porter waved away their concern. "No. I'm genuinely happy to be the only sad sap in our group. I love seeing these relationships I've rooted for coming to fruition. That's probably the main reason I kept it to myself for so long. I didn't want to crush the vibes."

Miriam said, "But we could have held more than one emotion at a time, Porter."

"Yes," Edith corroborated. "I'm a very complex person."

"No you're not, Edith," Porter said. "You have two emotions: intense devotion or intense anger. Not that complex."

"But I can intensely love you and your children while being intensely angry at your ex-wife. As I have proven since you finally gave me the chance."

The tiniest of smiles touched Porter's lips. Beginning to walk back towards the crowd, Porter wrapped an arm around each woman, squeezing in a brotherly side-hug. "I know the two of you can handle it. I just hate that you have to."

Miriam, laying her head on his shoulder for a brief moment, said, "Okay. But from here on out, we're in this together. You've got to let us in. Boone and I, Forrest and Lucy, Edith, Dr. Hubert - all of us, Porter. You've got to let us share your burden."

"Or your anger," Edith said. "I'm good at sharing anger."

Giving one final squeeze before he walked towards his kids, Porter said, "It's a deal."

***

Boone mingled with the guests. It wasn't in his nature to mingle, but Rubie had lectured him on groomsmen etiquette before he left the house, and she'd even face-timed with Travis to get his endorsement. Travis had agreed that, yes, Boone would need to be sociable at this event. Boone asked Rubie who the hell had taught her how to FaceTime. Apparently, there was a new librarian - a student worker from the university - who was so young that he was born in the current century. Rubie was milking all sorts of information out of this one.

Finally, having mingled with enough guests to satisfy Rubie's questioning later that evening, Boone headed towards Miriam. It was nearly impossible to keep his eyes off of her during the whole mingling ordeal. The deep purple (she'd called it eggplant, but he thought of it as Ebb Tide Floribunda Rose) suited her naturally tanned skin and chestnut hair.

Miriam was just finishing a conversation with someone's at-least-one-great uncle when Boone walked up behind her. As she turned to him, her face broke into a grin that Boone couldn't believe he sparked. He'd never thought of himself as someone who made others smile.

Wrapping her arms around his waist, Miriam said, "There you are. Do you have any idea how good you look in that suit?"

Realizing her arms were cold, Boone started rubbing them as he spoke. "Yeah. Unfortunately, I managed to find the one puddle of water on this campus - looks like a leak from a sprinkler -, and now I doubt they'll give me back my deposit."

Miriam looked down at his muddy left shoe with splatters halfway up the leg. Leaning her forehead on his chest, Miriam said, "You just can't help yourself, can you?"

"Nope." Boone's lip slanted in a grin.

Turning Miriam around in his arms so that her back was leaning against his chest, they watched as Forrest and Lucy smiled for the photographer who was finishing up the formal photos of them with various configurations of their family members. The wedding party would be next.

"My goodness. They do look happy."

Boone smiled at the wonder in Miriam's voice.

"It's going to be us next, Miri. Taking goofy wedding pictures in front of the greenhouse with Rubie dressed in a muumuu."

"And Travis and Paul with the babies."

Boone shook his head, still in disbelief. "Yes. Both of them."

"Your boots will be hopeless at the greenhouse."

"I doubt I'll make it to the church without them getting muddy."

"It's unlikely."

Boone's arms tightened around this person who had accepted with unquestioning love both him and his family. "Yes. And I know one thing for certain about that day."

"What's that?"

"Muddy boots or not, our wedding photos will have me smiling with both sides of my mouth."

Before he could exhibit just how thoroughly she made him smile, Miriam turned in his arms and kissed him with fervor just short of needing to get a room.

That was fine with Boone. He'd show her later.

About the Author

Librarian by day and crafter of cozy rom-coms by night, author Kalyn Gensic lives surrounded by stories. She resides in Texas with her charmingly grumpy husband, four precocious children, and two dogs who shed quite a lot of fur.

Connect Online

On Facebook & Instagram @
KalynGensicWrites
&
kalyngensic.com

Acknowledgements

Book 2 is in the books – pun intended – and I'm so grateful for the support of my friends and family as I've taken yet another step in this whole writing journey. It still feels surreal. What a strange hobby I have. But it is also real, and it wouldn't be real without my circle of people. To my family, thank you for putting up with me being distracted ninety percent of the time as my mind resides in a fictional world. To my friends, thank you for cheering me on. To Abilene, thank you for buying my book at 7 and 1 Books over and over again. To people not in Abilene, stop by 7 and 1 Books if you ever drive through. It's on North 2nd Street.

Speaking of Abilene, I would be remiss if I didn't thank the people of Heavenly Rest Episcopal Church. I walked into their vaulted nave with a trunk load of religious trauma. It's a good thing their rectors don't spook easily. Mother Miriam would love it there.

Telling the story of a female minister in a romance novel is a strange thing to do, isn't it? There isn't a deep stack of similar novels to establish tropes and set a framework. But I hope that you, the reader, found appreciating Miriam's story doesn't require adhering to any particular faith. Hers is a story that anyone can connect to who has ever felt called to a purpose while also being a little lost in life.

As for Boone Rutledge, when I think of him, the same part of my heart tugs as when I think of my beloved dog, Cash. His wounds mimic some of my own, and in writing him into existence, I shaped a guy I would be buddies with if only he were real. He is broken in the same way as many of my favorite people. May his story of love be uplifting to anyone who has ever felt like damaged goods. We are all broken, but we are all worthy of love.

I hope *Meet Me in the Greenhouse* made you think and made you swoon and made you laugh. If it made you cry a little, I apologize. But also, that's cool. I always wanted to make a reader cry. Regardless, if you made it here to the acknowledgements page, thank you so very much for taking a chance on Miriam and Boone's story.

Much love,
Kalyn

Printed in Dunstable, United Kingdom